ARES
KINGS OF MAYHEM MC TENNESSEE

PENNY DEE

Ares
Kings of Mayhem MC
Tennessee Chapter Book 3

Penny Dee

This book is a work of fiction. Any references to real events, real people, and real places are used fictitiously. Other names, characters, places and incidents are products of the Author's imagination and any resemblance to persons, living or dead, actual events, organizations or places is entirely coincidental.

All rights are reserved. This book is intended for the purchaser of this book ONLY. No part of this book may be reproduced or transmitted in any form or by any means, graphic, electronic, or mechanical, including photocopying, recording, taping, or by any information storage retrieval system, without the express written permission of the Author. All songs, song titles and lyrics contained in this book are the property of the respective songwriters and copyright holders.

Disclaimer: The material in this book contains graphic language and sexual content and is intended for mature audiences, ages 18 and older. There is content within this book that may set off triggers, you will find more information and help at the end of this book.

ISBN: 979-8845865489

Editing by Kay at Swish Design & Editing
Proofreading by Nicki at Swish Design & Editing
Book design by Swish Design & Editing
Cover design by Marisa at Cover Me Darling
Cover Image Copyright 2022

First Edition
Copyright © 2022 Penny Dee
All Rights Reserved

DEDICATION

To you, the reader.
Thank you for reading.

TENNESSEE CHAPTER

Kings of Mayhem MC
Tennessee Chapter Members

Jack (President)
Shooter (VP)
Ares (Sergeant-at-Arms or SAA)
Banks (Treasurer)
Doc (Medic)
Bam
Loki
Paw
Dakota Joe
Ghoul
Earl
Boomer
Venom
Wyatt
Gambit
Merrick

Munster
Gabe
Alchemy (Looks after the Still, the club's legit business)
Prospect one
Prospect two
Dolly (Clubhouse Bar Manager)
TJ (Tends bar)

ARES
KINGS OF MAYHEM MC
TENNESSEE

PENNY DEE

PROLOGUE

ARES

Twenty Years Ago—A small town outside Jacksonville, Florida

I was born a monster.

I killed my mom during childbirth.

Or so the kids at school say now they're old enough to know how to hurt me with their words. They know they can't hurt me physically, so they resort to poisoned words to do their bidding because they're afraid of me and don't know how to hide it.

I'm a freak.

A genetic mutant. Tall and strong. With eyes as dark as night.

And it isn't only the kids who are afraid of me, it's the adults too. I'm already taller than our teachers, and I can see the fear in their eyes whenever we make eye contact. No one wants to be caught alone with me, not even my teachers.

No matter what I try, I can't put their misguided beliefs about me to rest. I can't help being the size I am or the height I am, and it crushes me to see people shrink back in fear when they see me coming their way. I always thought they were wrong about me. But lately, I've started to wonder if they might be right because sometimes I feel my moods swing like a pendulum. Sometimes they soar from the highest of highs where I feel like king of the world, but then they plummet without warning to the lowest of lows where I can barely get out of bed.

But I never show it.

Never let anyone know about the storm brewing inside. I keep quiet and pull my hoodie down to hide my face and try to turn invisible. But invisibility is hard when you're already six foot eight at eighteen.

"Six-foot gazillion inches and built like a brick shithouse," my Uncle Frankie always jokes. Half the size of me and skinny as a garden rake, you never see him without a cigarette dangling from his bottom lip. "And more misunderstood than a frightened Pitbull."

He's right. I'm misunderstood by everyone.

Except for Uncle Frankie and Belle.

When Belle moved in next door, I had never seen anyone like her in the world. She is so beautiful my chest aches just looking at her. Blonde, with crystal blue eyes and a smile brighter than sunshine, I fell in love with her the moment she walked up to the front door of my father's mansion and introduced herself to me. She was with her parents, and to this day, I can still see the look on their faces when I opened the door and they saw me for the first time. I was smiling because they'd caught me on a good day when my moods were high. They were smiling too... until they saw me, and their smiles faded, and Belle's father not so discretely nudged his seventeen-year-old daughter behind him as if he needed to protect her from me.

The introduction was stilted and awkward. Her parents were quick to realize it was a mistake to introduce their daughter to the freak who lives next door.

Their eyes didn't lie— they were frightened of me.

But not Belle.

I could tell she'd felt that zip of lightning hit her when we met, and despite her parents ushering her away from me that day, it wasn't long before we started to meet in secret whenever she could get away from her father's watchful eye.

That's the good thing about your father hating the sight of you—he's never around to enforce curfews or ground you. And boy, did my old man hate me. He never got over my mom's death or the fact that I caused it.

That's why Uncle Frankie moved in with us after Mom's funeral. The man raised and treated me right when my cold-hearted father couldn't. He's the one I confide in about Belle and helps us meet in secret because he knows we have something special and that everyone has the right to experience it at least once in their life. *And who am I to say your time isn't now?*

It was Uncle Frankie who brought Belle the secret phone she keeps hidden under a floorboard in her bedroom so we can communicate without her parents knowing.

This afternoon, she sent me a message asking me to meet her at the abandoned theater just outside of town. That's why I'm here now, parking my bike around the back.

I find her in the old brick building, standing amongst the ruins and a hundred lit candles.

She looks so beautiful I can barely breathe.

"Belle baby... what's going on?"

She begins to unbutton the front of her dress, and I struggle to swallow. My mouth is a desert, my throat as rough as sandpaper. I've never seen anything as so lovely.

"I want you to be my first," she says, her glossy lips breaking into a soft smile.

Her dress slips to the floor, and all I can do is stare at her.

"Say something," she whispers.

I swallow deeply. "I've never seen anything so beautiful."

She smiles as she comes toward me and rises to her tiptoes

when she reaches me to wrap her beautiful arms around my neck. I have to lean down to meet her kiss. Her lips are sweet and gentle against mine, her tongue warm and velvety soft.

God, I am so in love with you, I think as I kiss her back.

But when my desire for her becomes too much, I pull away.

"Please don't," she says, reaching for me. She places my palm against her naked breast, and I shudder with longing. "I want you to touch me, Ares. I want you to do all the things to me that people do when they're in love."

She comes closer.

"I think about you at night…" she continues, "… when I'm alone in my bed. When no one can see or hear me." Her hands drift down her naked body, touching herself in all the places I want to touch her. One hand slides between her thighs. "I touch myself here and picture you, and it feels really good." She gasps as she slides her fingers inside, and I lick my lips because I'm so hungry for a taste. "But it always leaves me achy for more because I need *you*, Ares. I need *you* to take the ache away."

My body reacts to her words. To the sight of the girl I love touching herself. Behind my zipper, my erection strains to be released, but I resist reaching down to touch it. Instead, I go to Belle and collect her into my arms and kiss her wildly, my lust and need almost too much to bear.

But she takes control, pushes me back into an old armchair, and slides onto my lap.

"Are you absolutely sure about this?" I swipe her hair from her face. We've never talked about this moment.

Her smile is carnal and lusty as she reaches for my zipper. "I couldn't be more sure."

The moment my zipper is down, my cock springs free. Belle looks at the size of it, then back to me, her eyes wide.

She gulps. "It's so big."

I know I have a big cock. It's heavy and thick, and sometimes when I get hard and jerk off, I get dizzy because all the blood rushes south from my brain.

"I don't want to hurt you," I say.

She's tiny, and I don't know how all of me is going to fit inside her.

"Then you're going to have to get me ready for you." She climbs off my lap and leads me over to the makeshift bed she's made from old cushions and blankets she has brought from home and slides her panties down her firm thighs. Lying down, she opens her legs. I see her for the first time, and every cell in my body begins begging me for this.

She reaches for my hand and pulls me down to her. "Make me come with your tongue."

It's my turn to gulp.

"I've never done that before," I admit. Although, I've spent many nights dreaming about it with my hand in my shorts and my teeth biting into my lip, picturing my head between her thighs.

She pulls me closer, and my instincts take over, guided by her moans and the violent tugs on my hair as I lick, suck, and penetrate her with my tongue. When I find the little bud of nerves, I torment it with my mouth, and she falls apart beneath me.

Listening to her come, I'm so aroused my balls tighten with a need for release. But I want to make her come again, so I fuck her harder with my tongue until her legs shake and her tugs on my hair grow more violent, then she comes again.

Flushed, she looks up at me, and I feel so triumphant.

I've never made a girl make those kinds of sounds before.

Her eyes drop to my cock curving toward my navel and the tiny pearl of cum on the head.

"I want you inside me," she says.

"Are you sure you're ready?" My breath is ragged.

She guides my hand to where my tongue and mouth were, where she's swollen, supple, and creamy.

"See what you do to me?" she says. "I'm ready for you."

She's so pink and wet. *So fucking perfect.*

"I'll be gentle," I promise. But inside, I'm terrified I'll hurt her. She's so small, and I'm so big. "Tell me if I hurt you, okay?"

Belle's fingers trail down my abs as I place myself at her entrance. She inhales sharply as the broad head nudges inside her, then again as I gently ease into her. She cries out, and I pause, but she begs me to keep going. "Don't stop."

"But I'm hurting you," I say, easing back.

She grabs my wrist. "I want all of you, Ares. Every single inch."

I let out a harsh inhale. Every instinct in me doesn't want to hurt her, but we both want this.

Controlling the urge to plunge into her drenched pussy, I take my time and push in slowly, taking her virginity. She cries out, and tears spring at the corner of her eyes.

"You're crying," I whisper, suddenly worried that I'm doing something wrong. "This isn't right."

She grabs my face in her hands. "This is perfect. Yes, I'm crying because it hurts. But you need to understand that it's the most beautiful kind of pain."

She kisses me, the kind of kiss you feel all over your body, and I pick up a rhythm that rocks me deeper into her. We have to stop a few times so her body can adjust, and the stopping and starting is sweet agony, but it builds a euphoric tension in my balls.

After a few more strokes, without warning, the tension erupts in me with mind-altering euphoria, and I know exactly what's happening.

"Oh God, I'm going to come—"

I know I need to pull out.

We haven't discussed precautions.

Hell, we haven't discussed any of this.

All I know is that I'm inside her now, and what we're doing can get her pregnant.

"No, I want you to come inside me," she begs, tightening her thighs around my hips so I can't pull out. There is no time to argue because, at that moment, I'm hit with earth-shattering pleasure like warm water flowing over my body, and all my pent-up desire for her bursts from me in a series of violent jerks.

Caught up in the storm, I thrust harder and harder, sliding in and out of her slippery body until my body grinds to a sudden halt, and I shudder with a final, powerful release.

It's the most intense feeling in the world shooting out of me and into her depth.

I had read things, seen things on television, even watched things on the internet, but nothing could prepare me for the sensation coursing through my veins as I emptied inside her.

It's like all the electricity in my brain gathered in one place and then burst across it in an extraordinarily bright light.

I pant against her warm skin, not sure if I'm ever going to come down.

Finally, I collapse against her.

"Did I hurt you?" I finally manage to speak some words.

She shakes her head. "It was magical."

When my breathing evens, I roll onto my back, pulling her with me so she settles onto my chest. With a whimper, she melts into me, content.

We lay like that for hours, staring up at the starlit night through the broken window, talking about our future and our dreams. And when our hands find one another again, and the touching gets to be too much, I make love to her once more. This time more frantically because despite the pain and sting of me entering her again, she begs me to fuck her harder and harder, her cries ringing out into the darkness before she comes beneath me with the sweetest cry on her lips.

"Let's run away," she murmurs against my chest afterward. "Just you and me. Let's pack our bags and leave."

"You really want to leave your parents behind?" I ask, tucking her long blonde hair over her bare shoulder.

"They'll never accept you, Ares. They're mean and prejudiced, and it scares me." Tears well in her beautiful blue eyes. "I'd rather die than not be with you."

"Don't say that, baby." I cup her jaw.

"It's true. Truth be told, I hope you made me pregnant with your baby so we can run away and be a family. I want it all with you, everything."

The idea of putting my baby inside her makes me hard.

But it's getting late, and we have to leave before her parents get home from their church meeting and find her missing.

"I don't want to let you go," she says after we dress, and it's time to leave.

"It's only for a short while. When we finish school, we'll leave this all behind. It will be just you and me."

"Promise?"

She looks so innocent and sweet I have to kiss her again. "I promise."

Walking side by side, we push our bikes through the night and reluctantly head for home.

It begins to rain but instead of racing for cover beneath the bus stop, Belle lays down her bike and holds out her arms and begins to twirl in the rain shower.

I don't know it now, but later this will be the last thing I remember—her twirling in the rain with a beautiful smile on her face.

I don't remember what happens next because before I realize it, I'm waking up with the rain splattering against my face and a violent pounding in the back of my skull.

I'm lying on my back, and everything hurts.

Dazed, I blink against the raindrops hitting my face and try to remember what the hell happened. My head throbs, and when I reach up to touch it, blood coats my fingers.

I sit up, and pain shoots through my head and pounds at my temples. Blood mixes with rainwater in my mouth, and I roll onto my palms to vomit.

That's when I see her.

My beautiful Belle.

Lying skewed on the wet concrete, her dress is hitched up around her waist. Her head is turned and her half-open eyes stare lifelessly at me.

It takes a moment to register.

The roar that leaves me is desperate and violent, rushing out of me and dying on the tail of a flash of lightning through the stormy clouds.

Long nails of rain pelt from the night sky, drenching me as I kneel on the wet road with Belle in my arms, her body limp, her arms swinging lifelessly. I hold her to me. Blood mixes with the rain on her skin and swirls down her throat before disappearing onto the road.

I don't know how long I lay there with her because time has stopped. All I know is that the rain keeps coming down hard, but I won't leave her. I cry and scream, a part of me dying on the roadside with her.

Finally, a pair of headlights cut into the darkness and come to a stop only a few yards away. The door opens, and my uncle gets out. Rushing over to me, he looks down at Belle in my arms.

"Dammit, son," he cries. "What have you done?"

The court is at full capacity.

The trial is a media sensation, and outside the crowd is hungry for blood.

My blood.

The press is having a field day with clickbait headlines like *The Beautiful Teenager Brutally Murdered by The Weirdo Next Door* and *Beautiful Belle and the Brutal Beast.*

Before I even step inside this courtroom, I've already been found guilty by the court of public opinion.

Now, I'm in the witness box wearing a suit that is too tight and shoes that are too small.

After days of witness testimony and forensic demonstrations, the court has heard how I am a manic depressive with violent tendencies who raped and murdered the girl next door. They've heard about my obsession with Belle, how I kidnapped her when she rejected my advances, and took her to the abandoned theater, where I violated her before beating her to death.

My wounds—a concussion and a fractured skull that required seven stitches—are never questioned. Instead, they're used as evidence against me—proof that Belle fought for her life before I overpowered her.

I plead my innocence, but I can't give them an accurate account of what happened because I can't remember. One moment, we were walking in the rain together, laughing as the rain began to fall harder and then… nothing.

"And do you deny that the semen found in the victim the night of her murder was yours? That you attacked her so violently during the rape that you made her bleed."

"No, no, we were together. Yes, but it was our first time—"

"And for your first time you lost control and tore her apart? I beg you, please, Mr. Salvatore. You heard the forensic evidence. The rape kit showed bruising and vaginal bleeding not consistent with a first time, but with a violent and—"

"Stop!" I cry because I can't stand it. I can't stand the thought of Belle and the pain they say she went through. With a rush, I stand, and a couple of ladies in the jury look physically afraid. But I can't help it. The pain is too much, and I need it to end.

The prosecutor looks pleased with himself. "That's all, Mr. Salvatore, you are excused."

It takes the jury less than an hour to decide.

My lawyer tells me it can be a good sign that this case may get thrown out.

But even he doesn't believe his lie.

We are all told to rise, and I shoot a frightened look across to Uncle Frankie. My father declined to attend any of the trial, but Frankie has been with me every step of the way. He tries to hide his concern but fails, his furrowed brow a dead giveaway.

I'm scared.

The judge clears his throat and doesn't waste time handing down the jury's verdict.

"Ares Salvatore, the jury of your peers finds you guilty of the charge of murder in the first degree."

His words tear through me like a bullet, but I don't react. I'm a quick learner. There are so many cameras on me, any wrong facial expression, and they'll use it against me. But the horror taking place inside me is violent and terrifying. I don't have a chance to catch a breath before the judge looks over the piece of paper at me. "And for this, I sentence you to death."

CHAPTER 1

ARES

Five Years Ago—Somewhere near Jacksonville, Florida

There are three names on the list.

Two are already crossed off, and I'm about to cross off the third. Metaphorically, of course. Because there is no actual list, just three names tucked away in my brain since I learned them. Three names seared into my memory and tormenting me with every second I draw in a breath.

Two of them are buried in shallow graves, but the third is still breathing. Still going about his day as normal, still staining this earth with his presence, not knowing he is about to die.

I find him in the bar he frequents most weekends. It's a dive bar off one of the backroads near the county line, dimly lit and smoky with a tired country song playing on the jukebox. He sits at the bar, nursing one of many beers, a cigarette burning between his yellowing fingers. The years haven't been kind to him. In fact, it looks like they've run him down and backed over his unshaven face *repeatedly*.

I slide onto a stool next to him. Not too close but close enough to strike up a conversation when the time is right.

He glances my way, then takes an appreciative look, his eyes lingering over my long hair and muscles. He likes what he sees because he doesn't take his eyes off me as he lifts his cigarette to his mouth and takes a deep drag.

"Ain't seen you 'round here before," he says, that familiar voice striking a match to my hatred and igniting a fresh wave of fury inside me. Not that he would notice—hiding my emotions is my fucking superpower.

"Just passing through," I say.

Behind the bar, a blonde in denim shorts and a tight shirt with the name *Cheri* embroidered above her ample left breast takes my drinks order. She doesn't like the man sitting next to me. In fact, she despises him. Her body language and looks of disdain are dead giveaways. She can't hide her disgust, and it makes me wonder what he's done to her. Reading people's silent cues is another superpower and probably one of the reasons I survived prison for nine years.

"You in town on business…" His eyes slide down my body. "Or pleasure?"

It's time to bite back the revulsion and play the role.

"I'm here on business, but I'm open to some pleasure. You got something in mind?"

My boldness surprises him, and he chuckles. "Well, that all depends on what takes your fancy? If you like a little blow or little special K…"

"I don't do drugs."

"Hmm… then what kind of fun are you looking for?"

"I'm not opposed to some company." My eyes find his. "Of a particular kind… if you catch my drift."

Cheri brings me my beer, but I don't touch it because DNA is powerful evidence. And if anyone knows, it's me. I also don't pay with a card. Instead, I slide a few bills across the bar.

When Cheri notices my gloved fingers, she lifts her heavily lashed eyes to meet mine, questioning why I'm wearing gloves in this heat.

"Keep the change," I say.

With a tug of a smile on her lips, she turns away to silently put the money in the cash register, then moves away to wipe down tables, leaving my new friend and me alone.

"You got a name?" the man next to me asks.

"Name's Duquette. My first name don't matter."

He slides onto the stool next to mine. "Are you a cop, Mr. Duquette?"

"A cop?" I chuckle. "I fucking hate cops."

He studies my face, and I wait for him to remember me, but his brain has been marinated in alcohol for too long, and there is no recognition in his bloodshot eyes.

But he WILL remember.

He WILL remember everything he did in excruciating detail.

He relaxes.

His defenses are coming down, and it makes him easy prey.

"Well, I think it's your lucky night, Mr. Duquette."

"Oh yeah?"

"You know… for the right kind of money, a guy can have whatever he likes in this town. I can see to that personally."

"Is that so?"

His gaze drifts to my crotch, and he sucks in a shaky breath. His lips are wet and eager, his revolting eyes filled with sexual attraction and heat.

Leaning in, he runs the tip of his finger along my forearm seductively. "See, if you let me suck that anaconda I know you're packing in your jeans, then I'll let you fuck me for free. Normally, I charge thirty-five for a blow job or fifty for some backdoor lovin', but I have a suspicion there is something very impressive behind that zipper, and my curiosity makes me generous."

Despite the bile rising in my gut, I smile. "You think you can handle what I've got to give?"

Lust shimmers across his face. *Hook, line, and sinker.* "Meet me out back in two minutes, and I'll show you."

He leaves first. It's what he always does. I know because I've spent the last few weeks watching him from the shadows, absorbing his patterns and behaviors, and studying his quirks and mannerisms because that's what I do before I take down a mark.

Knowing a man's routine makes it easier to kill him. And I know everything there is to know about this guy. I know he beats his girlfriend when he returns to their trailer near the swamps full of alcohol and stinking of failure. I know he doesn't go anywhere without his flannel shirt and trucker cap fixed firmly over his greasy hair. I know he looks like a redneck and likes to suck cock, and that coming here to hustle every Friday and Saturday night is more enjoyable than he'd ever admit to his beer-swilling buddies down at the pool hall.

I wait the two minutes, then leave by the back door.

By now, he'll be rubbing himself through his jeans as he waits for me by the dumpster.

Stepping into the late night, the heat of the evening mingles with the scent of garbage and piss and the recent rain shower. I know this alleyway. I know there are no cameras or access to it other than the door I just exited from. It makes it a popular location to make some easy cash if you don't mind sucking cock in the shadows or getting fucked-up against the wall. But tonight, the rain has kept people away, and it's empty.

But, of course, I knew that too.

My earlier prediction was correct. My mark is rubbing the rigid outline of his cock through his grubby jeans.

"Oh, you're a beauty, you are," he says as he walks toward me. The asshole has a limp from an old football injury. He keeps rubbing the front of his jeans, and with a wave of nausea, I wonder if it's what he did on that night all those years ago when he raped and murdered my girlfriend.

Did he pleasure himself through his jeans as his friends held her down and did the unimaginable to her?

My hands fist at my sides, and I have to contain the rage and not let my emotion get the better of me. When you kill people for a living, you can't be a slave to your emotions. I want to rip this guy's head off and spit down his neck, but that kind of thinking leaves you open to mistakes.

No, I stick to the plan, knowing it's going to bring me immense satisfaction in the end.

"You're a big guy," he says, looking up at me. Desire rages in his expression, and he licks his lips. "You want to show me what you got hiding in those Levi's?"

"Sure." I start to unzip my jeans, and he shifts excitedly on his feet, salivating as he drops to his knees.

"Fuck, I need to taste you," he says. "I'm going to suck you like a goddamn lollipop."

He slides his palms down my legs and licks his lips again. He's eager, right up to the moment when my knee collides with his jaw and sends him flying backward, falling onto the wet concrete.

Stunned, he looks up at me. "What the hell?"

I rezip my jeans as he rubs his jaw.

"What the *fuck* is your problem?" he yells.

I haul him to his feet by his collar so his face is up real close to mine. I can almost see his mind racing. His eyes dart about, his lips quivering in fear and confusion.

Not so tough without your buddies now, are you?

"You want to know what my problem is? It's you, you pathetic piece of shit." I let him go. He must still be dazed, or he'd be going for the piece he keeps in his jeans. "We're going to play a game.

It's called... Let's Walk Down Memory Lane."

Blood drips from the corner of his mouth, and he wipes it with the back of his hand, his mind still frantically trying to make sense of the situation. "It's called fucking what? Who the hell are you, man?"

I step closer, and he has to look up because I tower over him.

"Take a good look and think about it," I growl through gritted teeth.

It takes him a moment before the recognition slowly seeps in, and he remembers. His pupils dilate with fear. It's the instant he realizes this isn't going to end well for him.

Now, he'll do one of two things.

He'll go on the defense and think he'll be able to talk me out of what he knows is coming next.

The first name on the list did that—tried to tell me it was a bit of teenage fun, harmless and juvenile. *Until it wasn't*. He shut up when I wrapped my hands around his throat and squeezed the life out of him.

The second option will be to go on the offense and do something stupid like grab for the pistol in the waistband of his jeans. Which is exactly what he does, but my instincts are faster and my body a hell of a lot stronger. I have him disarmed and pinned to the wall with his throat crushed beneath my forearm before he has a chance to think *I'm fucked*.

He knows he's about to die.

But I want to draw it out a little longer.

I want those wide, terror-drenched eyes to beg for mercy a little longer.

I want him to know what real fear feels like right before his heart stops beating.

I want him to know why he's going to hell and why I am sending him there.

With my free arm, I remove Belle's picture from my back

pocket and shove it in his face.

He tries to look away, which only infuriates me more, and I press my forearm deeper against his throat so he will look. He doesn't get to look away from her. He never showed her any respect the night he raped and murdered her. But he will fucking show it to her now.

He's terrified, but even in death, his depravity gets the better of him. A darkness known only by the truly depraved enters his eyes. "Oh yeah, *her*... that ripe piece of pussy in Jacksonville."

Rage flies through me. I shove Belle's picture back into my pocket and slide my knife from the sheath on my hip.

It was his semen found inside Belle.

It was his semen found in her mouth.

Not that the court ever heard about it.

"You will *not* disrespect her again. Do you *fucking understand me*?" I push harder on his throat and slide the blade of my knife down his cheek. "Now before I lose my patience, I want to hear you say that you're sorry."

His eyes widen with fear. "W-what?"

"Don't make me tell you twice, motherfucker. I want to hear you say, I am sorry for raping and killing that innocent seventeen-year-old girl back in Jacksonville all those years ago."

"I'm sorry, I'm sorry," he cries.

Of course, he's not sorry for what he did. The only thing he's sorry about is me knowing it was him and his two buddies who stumbled across Belle and me shortly after we'd left the abandoned theater.

How I know... they hit me from behind with an iron bar, knocking me out instantly.

That I know... every graphic detail of what they did to her as I lay unconscious on the roadside, useless and out cold.

That it was him who snapped her neck after they'd had their fun.

I dig the tip of the blade into his cheek, drawing first blood, and he winces.

"I said I was sorry," he blubbers. "What... what do you w-want from m-me?"

"I want you to *beg*," I growl. "Just like she would've begged for her life when you were violating her."

His eyes cloud with panic. "Let me go, and I'll make it worth your while. I've got money. Back at the trailer. It's yours, all yours. Just don't fucking kill me."

"Go on."

"I can get you whatever you need. You name it. My name means something around here." *It doesn't.* "You want grade-A pussy or cock? Money? Blow? Tell me. I'll get you anything you want."

"Anything?"

"Yes. Anything. Just, please don't kill me."

I ease my hold on him a little. "Fine. I want you to say *I am a raping son of bitch, and I deserve to go to hell for what I did.*"

"W-what?"

I grit my teeth. "Say it."

"Okay... okay... I'm a raping son of a bitch, and I deserve to go to hell for what I did."

"Again."

"W-what?"

"Say it again, asshole." I drag my knife down his cheek.

"I'm a raping son of a bitch, and I deserve to go to hell for what I did." He's shaking. "There, I said it. I did what you asked, man."

"I haven't finished. Now, I want you to *beg* for your life."

"Please don't kill me. I'm sorry. I am. I was just a kid, man. We didn't know any better."

I sigh. "You're not very good at the whole begging thing, are you? I want tears, loser. I want to see you ugly cry." I dig the blade into his cheek, nothing deep, just enough to draw blood and cause pain. "I want to hear you beg."

He starts to sob. And ugly cry. *And I mean real ugly.*

But I get bored.

"Yeah, I'm just toying with you, asshole. No amount of begging is going to save you. I just wanted to make you beg for life a little while."

"What the fuck is wrong with you? You got fucking problems, man."

"Not from where I'm standing. I'm not the one with the knife to my throat, asshole."

I've been doing this a long time and what I've learned is that there is this one moment when the mark realizes he's totally fucked, so he might as well go out with a bang. He'll challenge your manhood, your toughness, your prowess, or he'll sink low and defame your mom, or your sister, or your loved one. It's one last insult for the road. Not all marks do it, but it's surprising how many do.

This human stain is one of those.

He knows he's leaving for Hell any minute and figures he might as well end his time on earth with some good old-fashioned torment.

His body relaxes, and a defiant gleam enters his eyes as they lock onto mine. "You know what? Yeah, I remember that night. And I remember her. I remember her *real* well. That tight little pussy. Her hot little mouth wrapped around my—" His eyes bulge as my knife enters his chest. The wound isn't enough kill him, not right away, but it's enough to hurt like a motherfucker.

"Her name was Belle, and she was eighteen years old. She was my girlfriend. She was sweet, gentle, and an angel who never got to enjoy her life because of you and your buddies. She was kind and loving—"

He bares his yellow-stained teeth. "And she loved every second of it."

Another strike of my blade pierces his insides, and he winces. I put the blood-soaked blade to his throat. "I'll see you in Hell, asshole."

My blade slides across his neck, and the rise of blood is quick. I don't move. Instead, I keep looking into his eyes until they go vacant and savor the moment I see him leave his body.

Satisfied he's dead, I let him go, and he slumps to the ground in a heap.

The truck I stole from an alligator farm up the road is parked a few yards away, cloaked in darkness. I drag the lifeless body—of the third man who raped and murdered my girlfriend and left me to do the time in prison for her death—over to it and dump him in the back. Within the hour, the truck with his body inside disappears into the murky swamp waters. Chances are he'll never be found. If the alligators don't get him, time will. His skin will slowly slough away, and his muscle tissue and tendons will disappear with the tide, leaving only the bones behind. If by chance they are ever discovered, there won't be any stab marks to indicate the cause of death—I've been doing this too long to ever leave a story behind. They'll assume he stole the truck, drove home drunk, and took a wrong turn.

I leave on foot and another summer shower covers my footprints, almost as if Belle is smiling down on me for a job well done.

The three names on my list are now crossed off, and I can go back to my day job.

I fly back to Boston immediately.

I am the Angel of Death for the De Kysa family, one of Boston's biggest crime syndicates. They pay me handsomely to rid this earth of their enemies. I kill men for them—bad men—men who have done the despicable and the deviant. But there is no emotion behind their deaths. Their lives are wiped out by a single bullet paid for by my employer, and I think nothing more of it.

Unlike tonight.

Because tonight was very, very personal.

And I enjoyed every second, every morsel of his death.

Like I've said before...

... I was born a monster.

Leaving the airport, I step onto the busy Boston street and hail a cab.

When I left prison, I didn't plan on killing men for a living.

And somewhere beneath the layers of grief, heartache, and the disdain for men who thrive on depravity, I know it's wrong to kill even if I am killing a villain.

But the thing is, I fucking like it.

CHAPTER 2

ARES
Present Day—Flintlock, Tennessee

The moment the set of knuckles connect with my face, I feel my eyebrow split open, but I don't let the pain register. Instead, I take out my opponent with a powerful right hook, followed by a jaw-breaking left upper cut. He drops to the floor in a bloody, crumpled heap, instantly knocked out cold. The referee raises my arm in victory, and the crowd gathered at Oscar's Gym roars with pleasure. Some of them have just made a lot of money.

My opponent, Sven 'Scorpion' Slott, has never been beaten. I was the underdog, despite my size and strength and the fact I have never been beaten. But Scorpion has more fights behind him and is freakishly fast on his feet, making him a favorite with the crowd.

Once a week, I come here and toy with my opponent before sending him to sleep with my fist. It earns me five hundred dollars per fight, seven hundred and fifty if I knock him out. It's not going to make me rich, but it fucking makes me feel good.

Coated in sweat and with blood dripping down my face, I

leave the ring, and immediately two girls step in front of me. They're blonde and cute, their full lips pink and glossy, their eyes sparkling with interest and maybe a bit too much alcohol. Despite the sweat and blood, they attach themselves to me, one sliding her hand up my chest, the other licking her lips as she curls her arm around my bicep. They're circuit groupies—women who follow the underground fighters from fight to fight, hoping to warm their beds for the night. They make their interest crystal clear, but I'm not interested in what they're offering. Just like I don't indulge in the club girls back at the Kings of Mayhem clubhouse, I don't touch circuit groupies. If I need to satisfy an itch, I scratch it at The House of Sin just out of town because no strings are how I like to roll.

"You were amazing out there, Ares," says the girl wrapped around my bicep.

"So big and strong," says the one running her hand up my chest. "I love a man who's hot and sweaty." She presses her body tighter to mine. "If you come with us, I can show you just how much."

She bats her long eyelashes. She's pretty, cute, and a college girl.

But it's not going to happen.

I won't mess with fans, and I'm not in the market for a girlfriend. Sex is a complication I don't need right now.

"Sorry, ladies, I've gotta hit the showers."

"We can come with you," bicep girl says eagerly. "We can wash your back and anything else that pops up."

She digs her teeth into her lower lip, and out of nowhere, I'm tempted. She's gorgeous and sexy and after a fight—especially one that's inflicted a little pain on me—I'm turned on. I'd planned on taking care of my arousal in the shower, *alone*, but maybe a little assistance could be enjoyable.

But then I think about King Pin.

We used to fight together in the underground circuit. He was a champion who liked to indulge in the circuit girls. *Lots of them.* Unfortunately, one of them became obsessed with him after a one-night stand, and when he didn't return her interest, she shot him dead a few months later.

Just another reason I avoid female company.

It's too unpredictable.

My right hand isn't.

"That's a real sweet offer, but not tonight," I say with a wink.

"Maybe we could come and see you at the clubhouse," the other girl suggests. "Keep you company for the night?"

Okay, that makes me pause.

How do they know I belong to a motorcycle club?

I keep my private life separate from my underground fighting. I don't tell anyone I'm a King. But these girls have clearly done their homework, and that's a red flag.

I untangle myself from them both. "Maybe another time."

Not hanging around to hear their protests, I make my way through the bar toward the locker rooms where the fighters can shower and change.

Inside, Doc, Jack, and Paw are waiting for me.

"Scorpion got you good," Paw says when he sees the blood on my face. He grins happily. "You losing your touch, big fella?"

Paw likes to tease.

"A bit of pain is half the fun," I reply, crossing the locker room to where the benches line the wall.

I sit, and Doc takes a look at my eyebrow.

"Yeah, well, that fun is gonna get you four stitches," he tells me.

"Do your worst," I reply.

When he opens his medical bag and tries to stick a local anesthetic into the area surrounding the wound, I stop him. "No drugs," I remind.

Doc shakes his head. "You know this is going to hurt like a motherfucker."

"I said… no drugs."

Truth is, I like the pain. Call me a psycho, call me what you will, but I am what I am, and I like a little physical pain.

Across the room, neither Jack nor Paw are surprised.

"Crazy sonofabitch," Jack mutters with a shake of his head.

Jack is President of the Kings of Mayhem Motorcycle Club, Tennessee Chapter.

Four years ago, he found me at The House of Sin during one of my benders. I was high and drunk on just about everything, and by the time Jack roared in on his Harley, I had been through one girl after the other, sometimes two or three in a night.

But Antoinette, the owner of the House of Sin, was getting worried about my lack of interest in leaving and was worried I might become a problem. She asked Jack to swing by the brothel to show me who I would be dealing with if I started any trouble. Not that she had anything to worry about. I was only there to blow off some steam and work out my next move. Since leaving the De Kysa, I had no direction, no place to be. I didn't belong anywhere. To cope, I indulged in a lot of fucking, drinking, and doing blow.

But I was never a threat to them.

When Jack was there, a wild storm hit, and we were all trapped for two days, which if I'm real honest, there are worse places to be stuck than a brothel with a lot of beautiful women during bad weather.

Jack and I bonded over a chess board as lightning lit up the room and thunder rumbled in the sky, and the next day he invited me to join the Kings of Mayhem.

Figuring I had nothing else, I bought myself a Harley, threw the bag containing all of my belongings over my shoulder, and joined the club.

Now, they're my family.

"Never met anyone with such a hard-on for pain," Paw says. "Not sure if I should high-five you or call a psychiatrist."

And Paw, I guess you can call him my best friend—he's a smart motherfucker. He jokes that I'm the brawn and he's the brains in our friendship, but he's right. His real name is Malcolm, but we call him Paw because of the deep claw marks on the side of his face. In his previous life, he used to be in the FBI. One day he was attacked by a mountain lion when he was on a case, which left him badly scarred. If the scars bother him, he doesn't let it show. Now he takes care of our club's security and all the technology we use daily. He still has contacts in the FBI which has gotten our balls out of the frying pan more than once.

"Some people have a higher threshold to pain than others," Doc says, sewing my eyebrow back together.

"While some just like it," I declare.

Paw pulls a face. "You mean that needle ain't making your insides roll? Because just watching it is making me queasy as hell."

They think I don't feel because I'm quiet and silent, and barely react to things that most men would look away from.

But they're wrong.

I feel fucking everything.

"Who's coming over to Aces?" Paw asks.

After every fight, we head across the road to a bar called Aces High.

It's owned by Oscar, who runs the underground fights at his gym. He'll slide an envelope of cash across the table and buy us a drink. Afterward, my brothers and I will shoot some pool, then we'll head back to the clubhouse, where I'll retreat to my room alone, jerk off to drain any residual energy coursing through my veins, and start praying that insomnia doesn't set in.

"I have to sit this one out," Jack says.

His wife is heavily pregnant with their second baby, and he wants to spend more time at home.

"How is Bronte?" Paw asks.

"You know, she takes everything in her stride. It's Friday night, so she's expecting popcorn and foot rubs. But I want to check in on Gabe before I head home."

Gabe is back from Las Vegas. After three months of marriage to a showgirl he married within two days of meeting, he walked in on her and a male dancer going at it in their bed. After a lot of screaming, she told him it was over. She had made a mistake, she said. She wanted a divorce.

Heartbroken, he came home to Tennessee and the club and has been finding solace in one whisky bottle after another.

"Well, I'm feeling lucky tonight," Paw says, shoving his phone into his back pocket. "I'm going to have a drink, shoot some pool, and hopefully meet the future ex-Mrs. Paw. What about you, Ares?" He pats my shoulder.

"I don't need a distraction. Not until after the fight with Punisher."

"You need to lighten up and indulge in some relaxation time." Paw shoots a raised eyebrow at me and says, "You're allowed to get close to a woman, you know. They don't bite. Well, if you're lucky, they might. Might even let you spank them a bit. Hell, if you're real lucky, they'll want to spank you back. But my point is, you need to at least get close to one first. It'd be even better if they were naked."

I frown at him.

Jack leans in. "In other words, do yourself a favor and go get laid."

CHAPTER 3

RORY

I wait patiently for him to arrive.
Alone in a booth, nursing a vodka and soda, my nails tap the side of the glass in time to Quarterflash singing "Harden My Heart" bleeding through the sound system.

The bar is filling with people who watched the fight across the road at Oscar's Gym. The booth beside me is full of women on a bachelorette night, and they're getting nice and toasted. The bride-to-be is dressed in a tight, white dress and heels with a sash draped across her and a veil covered with cheap plastic beads. She's drunk as fuck on sparkling wine and keeps banging the table with her palm every time her girlfriends make her laugh.

I glance past her toward the doorway, waiting to see the familiar big frame fill the space, but he still isn't here, and I'm beginning to worry he might not come tonight.

Be calm. He always comes after his fights.

I clear my throat and think about my game plan.

But my concentration is interrupted by the ladies in the booth beside me.

The bride-to-be, who I now know is called Leah, has had too much wine and starts to cry because the idea of spending the rest of her life with Brad scares her, and she really wants to have sex with Luke from the gas station, and if she's really honest, she hasn't gotten over Travis, the hot quarterback in high school who took her virginity and then dumped her for the cheer captain.

When one of her friends—a sweet girl with a short black pixie cut—tries to console her, Leah snaps at her and questions why she should listen to her when she's never even been on a date.

Breathe, bridezilla. Breathe.

There's more sobbing as her girlfriends all rally around her before she dramatically disappears to the bathroom with the pixie-cut girl in tow.

That's when *he* walks in, and it's like all the air leaves the room.

Every head turns as the six-foot-something of pure muscle and testosterone follows his friends across the room and makes his way to the bar. I look away and turn my attention back to my drink.

The women in the booth beside me start to giggle, one of them declaring what she'd like to spend the night doing to him, another wondering if he's as big in his boxer shorts as he is everywhere else. The third mentions she heard a rumor that he has eleven inches behind his zipper, to which all her friends sigh dreamily.

I can't help myself. I steal another look at him. His hair is long and dark and falls past his wide shoulders in wild, messy waves. The shadow of at least two-days growth creeps along his sharp jaw, and his lips are impossibly full. But it's his eyes that are the showstoppers. They're dark and heavily fringed with long, dark lashes, and their beauty softens the sharp edges of his good looks. He might be an almighty god in the ring, but his eyes suggest he is more than that.

Not that I care about that, but it's hard not to notice them.

Someone as hot as him probably knows it.

Which is a total turn-off.

But as I steal glances at him, I don't see any arrogance in the way he moves or acts. He's not cocky and self-assured but quiet as if he would rather be a part of the shadows than somewhere in the light.

His name is Ares, and I know this because I know everything about him. I know who he is and what he's done. I know he belongs to a motorcycle club and fights once a week at the gym down the road, followed by a few drinks at this bar afterward.

I also know he has killed people... which is why I am here.

The music changes to another old favorite. Pat Benatar's "Heartbreaker."

Which is kind of fitting.

I look up from my vodka and soda to take in his broad back and thick arms, my gaze drifting down his thick, muscular body.

He is so much man I feel my body tingle in places that haven't tingled in a long time.

Apparently, it's a feeling shared by the women in the booth beside me.

"Jesus, my ovaries are crying," says the brunette, who I've since learned is called Janey.

"My pussy is wet just looking at him," says a blonde they call Vivian and who I will now refer to as TMI Vivian.

"God, I want to eat him with a spoon," Janey says creepily.

"I want to lick every inch of that golden skin and then ride him like a pony," says the redhead, whose name I haven't learned yet.

"Back off, ladies, I saw him first," TMI Vivian warns.

"It's every woman for herself," Janey says, quickly finishing her drink and standing.

"Don't you dare!" TMI Vivian protests, standing just as quickly.

Not to be left out, the redhead stands too. "Hey, I'm interested in him as well."

And before I can say *these women are going to cause a spectacle*, all three start arguing over the top of each other, drawing attention from everyone around us. Even Pat Benatar can't compete with them.

"Fine!" TMI Vivian finally snaps, narrowing her eyes at her friends. "Paper-Rock-Scissors?"

I lift an eyebrow. Are they really going to *rock off* to see who can approach him?

After a minor pause, the two other women nod, and TMI Vivian counts them down—*three, two, one.*

"That's not fair!" TMI Vivian cries when Janey's *paper* beats her and the redhead's *rocks*.

"That's the rules," Janey reminds her friend smugly, already digging into her purse for some lip gloss. After applying a thick layer, she lets out an excited giggle. "Don't wait up for me, ladies."

I turn back to my drink. It's empty of alcohol, but I suck water from the ice through my straw to get the distaste out of my mouth.

I glance over at Janey, who is making her way across the bar toward Ares. She's tittering on high heels and trying to pull down her incredibly short dress as she makes a beeline for her target.

"She's such a bitch," the redhead complains, shoving her arms across her chest and slumping back in her seat.

"Don't worry," TMI Vivian says. "He's way out of her league. There's no way he's going to go for her. What is she even wearing?"

Turns out TMI Vivian is a mean girl.

The redhead laughs as she holds her fingers up to her ear like a phone. "Hello, Janey, this is the nineties calling, and we want our hair back."

Correction, both of them are mean girls.

"And our shoes," TMI Vivian adds.

They both roar with laughter.

I tell myself not to watch because I know it's going to be a train wreck. For weeks I've watched women approach him, and not once has he ever shown any interest. It intrigues me because this guy could have any woman he wanted, and he chooses none of them.

He doesn't have a girlfriend.

Yeah, I know that about him too.

And when he's here, he likes to keep to himself, even when he's with his friends. They usually sit quietly at the bar or shoot some pool.

When Janey reaches him, she goes for it. She launches into some serious hair flicking, lip licking, and flirty looks. But as suspected, Ares isn't interested, and he turns her down. Obviously not one to admit defeat, Jane keeps going for it, even running a long nail up his thick forearm until Ares eventually tells it to her straight. Her face drops, and I feel her friends' smugness seep over the top of their booth into mine.

I feel sorry for Janey.

Her friends are mean.

I don't watch her walk of defeat back to them. Instead, I open my purse and pull out a photograph. In the picture, two little kids are standing in ankle-deep water at the beach. The little boy is holding the little girl's hand, their backs to the camera. A surge of sadness rolls through me, and I swipe my thumb over the image before returning it to my handbag.

Feeling a new wave of determination, I leave the booth and make my way across the bar to Ares.

CHAPTER 4

ARES

The first time I notice her, she's sitting alone in the booth next to the bachelorette party. Long blonde hair. Big doe-eyes. Flawless throat. Lips that deserve to be kissed nonstop. She doesn't look my way when I walk past, which is good because I have a feeling if our eyes meet, something would ignite inside me, and I don't need the temptation.

The second time I see her, I've gotten rid of the annoying brunette who couldn't keep her hands to herself or get the message that I wasn't interested. She has just left when I look up from my bourbon to see the beauty walking toward me, and I'm unable to look away because this woman is something else—blue jeans, boots to her knees, and a tight tank that shows off her polished shoulders and the deep tan of her skin.

And I'm not the only one who notices her.

Beside me, Paw blows out an appreciative whistle before moving off to play pool.

At first, I think she's going to walk right past me. But as she gets a few feet away, her gaze finds mine and a small smile plays at the corner of her mouth. I immediately know she is heading my way, which makes me a lot happier than it should.

She stops next to me at the bar.

"Hey," she says.

But I only offer her a polite nod.

I don't want to engage.

I shouldn't engage.

But…

"I saw the fight. That's some mean upper cut you have," she continues. When she talks, I'm drawn to the two dimples pressed into her cheeks.

"You know your upper cut from your right hook," I say.

"And my jab from my cross."

"I'm impressed."

My gaze drops to her mouth. I was right. This girl has lips that should be kissed all night long.

"My uncle owned a gym, and when I was a kid, he let me hang out there." She shrugs. "I watched and listened and eventually learned."

Her accent is pure Boston. I lived there long enough to know the distinctive dialect when I hear it.

"Did you get in the ring?" I ask.

"When I was younger. But not professionally or anything. My uncle used to have me spar with some of his younger professional fighters."

I do a subtle sweep of her body. She's fit and strong, and even with her small frame, she looks like she could take care of herself.

She catches me checking her out and looks at me through heavy lashes, and something takes off inside me.

Just because I won't indulge in one-night stands doesn't mean I don't notice women. And I'm noticing everything about this woman. And I'm trying to ignore it but failing. I'm not ready to end our conversation. When she orders a drink, I signal to the guy behind the bar that it's on me.

"Thanks," she says, offering me a dazzling smile.

Christ, what I could do to that mouth.

"Your uncle's gym, was that in Boston?" I ask, dragging my bourbon to my lips and taking a mouthful.

Surprise shimmers on her face.

"It's your accent. I used to live there," I explain.

Her smile is beautiful.

"Geez... kickass in the cage *and* smart," she says.

It's cheesy, and because we both know it, we laugh and the ice starts cracking. She accepts her drink from the bartender and takes the stool beside me.

She offers me her hand. "My name is Rory, by the way. Rory Jones."

"Ares."

"I know." Her smile is beautiful, her grip hard as we shake.

I glance over at Paw showing a brunette in a Ramones T-shirt how to line up a shot. He's got her bent over the table as he guides the pool cue through her fingers. When she sinks the ball, she turns around and crushes her red lips to his.

When I turn back, I ask, "So what are you doing here tonight, Rory?"

"I've come to see you."

"Me?"

"I've been watching your fights. I wanted to meet you."

"You have? Why?"

She tilts her head, exposing her throat. It's flawless and creamy, and I can't help but picture my teeth grazing along the soft flesh.

"You intrigue me." She glances over to the bachelorette table, then back. "But then, I guess I'm not the only one."

She's forward—I like it.

"You saw that, huh?"

"Saw it. Heard the plan. But I knew you wouldn't go for it."

"How so?"

"You never do."

The fact she's obviously been watching me for a while should make me shut this down. But I'm too distracted by the way she bites into her cushiony lips to worry.

Both me and my dick.

Paw interrupts and leans over my shoulder. "I'm heading back to the clubhouse. Don't forget to pick up tonight's check from Oscar on the way out."

Behind him, the girl in the Ramones T-shirt is licking her lips as she checks out his ass.

"I'll catch you later," I say to him.

"I won't wait up." His eyes bounce between Rory and me, then he leans down and whispers, "Remember, if she wants to spank you, let her." Straightening, he gives me a wink and walks out with his new friend.

When I look back at Rory, her big blue eyes are watching me as if she's trying to figure something out. Then her lips go over the straw in her drink, and a new wave of heat hits me.

"Listen, there's something I want to talk to you about," she says as she finishes her drink and puts the glass on the bar. "I have an offer."

My eyebrow goes up. "What kind of offer."

"Maybe we could go somewhere a little more private to talk?"

Christ, I'm so tempted.

I picture dragging my tongue along the smooth contours of her throat, and my cock busts against my zipper.

"I need help with something, and I have a feeling you're the man for the task."

Our eyes lock.

"Is that so?"

"Yeah, but it's dirty work," she rasps.

I want to look away but I can't.

"Dirty is good," I say roughly.

The ways she bites into her lip is tantalizing.

"I think you'll find it *very* satisfying," she whispers.

I fight back a groan because I'm one more lip bite away from crashing my lips to hers. "I can imagine I would."

I want nothing more than to take her back to my room in the clubhouse and spend the night making her scream my name.

Fuck, just thinking about her stretched out on my bed all naked and creamy is doing shit to me.

But I come to my senses and decide to shut it down before things go too far.

I clear my throat. "Listen, you're sweet, and I'd be lying if I said I'm not tempted, but this isn't going to happen."

For a moment, she looks confused, then her eyebrow shoots up. "Whoa, there, cowboy. You're getting ahead of yourself." She puts her hands up and takes a step back. "No need to turn down what I'm not even offering."

Now, I'm confused.

She gives me a pointed look. "I'm not asking you to sleep with me, *Prince Charming*, I'm asking you to kill my stepfather."

I don't react to what she says.

Instead, I remain calm despite my head scrambling to make sense of what she's just said.

Does she know about my past?

I take a look at her—a good look this time.

No. She doesn't know who I am and what I used to do for a living.

But she comes from Boston.

"And why the fuck would you ask me to do something like that?" I ask calmly.

"I've seen you fight... I know a man who's killed before."

While she's talking, my mind is scrambling, pulling back the layers of memory to see if she is in there somewhere.

Did I know her when I was working with the De Kysa family in Boston?

"And how would you know something like that?" I question.

"Because of the man I want you to make unalive. He killed my mom and tried to hurt me."

"You came all the way from Boston to ask me to kill your stepdad?"

"No, I came all the way from Boston to get away from him." She points between us. "This is pure chance. A couple of friends of mine from the bar where I work went to one of your fights a few weeks ago. I've been to every one of your fights ever since."

A kick rattles in my heart knowing she's been watching me each week. I like the idea of those almond-shaped eyes focused on me.

Which is dangerous.

For both of us.

"Listen, sweetheart, you're barking up the wrong tree. I'm not a hired gun."

"You're in a motorcycle gang, aren't you?"

"Meaning what? And for the record, it's a *club* not a gang."

"Meaning, I thought this would be something you could help me with. I've heard about the Kings of Mayhem. You help people out in this town when they need it. Well, I'm one of those people."

I stare at her a moment longer. She really is beautiful, but all I can see is trouble.

"Sorry." I drain my glass and stand. "I'm not the guy you're looking for."

She looks away and bites into her lip, and heaven help me because it's distractingly sexy, and I'm seconds away from throwing her over my shoulder and taking her back to the clubhouse with me.

"Why do you want your stepdaddy dead, anyway?" I ask and immediately regret it. I should be walking out the door, not engaging with her. But she's got my attention, and for reasons beyond my understanding, I'm finding it hard to walk away.

"Because he hurt me."

Her words send a sharp sting into my very core.

She doesn't need to explain any further. The pain in her voice tells me what he did to her. But as much as the thought of any man hurting a woman in that way sends a wave of red-hot anger through me, I can't be drawn in by it. Because those days are behind me, and when I left Boston, I swore they were behind me for good. So I'm not the guy she's looking for.

"I'm sorry," I say.

"I don't want you to be sorry, I want you to help me."

She's trying to cover her pain with her fierce expression and ballsy body language, but she can't hide it from her vibrant eyes. The blue fire in them burns bright.

But I have to walk away—I *need* to walk away.

"It's been a real pleasure meeting you, Rory," I say softly. "But I can't help you."

Her face is tight, and I can read the rejection in her expression. But she doesn't try to sway me. I have a feeling this girl would set fire to herself before she begged anyone for anything.

With a simple nod, she slides off her stool. "Thanks for the drink."

I watch her walk away before I settle the bill and collect tonight's earnings from Oscar.

Outside, light rain is falling.

From the corner of my eye, I see Rory crouched by her car, attempting to change her tire. She's trying to get the nut off, but her hand keeps slipping off because of the rain.

Keep walking, my instincts say.

Just. Keep. Walking

But that's not who I am.

Despite being someone who puts bullets into men's skulls, I also happen to be a gentleman, and it just happens that helping a woman in distress is hardwired into my DNA.

I walk over to her. "Need help?"

She doesn't bother to look up, and it's obvious she's pissed at me. "Nope."

Again, her hand slips when the stubborn tire nut refuses to budge.

"That's one way to break a wrist," I say.

Which she ignores.

Yep, she's pissed at me.

It starts to rain harder, and within seconds, she looks like a drowned rat, but she keeps battling with the nut.

"Look, let me help you."

"Oh, so *now* you want to help me?"

"If you'd stop being a stubborn ass and let me, yes."

She straightens and glares at me. *She really is cute.* "Oh, that's rich, now *I'm* the stubborn ass." She goes back to battling with the tire nut, and again, it slips. Any second and she's going to bruise or break something.

With a growl, I hoist her up into my arms, and before she can start kicking and screaming, I plonk her onto the hood of her car.

"What the hell do you think you're doing?" she yells.

"Saving you from your own stubborn ass."

"My stubborn…" She slides off the hood and thrusts her hands to her hips. "For your information, *Thor*, I don't need saving."

"Kind of looked like you did. And the name is Ares." I flick the nut off and rise to my feet. "But both were Gods, so I can see where you'd make the mistake."

Her eyebrow lifts, and she folds her arms. "Arrogant and stubborn, how lucky can a girl get?"

"Listen, sweetheart—"

"Rory, my name is Rory."

"Listen, *Rory*, this can go one of two ways. We can stand here arguing in the rain all night, or you can say *thank you kind stranger for helping me out* and let me get the fuck on with it. Either way, I'm changing this goddamn tire."

She finally sees reason and backs down. "By all means, knock yourself out." She folds her arms. "And by that, I mean literally."

Her glare is adorable.

"Stubborn *and* hilarious," I mutter as I crouch beside the car.

In minutes, I have the tire replaced and the flat stored in the trunk.

We're both soaked now.

"Thank you," she says.

I mock gasp. "I'm sorry, what did you say?"

She rolls her eyes. "Now who's hilarious?"

Suddenly conscious of her wet tank top and how it clings to her firm breasts and taut nipples, she folds her arms across her chest..

But it's too late. I've already noticed.

"Just so you know, I'm still not asking you to sleep with me," she says.

"Good, because I'm still not interested."

A smile tugs at her lips.

And surprisingly, one tugs at mine.

Her smile turns into a grin. "But I am grateful, thank you."

"Pleased to be at your service."

She opens the car door but pauses. "Want to grab a coffee? It's the least I can do to say thank you."

I think about it for a second or two. I want to but I shake my head. "Maybe next time."

She doesn't seem upset—just smiles and climbs in. "See you around, Thor."

And closing the door, she drives out of the parking lot and disappears into the rainy night.

CHAPTER 5

ARES

"They are the hairiest, fattest fucking buds I've ever laid eyes on."

Gambit holds up the cannabis buds to the light.

We're in Church, and all twenty-two Kings are staring at the samples Jack has had brought over from the cannabis crops.

"And sticky," Venom adds.

Dakota Joe holds a big purple bud up to his nose. "That's some potent shit. The smell alone is like a kick in the face. How much are we looking at?"

"Street value of just over one million," Jack says.

"I think this is cause for celebration, boys," Merrick declares with a grin. He's always ready to party, and our harvest parties are legendary.

Hands bang on the table in agreement.

"Let's not get ahead of ourselves. Before we party, we pick." Jack looks around the long table at all the faces seated there. "The crop is ready for harvest tomorrow. It's all-hands-on-deck. You all know what you got to do and where you gotta be."

We don't harvest the crop ourselves, but we all have our responsibility. Jack runs a tight ship. You want to eat, you have to help stir the pot.

This season is set to be our biggest yet, and the Soulless Sons are in place to handle the distribution." The Soulless is a smaller club based in Cooperville. I wouldn't call us friends, but we're not rivals anymore, either. They have a good distribution line, so Jack struck a deal with their president, a hardhead called Zed. We supply the merchandise, and they distribute for a certain percentage. It means we don't have to fuck about with dealers and all the other people who come out of the woodwork when you have A-grade gear to peddle.

It's also good to have some kind of relationship with the Soulless.

"I ain't promising anything yet, but if it's as good as we're predicting, y'all are going to be receiving cash-fat envelopes at the end of the month."

The room fills with whistles.

Alchemy, who runs our more legitimate business, the Kings Pride distillery, gets up and picks a bottle off the shelves across the room. He pours us all a shot.

Jack raises his glass. "To a fucking profitable crop harvest."

A hum of agreement rumbles around the table as all the Kings throw back their shot of Kings Pride moonshine.

It's a face melter.

Even I react to the burn as it sears a path down my throat and into my chest.

"Before I call time on Church, there's one last matter to attend to. Lacey from the Spicy Crawdad said three thugs paid her a visit and said if she didn't start making weekly payments, quote, *bad things could happen to the club and the people who run it,* end quote."

The Spicy Crawdad is a strip club the Kings own in town. It's open twenty-four-seven and is the most popular club in town. Lacey is the feisty manager. As tough as an old leather boot up the ass, she isn't easily rattled. She's more likely to blow holes in you with the 12-gauge she keeps behind the bar than quake in her boots. But when something like this happens, it's protocol to let us know.

"A protection racket?" Shooter asks. "They linked to anyone we know?"

"No, I looked into it this afternoon after Jack got the call," Paw says. "Luka Silvaro is a gutter-feeding amoeba trying to break into the protection game. But he's not connected. He's small time with big dreams. Besides the Crawdad, he's hit seven other businesses nearby."

"Bam and I will take care of it," Loki says with a grin. He's the oldest of Jack's twin sons, and to call him a player is an understatement.

"No fucking way," Bam says.

"Why the fuck not?"

"Because the last time we visited the Crawdad on business, you brought home three girlfriends."

Loki gives him a shit-eating grin. "And your point is?"

The twins are complete opposites. Loki is a long-haired musician who doesn't hide a penchant for hot girls while Bam looks like he stepped out of a college debate championship. Glasses. Short hair. He's more reserved than his outgoing twin brother.

"My point is... if I have to hear you make anyone else scream as you listen to George Michael's "Freeek!" on loop again, I'll burn the goddamn house down."

"Freeek!"?"

"Yeah, the girl with the pink hair insisted you keep playing it. Over and over and over again."

"Oh yeah." Loki's grin grows huge as he remembers. "I forgot about her."

"How? I'm pretty sure she was the one who kept screaming, *do me, daddy, do me.*"

Loki looks smug and lifts his arms. "Well, when you've got it, you've got it."

Bam throws a pack of matches at him.

While the exchange amuses the rest of the bikers in the room, Jack clears his throat. "I could've gone the rest of my life without hearing that," he states, giving his son a pointed look. His eyes shift to me. "I want you to ride out there and let this asshole know what the Kings think about his latest business venture. Pick-up is supposed to be at eight-thirty tonight. You can take Shooter and Dakota Joe."

"I'll go alone," I say.

I need to ride off this restlessness, and the Spicy Crawdad is across town near the state line leading into the Appalachian Trail. I can take my Harley for a ride into Virginia and back after taking care of Luka fucking Silva.

Jack calls time on Church by bringing down the gavel, and we all disperse.

As I leave the clubhouse and ride toward the Spicy Crawdad, my mind slips back to Rory, and those wide, almond-shaped eyes have haunted me ever since.

Common sense tells me I should be concerned that she hit me up to be a hired gun. If I'm honest, there's always a concern my past might catch up with me someday, and when a beautiful girl approaches you in a bar and asks you to kill her stepdaddy for putting his hands on her, well, you have to wonder if she knows more than she is telling you.

But even with all of that in mind, it's those big eyes and full, plush lips that come to mind first.

I arrive at the Spicy Crawdad a little before eight o'clock. Lacey leads me through the club toward her office out back. The club is filling up. Warrant's "Cherry Pie" blasts from the speakers as a girl in a tiny pair of Daisy Dukes and a white tank top dances on stage.

"Like I told Jack, I'm happy to take care of this freeloading piece of shit myself. You know I've got plenty of kin who are only too happy to make a body disappear." Lacey comes from a long line of Appalachian bootleggers. She has family all over the trail who know how to dispose of a body. "But I know I've got to clear it with him first. If he says he'll take care of it, well that's good enough for me."

"Luka Silvaro won't be bothering you once I've finished with him."

She stops walking and looks at me. "Just don't get blood on my carpet."

I walk past her. "I don't make promises I can't keep."

Inside her office, I take a seat behind her desk and wait while Lacey disappears into the storeroom.

With my back to the door, I watch Luka and two of his men enter the room on the surveillance setup Lacey keeps behind her desk.

Luka Silvaro is a two-bit wannabe gangster and a real pain in the ass. He struts in like he's king shit. Gold chains. Tight suit. Shiny shoes. Slicked back comb-over.

He tugs on one of his jacket sleeves. "So, where's my money?"

When the chair turns around and he sees me sitting there instead of Lacey, his face pales. But he quickly recovers. "Who the fuck are you?"

When I rise to my feet and walk around the desk to stand in front of him and his thug sidekicks, his eyes follow my every move. His rat brain is scrambling to work out who I am and what the hell I'm doing there.

"I'm the guy who's come to let you know you've got two minutes to get out of this club and never come back again."

He scoffs, but it's nervous. "Oh, yeah, and why would I do that?"

"Because I'll break every bone in your face if you don't."

He smirks as he looks at his two friends, then back at me. "There's three of us and only one of you."

I tilt my head. "Then you haven't brought enough men."

His smirk drops. He shifts nervously on his feet. "Where's my money?"

"There's no money for you here. Walk away while your balls are still intact."

This loser should recognize I'm doing him a favor. I could've shot him and his thugs the moment he stepped foot in here and then sent the bodies to a hog farm to disappear.

But he doesn't.

Because he's a fucking idiot.

"This isn't going to end well for you, my friend," he drawls.

"I guess that depends."

"On what?"

"How quick you are."

One of his goons, an ugly shit with yellow teeth and bad skin, pulls his gun on me, but I knock it out of his hand and break all his fingers before the others have time to react. The second guy fares no better. When he comes at me, I break his fingers *and* an arm, sending him whimpering to the floor beside his friend.

I step toward Luka, and he takes a frightened step back.

"This is the Kings of Mayhem's territory. When you come around here trying to bleed money out of people for protection, you poke the bear. A *very... fucking... big* bear with a *very... fucking... bad* temper."

"I didn't know this territory's been claimed."

"Everyone knows."

"I swear I didn't." He holds up his hands. "Hey, it's just a misunderstanding."

They all say that.

Right before they—yep, he pulls his gun on me.

"Fuck," I growl. Why do they always think they're the one who is going to take down the giant? Now I'm going to have to hurt him too.

Before he can get a shot off, I have his gun in my hand and him on his knees in front of me, shaking like a leaf. I shoot a knee into a mouth full of capped teeth, breaking thousands of dollars' worth of porcelain veneers.

"That's for putting your hands on Lacey." I send another knee into his face, flattening his nose. "And that's for trying to extort money from the MC."

I hoist him to his feet, but I have to slap him across the cheek to stop his blubbering.

"Stop crying like a baby," I growl.

"I'm sorry, I'm sorry. Don't hurt me."

Blood drips from both nostrils and his lips. His nose is flat against his cheek, and his front teeth are nothing but jagged little lumps of enamel.

"You brought this on yourself the moment you stepped into *our territory*. Now get the fuck out of Flintlock and don't look back. Consider this your first warning." I loosen my hold on him, and he relaxes. But then I lunge at him, and he falls back into a pile of archive boxes. "If you're smart, you won't make me give you a second warning. Now… *get the fuck out*."

Luka and his goons limp out of the club and escape to their car parked in the alley. Lacey joins me from the back room, and we watch them on the surveillance screen as they skid off into the night.

"Do you think that's the last we'll see of them?" she asks.

"Probably not. But we'll increase security around the club, and if they come back, Jack will pay him a visit."

"I appreciate it." She pats my shoulder. "Come on, let me buy you a drink."

We leave her office, and I follow her into the club.

As strip clubs go, the Spicy Crawdad is clean and tidy with a bit of style. Blue neon lights run the length of the ceiling casting the club in an ethereal light.

Lacey pours me a bourbon, but just as she slides it across the bar, the sound of Def Leppard suddenly bursts into the club, and the energy in the room intensifies as a new dancer appears on stage.

My drink pauses at my lips when I see who it is.

The gorgeous blonde from the night before.

And she looks incredible.

Leaning against the bar, I ask, "Who's the new girl?"

"That's Rory. Nice kid. Great body. The regulars love her."

"She been here long?"

"She started a few weeks ago. Can't pour a drink to save herself, but I can't fault her dancing."

Neither can I.

She's goddamn mesmerizing on stage.

Legs for days. A body that doesn't quit. A deep golden tan that's a stark contrast to the white bikini she's barely wearing. She moves in perfect synchronicity to the music, the sway of her hips and flick of her long, blonde hair intoxicating to watch.

"Where did she come from?" I ask, spellbound.

Lacey lights a cigarette. "Not sure. She just turned up one day wanting a job. Said she was new in town. It's a shame she's thinking of leaving."

"Leaving?"

"When she came in tonight, she mentioned she might head back to—"

"Boston," I say without thinking, my eyes still glued to the stage.

"Yeah, how'd you know?"

"Why?" I ask, ignoring her question.

"Why what?"

"Why is she thinking of leaving?"

"Do I look like her mom? How the hell do I know?" She takes a drag on her cigarette and shrugs. "Kind of feels like she came here looking for something but didn't find it, so she's packing up sticks."

Watching Rory slide her lithe body around the pole is making me hard.

"It's not like you to look twice at any of the girls here," Lacey adds.

I straighten and drain the rest of my drink. "And I'm not starting now."

But Lacey gives me a knowing look. I must have *interested* written all over my face because I can't tear my eyes off Rory.

"Can I suggest that if you *were* interested in making her acquaintance, tonight would be a good start," Lacey suggests. "Although, you might have to get in line. Plenty of boys around here have tried, but she shoots them down like ducks in a barrel."

I don't say anything as I walk away and head toward the stage.

I can't help it.

It's like my feet have minds of their own.

I'm trapped in the light of the glitterball and being pulled toward something.

Not just her.

But something much bigger than both of us.

Need.

CHAPTER 6

RORY

I love my job as a dancer.

Whenever I'm on stage, I see nothing but the twirling sparkles of the glitterball across the room and the spangle of light from the light show.

But I feel everything.

The pulse of the music thrumming through my veins.

The throb of power as I move my body to the beat.

The pull of strong muscles as I hook my leg around the pole and begin my routine.

There is something powerful and liberating when your body is syncopated to the music and your limbs move in harmony to the songs booming out from the sound system.

I never thought I'd be a dancer.

But when I moved here four weeks ago, I applied for a job as a bartender. Unfortunately, it turns out I suck as a drink slinger. I don't know my Jack from my Jimmy, and that's kind of important to folks around here. Lacey, the owner, fired me the first night. But I was desperate for money, so when she asked if

I could dance, I figured I'd give it a go.

Turns out I *can* dance.

And I like it.

Tell people you're a dancer, and they get that amused gleam in their eye like it's something dirty and seedy. That you're somehow a lesser person because you dance for cash. But I flip that stigma the bird every time I go on stage because I enjoy it, and I'm proud of what I do out there.

Hell, why shouldn't a woman be proud of her assets? And if those assets earn them a decent wage, tell me where the problem is because I'm not seeing it.

Tonight, I weave my magic around the pole to Def Leppard's "Pour Some Sugar On Me."

I'm halfway through my song when I see him.

Ares.

Standing back from the seated area. Almost seven feet tall with arms as big as my thighs and the face of a god. He's watching me just out of view of the light, lingering in the shadows, his eyes taking in every move I make.

My skin tingles knowing he is watching me.

Our eyes lock, and suddenly, every move is for him, and I feel myself getting more and more turned on with every beat that passes. I don't ever make eye contact with the patrons, but I can't look away.

And he doesn't look away from me.

He doesn't even blink.

Just sears that dark gaze onto my skin.

When the song ends, I leave the stage, but instead of heading back to the dressing room, I exit stage left and descend the steps to where the patrons nurse their drinks as they wait for the next performance.

Dove Cameron's "Boyfriend" starts, and Layla, one of the other dancers, begins her routine as I make my way toward

Ares. But before I get to him, a fat hand grabs me by the wrist, and I'm pulled onto the lap of one of the creepier regulars. His name is Boz, and he smells like stale liquor, body odor, and desperation.

"Where you going so quick, baby?"

His erection pokes into my thigh, and it makes me want to puke. "Let me go."

"Oh, don't be that way, baby. I just want to show you my appreciation for the dance."

"With your hands?" I shove him in the chest. "I don't think so—"

I don't get to finish because strong arms rip me away. It's Ares, and he's mad as hell. He plants me on my feet before turning back to Mr. Grab-A-Lot. Lifting him by the collar, he drags Boz to his feet and pins him to the wall. His face is murderous. His bulging biceps are a huge distraction despite the seriousness of the situation.

He looks like he's about to snap Boz like a twig.

"The lady said *hands off.*"

"What the fuck, man?" Boz shoves his arms up in surrender while I'm still in awe of Ares' strength and those mesmerizing biceps.

"You touch her again, and I'll cut both of them off." Ares leans even closer. "And jerking it won't be much fun after that."

"Okay, okay…"

Ares drops him to his feet, and Boz takes off.

I have to crane my neck to meet Ares' dark eyes. "You didn't need to do that."

"No?"

"No, I had it handled."

"Didn't look that way to me."

"What is it with you trying to be my knight in shining armor anyway?"

"You know… a simple thank you would suffice here."

"He was a good tipper."

His expression turns serious. "No amount of money is worth him putting his hands on you without permission. And from where I was standing, you weren't granting him permission."

He's right.

Don't get me wrong, I am grateful for the help.

My testiness has everything to do with me, not *him*.

Because ever since I saw Ares fight at Oscar's, I can't get the wall of muscle out of my head, and I've been going back to every fight because of it.

And that's not the plan.

It's also dangerous.

The other night when I approached Ares at Aces High and told him I wasn't there to hit on him, I was telling the truth. I was there to ask him to kill my stepfather.

But if I'm being real honest, I *do* want to kiss him.

And I mean *really* kiss him.

I'm talking the kind of kiss where you feel every emotion, every need, every desire.

One that you don't ever want to end because it feels too good.

Even now, standing here wearing nothing but a glittery bikini in the middle of a strip joint, I want to taste those lips. But if I reach up and brush my lips against his, we'll end up fucking, and that's not *why* I want to kiss him. I want to because his mouth is perfect and soft, and I haven't ever been kissed into nirvana before, and I know Ares would be able to do that.

Effortlessly.

Fuck. What the hell is wrong with me?

This has already gone too far, and now I'm thinking about magical kisses?

Time to pull back.

"So have you reconsidered?" I ask him.

"About sleeping with you?"

"What? That's not what I meant. And for the record, that offer was never on the table."

"Oh, you mean the other thing."

"Yes… the *other thing*."

"No."

"Then why are you here?"

"This is a Kings of Mayhem club. I'm here on business."

In the ethereal blue light, he looks almost angelic. But I know he's more demonic than divine.

And it excites me.

Even though it shouldn't.

"I can help you with a lot of things. Just not that."

I picture his big hands roaming my body, and a wave of heat sweeps over me.

"I bet you could."

His eyes flare, and the air crackles between us.

I get the feeling he doesn't want to be here, but he can't help himself. And that excites me further.

"You're a good dancer," he says. "Every man here couldn't take his eyes off you."

"Including you?"

His jaw works heavily. "Including me."

He's losing whatever battle he's fighting in his head, and it's a turn-on.

"I liked you watching me. Is that bad?"

"Yes," he rasps.

My pulse picks up.

"Why?"

I lick my lips, and his gaze drops to them.

"Because you shouldn't want that."

"I shouldn't want chocolate either, but I still do."

His dark hooded eyes don't blink. "I'm not as harmless as chocolate."

I give him a wicked smile. "Neither am I."

He opens his mouth but then shuts it again.

"Well, I should go shower." I bite my lower lip, and a look of hunger crosses his face. "I guess I'll see you around."

His voice is thick. "I guess so."

Our eyes remain locked, and neither of us moves.

But then Layla's routine finishes, and the "Six Days" remix by DJ Shadow and Mos Def blasts into the club and breaks the spell.

I smile softly. "See you later, *Thor*."

I walk away without a backward glance, but I can feel the heat of his scorching gaze heat my skin, and there is an enormous part of me that wants him to throw me over his shoulder and drag me into whatever dark and depraved cave he climbed out of and do unspeakable things to me.

Thankfully, I come to my senses back in the dressing room, where I shower and change into a pair of cut-off shorts and a tank top before pulling my hair into a ponytail. Gathering up my belongings, I pause to look at the photograph in my purse.

I won't forget, I say, brushing my thumb over the crumpled picture.

Shoving it back inside my purse, I leave the club and exit through the back door and out to the car park.

But on the steps, I come to a halt.

Leaning up against his bike waiting for me is Ares.

He meets my gaze. "How about that coffee?"

We tumble through my apartment door, kissing fiercely as we tear at each other's clothes, desperate to get naked.

I don't know why this is happening.

It's definitely not part of the plan.

We had been coming back here for coffee, but then he had stopped me on the stairs, spun me around, and kissed me until my knees were weak and my bones were liquid.

And well… here we are.

Like I said, not a part of the plan.

But his kiss is like catnip, and I can't get enough of it.

Maybe I'm still turned on by the way he watched me dance.

Or maybe it's because I can't remember the last time I was touched, and I want something other than my battery-operated boyfriend to make me come, and I'm pretty sure this guy will do that well.

Once inside the door, he shrugs off his leather cut and lifts his T-shirt over his head, revealing the muscled body of a god. He's so rock-hard and built like every woman's fantasy, it sends fire into every erogenous zone in my body.

I stand rooted to the spot, absorbing the inked monster in front of me.

His abdomen is a patchwork of tight muscle and deep grooves that flex with each fluid movement. His skin is dark and smooth, his hair flowing past his shoulders, tattoos inked everywhere. I soak in his broad chest, the six-pack, and the way the sharp V of his obliques disappears beneath the waistband of the jeans hanging low on his hips.

My mouth is suddenly dry.

Fuck the coffee.

Our eyes lock, and all common sense leaves me.

I want this.

God, I want this.

I want this so bad nothing else in the world matters.

Shirtless and in nothing but jeans, he lifts me into his arms and takes me toward the bedroom. He sets me down, and his big hands remove my clothes slowly, piece by piece, his blazing eyes not leaving mine until I'm standing before him in nothing but a pair of lace panties.

A smile of appreciation touches his lips. "You're fucking beautiful," he rasps.

I yank him toward me by the waistband of his jeans.

"And you have too many clothes on," I say.

Wickedness gleams in his eyes. "Best you take them off me then."

I reach for the button of his jeans. He doesn't move as he watches intensely, his gaze searing into my skin as I lower the zipper. He's hard, and when I see the rigid outline of his cock, my skin flushes with heat and excitement, and I swallow thickly.

The rumors are true. His cock is huge.

He steps out of his jeans and underwear and again I'm rooted to the spot, wondering how the hell I'm going to fit him inside me.

"I didn't bring any protection," he says. "Do you have anything?"

My stomach drops. "I don't."

Oh god, why don't I?

I haven't seen a dick in months, hell, maybe even a year, and I need to get laid.

But sex without protection is a no go for me.

My body weakens with frustration, but my disappointment doesn't last long.

Ares takes my face in his big hands, his smile wicked. "Don't look disappointed, little one. I don't need to be inside you to satisfy you."

He pushes me onto the bed and slowly crawls over me. Pushed up on his knuckles, he leans down to drag his tongue from my neck to my shoulder, and I shudder beneath his touch. His tongue is velvety soft against my skin, his breath hot, the heat from his muscled body radiating around us as he descends further down my body.

"You taste so fucking good," he murmurs, sliding lower.

Skillful lips close around one nipple and then the other, applying enough suction and pressure to send a heat of lust to my clit. I arch my back as his tongue continues to weave a trail along my skin, thinking I'm going to die from the sensation. His mouth finds my clit, and my hips shoot off the bed. Big hands reach up and hold them down while he fucks me with his tongue. *Like a tongue-fucking expert.*

It doesn't take long.

"Oh God…" My moan is long and drawn out as I surrender to the pleasure. "I'm going to come."

He tongue fucks me harder, and I fall apart. I come in sweeping waves while clinging to the headboard behind me.

"That's it, little one. Come on my face."

He licks, sucks, and plunges his tongue in and out of me until I'm a rag doll, and I sag into the mattress. When he lifts his head, his dark gaze sweeps along my naked body.

He crawls over me and leans down, claiming my mouth with a searing kiss that is a mix of him and me.

But I pull away from his kiss, suddenly needing more.

Through half-lidded eyes, I see his erection hanging heavily between his thighs, and it's all I can take. I want him inside me, but the protection thing is a real bummer. I at least want him rubbing up against me.

I grab him and pull him down, tightening my thighs around his hips, then begin to rock against his cock, needing the pressure against my aching clit. His kiss turns wild, and his big hands dwarf my face as he holds it tight to his. His tongue, lips, and hot mouth punish mine. It's all too much. I want to come again. I *need* to come again. So I rock harder against him, the friction threatening to set off fireworks but not getting me there.

"We gotta stop," he rasps.

But I grab his wrist. "Not yet." My breath is ragged. "Don't stop… I'll fucking die if you stop now."

I'm on the brink of orgasm number two, and I'll implode if he pulls away.

Taking him by the base and guiding him toward the saturated place between my thighs, he drags in a ragged breath.

His brows draw in. "I'm not sure this is a good idea."

"I just want to feel you there." I know I'm playing with fire, but I'm drunk on desire, and it's making me reckless. It's been months since I've seen action, and I'm about to burst with need. "Kiss me."

I feel the weight of his cock between us as he leans down and kisses me into a dangerous stupor. He rocks his hips against me, and I part my thighs further, needing more pressure to soothe the throbbing ache.

I've heard that the logical side of your brain can shut down during sex, and right now, I'm proof of that fact.

He grinds against me, his erection rubbing over my clit and his groans stealing the last of my common sense and turning it to ash.

The moment gets away from us. Not thinking, we both let it happen. One second, I'm rocking beneath him, and the next, he's sunk deep inside me, and I don't even care because I'm distracted by the thick column of flesh that stretches me to a point that's almost painful.

I've never felt so full in my life.

Sweet Mary and Joseph.

My eyes roll into the back of my head. My lips part with a deep moan that comes from somewhere deep inside me. "Oh, God…"

Resting on his strong forearms, he leans down. "God isn't going to make you come, baby…" His lip brushes my ear. "I am."

One more powerful thrust and I unravel beneath him. And this time, it's going to blow my mind even more.

My back arches and my nails dig into his muscular shoulders as he grinds hard into me.

But I'm not even here anymore.

I don't know where I go.

I cease to exist.

Swept away by the storm.

Mind successfully blown.

He kisses me back to reality.

"I love hearing you come," he mutters against my lips. "I love the way your pussy tightens against my cock." I clench, and he groans. "Yeah, baby, just like that."

High on dopamine and oxytocin, I ease up onto my elbows to watch his thick cock sliding in and out of me.

Over and over again.

But it becomes too much for my senses, and I fall back to let another orgasm consume me with its delicious, sweet heat. I lose myself in sensation after sensation as he goes on to give me one orgasm after another without showing any signs of coming himself.

My body is on overload. Thank the Almighty for not giving me a refractory period. Because just as I get over one orgasm, he conjures another with his magical cock.

This man has stamina.

"Get on your knees," he commands, pulling out.

My legs are shaky, and my pussy throbs. I've come so many times I've lost count.

He guides me onto all fours.

"You're so goddamn beautiful." His voice is smooth. "Look at that pussy, so pink and tight."

He notches his cock to me and eases in slowly, letting out a low groan. "You're so fucking wet, baby. You know what that does to me? Feel how fucking hard your pussy has got me." He thrusts in, deep and hard, and my head drops as pain collides with pleasure.

He continues to rock with a punishing rhythm, his cock so big it hits me in places no other cock has come close to touching. I grip the bedsheet and moan because no one has ever fucked me this good.

"Oh fuck, your pussy... you're so fucking perfect..." Ares lets out an urgent growl and slows his pace. His hands grip my hips as his head falls back. "I'm going to come..."

Deliciously drunk on my post-orgasm highs, I watch over my shoulder as he pulls out and runs his palm up and down the thick shaft, unleashing a deep, primal groan as streams of cum rain down on my ass.

When he's done, he eases down beside me, his rock-hard chest heaving. His eyes close, and his pulse races in his throat as he tries to catch his breath.

This isn't what I came here for.

But I'd be lying if I said it wasn't exactly what I wanted.

He's a killer, and it excites me.

So does the way he uses his cock and the orgasms he gives me.

I want more, and anything else can wait until I get my fill.

I'm selfish that way.

I'm also out of my fucking mind.

CHAPTER 7

ARES

In the morning, I wake up to the sound of soft rain against the window and the bed empty beside me. I hear the shower going and roll onto my back, every muscle in my body soft and relaxed. I'm so damn comfortable, it's crazy. I haven't slept like that in years.

From the cocoon of warm bedsheets, I gaze around the room. It's sparsely furnished with a dresser, mirror, and a bedside table and lamp on either side of the bed. By the bedroom door are a pair of Doc Marten boots and running shoes, and a leather belt dangles from a hook on the wall. Other than that, there isn't much in the room. No photographs. No personal items that tell me anything about the girl I spent the night inside of.

I close my eyes and listen to the rain outside.

Usually, the only thing to relax me like this is a punishing session at the gym with a punching bag and weights, and sometimes I'll take hours to drain the restless energy from my body. And sex can leave me edgy and charged with energy even after I've come.

But this morning, I'm on freaking cloud nine.

Every muscle is relaxed.

Every nerve and fiber is loose and satisfied.

I don't want to move, but my body clock tells me it's time for coffee.

Forcing myself up, I push back the covers and start to dress. But as I shove my feet into my jeans, the soft sounds of Rory singing in the shower drift into the bedroom, and I stop what I'm doing.

I'm not ready to leave.

Not by a long shot.

I'm expected at the clubhouse for Church at midday, but until then, I'm free as a bird. So I step out of my jeans and walk toward the bathroom. She doesn't hear me enter until I open the shower door. She has her back to me and looks like a vision of perfection beneath the glittering stream of water.

She looks over her shoulder at me, her long wet hair hanging like silk over the subtle curves of her shoulder blades and down to the arc of her waist.

Her gaze sweeps over me, and a dark heat enters her eyes when she sees the heavy erection hanging between my legs.

"Like what you see?"

She quirks an eyebrow. "Maybe."

I step inside and stand behind her, and she bites down on her lower lip.

I love how tiny she is in comparison to my size.

My lips graze her shoulder, my tongue trailing up to the sensitive spot behind her ear. She shivers and tilts her head, exposing the full curve of her throat. My teeth sink into the flawless skin, and she lets out a whimper that sends all kinds of crazy to my cock.

I guide her hands up to the wall and press her palms against the tiles.

We didn't use a condom last night, and it's the farthest thing from my mind when I rock my hips forward and slide my cock inside her. With a groan, she braces herself against the tiled wall and sinks her teeth into her lips.

Her sweet pussy tightens around me, and it feels so good, the effort not to come straight away almost kills me.

I'm high on all the sensations hitting my brain at once. The sound of her sweet moans. Her soft milky body bending against mine. Her wet pussy as it suckles my cock. The warm shower water hitting my skin. It all feels so good I know I'm about to explode.

Reaching around, I begin to rub her clit, and her knees buckle.

"Oh God, Ares, don't stop," she begs. She sags against the tiles and gasps for breath. "I'm so close. So… fucking… close."

I pick up the pace.

Both my fingers and my cock.

She trembles and cries out as she comes. Her sweet pussy contracts violently around my cock and fuck me, out of nowhere my orgasm hits me like a brick in the face. It crashes through me, but I don't stop thrusting until we both ride the wave all the way to the end, and our cries are swallowed by the warm stream of the shower.

Panting, I turn her to face me and take her by the throat. I claim her mouth and kiss her until my racing pulse begins to calm.

This woman.

Fuck.

I could get fucking addicted to this.

Leaving the shower cubicle, we towel off the water and dress.

Once in the kitchen, Rory makes us coffee.

"About last night and this morning," she says candidly, handing me a cup. "I don't want you to worry. I had a full medical last month for work, and I got a clean bill of health."

I never take a pussy unprotected, but somehow all rhyme and reason left me last night. *And again, this morning.*

"It's not how I usually roll," I assure her. "And I have to have medical clearance to fight, so you're safe."

She smiles at me over her coffee. "Then we should be okay."

She's fucking cute when she smiles.

Especially when she's standing there in a tiny pair of shorts and a sweater hanging off one shoulder.

Before I realize it, I'm smiling back at her.

She notices the patch on my cut. "What does it mean to be a sergeant-at-arms?"

"It means I enforce the things my president wants enforced."

Her eyes narrow with intrigue. "Sounds dangerous."

She licks her lips, and I know I want to taste them again.

"Sometimes," I say.

As SAA, I work closely beside my president and VP to make sure the club and their families are safe and that the interests of the club—like the cannabis crops—are protected. Sometimes that means getting blood on my hands.

The mood takes a strange turn.

"If I ask you something, will you answer truthfully?" she asks.

"I don't lie."

"How many men have you killed?"

The question should catch me off guard, but strangely it doesn't. It makes me curious.

"You don't ask *if* I've killed a man. Instead, you ask *how many* I've killed?"

"Because like I said to you last night, I know a killer when I see one."

The harshness of her words is in complete contrast to the calm tone she uses.

"And where do you come from that you would know such a thing?"

"A lot of different men used to visit my uncle's gym. Good guys. Bad guys. A few in between."

"What constitutes a bad guy?"

"The ones who lie and said they're good guys. When really, they should be honest and own it. *I'm bad. I do shitty things.* I'd have more respect for them if they did."

I love how frank she is.

I also decide that I love her dimples.

They press into her sweet face when she smiles.

I think a moment and then answer her question, "Being sergeant-at-arms means you have to do things you might not want to. Some of it is ugly."

She raises an eyebrow. "That's the most indirect *yes* if ever I've heard one."

When I don't say anything, her eyebrow drops, and for the first time, I see the uncertainty enter her beautiful eyes.

She pauses then asks, "Were any of them women?"

She's direct, and I like that.

But that question—it's loaded.

I recall what she said about her stepdaddy and how he hurt her and her mom.

I take a step closer, towering over her. "A man who lays a hand on a woman is not a man. He's a coward, and I'm no coward. I especially hate that a coward hurt you." I find the gentle curve on her face with my hand. Her throat works as she struggles to swallow, and she presses her face against my palm, closing her eyes. "I would never hurt you," I say, hating that she would even need to hear me say it out loud.

She nods, and when she opens her eyes again, her kiss-swollen lips break into a soft smile, and I know I want to taste her plush lips again, just like I want to run my tongue along the creamy column of her slender throat again.

I step back, pick up my cup of coffee, and drain it.

I'm stalling, and I don't know why.

"Why do I get the feeling that you're every man my mom warned me about rolled into one?" she asks.

"Because I probably am. Does that frighten you?"

"Should it?"

Yes, little one, it should.

I place down my cup. "I should go."

She hugs her arms around her waist as she watches me, her eyes hungrily taking in every move.

Attraction crackles between us. It's surprising because after the number of times we've both come in the last twelve hours, we should both be exhausted.

Rory gives me a shy smile as she lifts her cup to her lips. "Thanks for a memorable night."

I think about what we did the night before and again in the early hours of this morning. Not to mention, twenty minutes ago in the shower. I should be exhausted, but my body reacts, and I begin to question why the hell I'm even leaving.

"Maybe I'll see you at another fight sometime."

"Maybe." She gives me a coy look, her hair falling around her lovely face in icy blonde waves.

I can't help myself, she's beautiful, so I take her cup and lean down to kiss her. When she kisses me back, I walk her backward toward the bedroom.

"I thought you were leaving," she says between kisses.

I cup her jaw and keep kissing her. "Pretty sure I left something in the bedroom."

"Oh, really? What?"

I lift her and throw her onto the bed. "You."

By the time we say goodbye, I've spent the last hour eating her pussy and making her come, and she's reciprocated by giving me a blow job that will keep my knees weak and my body humming for damn hours.

Penny Dee

I leave her spent amongst the tangled sheets on her bed and step into the early morning light.

We won't see each other again.

Because it's better that way.

CHAPTER 8

ARES

The punch lands directly on my face.

The right hook makes contact with my eye and sends me stumbling backward. I manage to recover but the blow has left me seeing stars. I cover my face and regroup, collecting my opponent in the gut just as the umpire calls time on the round.

We're three rounds in, and I've collected more blows to my body tonight than in all my fights put together.

I retreat to my corner, where Paw and Doc are waiting.

"What the hell is wrong with you?" Paw asks, wiping my face with a towel. "You're fighting like a fifth grader in the playground."

"You're distracted." Doc squirts water onto the freshly reopened cut in my eyebrow. It stings, but I barely feel it because my body is flooded with adrenaline. "You need to focus on what you're doing because if he gets you down, he'll shove his knee so deep into your face you'll be knocked out before you can say, *I'm on my ass because I wasn't paying attention to what the fuck my opponent was doing.*"

"I got this," I assure them, adjusting a loose piece of tape across my knuckles.

"Then start telling *him* that." Paw nods toward my opponent, a six-foot Samoan named Punisher. "Preferably with your fists and a couple of round kicks."

Blood from the reopened cut in my brow streams down my cheek, and I taste the metallic tang on my tongue.

Doc dabs something on it and says, "This isn't like you. Whatever is on your mind will have to wait until after the fight unless you want your ass kicked. Then, by all means, keep doing what you're doing."

I raise my unwounded eyebrow at him. "I said *I got this*."

But he's right. I *am* distracted. Because the moment I stepped into the cage tonight, I started searching for *her* in the crowd, and when I couldn't find her, my mind spun chaotic thoughts in every direction. Even now, blinded by all the blood dripping in my eyes, I'm still searching the crowd for her familiar face.

Why isn't she here?

And why the fuck does it matter so much to me that she's not?

By the time I stand and meet Punisher in the center of the mat, I've already made up my mind. After the fight, I'm going to swing by her apartment, but that means dealing with Punisher first.

When the bell sounds for the round to start, we grapple, and I send him unconscious to the floor with a double collar tie followed by a flying knee to the chin.

"Now that's what I'm talking about," Paw adds as I leave the cage, victorious not five minutes later.

Doc says nothing but eyes me suspiciously—he's trying to figure out what's going on with me.

They follow me into the locker room, Paw even following me into the showers, wanting to know what has gotten into me.

"You seriously going to watch me shower?" I ask.

Ares

"If it means I find out what the fuck that was," he says, pointing in the direction of the cage.

"What the fuck are you talking about?"

"You never let your opponent make contact more than once or twice, but tonight you let Punisher put his hands all over you. Are you thinking about that girl?"

"Are you leaving? Or you planning on joining me in the shower?"

"I'm not going anywhere until you answer the damn question. Is Ares the Giant pussy-whipped because if he is, you gotta get that shit under control, my friend."

I'm not shy, so to avoid answering the question, I shove off my shorts and underwear.

When Paw sees what's hanging between my thighs, his eyebrows disappear all the way up his forehead. "Well, I'll be goddamned."

He turns away.

"Didn't take you for the shy type," I say, stepping into the shower.

"Is that thing fucking real?" He shakes his head. "How many women have seen that and run away?"

"I haven't had any complaints."

In the shower, I lather up the soap to wash away the sweat, blood, and the dull ache lingering in my muscles and joints.

All the while, Paw keeps at me.

"You've got the fight with Raptor in a couple of weeks. If you want to keep your teeth, I suggest you do whatever it takes to get this distraction out of your system."

He's preaching to the converted. That is exactly what I plan to do. Tonight, I'm going to spend the night fucking this need out of my body.

"Don't worry. I'll be ready for Raptor."

But Paw doesn't let up. Even as I step out of the shower and wrap a towel around my hips, he follows me back into the locker room, where Doc is packing up our belongings and shoving them into a large canvas bag.

"Why am I not convinced?"

"Because you're ex-FBI, you'd be suspicious of your own grandmother."

"Hey, that suspicion has kept me alive." He shakes his head. "No, I'm not convinced because I've never seen you like this over a girl before. Hell, I've never seen you *with* a girl, period. Those club girls flutter their eyelashes at you, and you walk in the other direction. But this girl… she's got to mean something for you to get this distracted."

"She means nothing." I tower over him as I reach for my clothes neatly stacked in my locker. "Now, are you going to keep nattering at me like an old hen, or are you going to leave me in peace so I can get dressed?"

Thankfully, both he and Doc leave, and I dress in silence, but inside, my head is chaos. Paw is right. I need to get this distraction under control. Raptor is a mean sonofabitch, and he almost matches me in size. I can't enter that cage thinking about a pair of bee-stung lips and a face you get lost in or he'll make a meal out of me.

Feeling more determined to get her out of my system, I leave the gym and walk in the opposite direction of Aces High.

"Hey, where are you going?" Paw calls out from the pathway leading to the bar.

"To work on my distraction," I call back.

"What about the money for the fight?"

"Tell Tony I said to give it to you."

Despite the curious looks of my brothers, my aching body, and the blows to my face, I climb on my bike and disappear into the night, pointing my Harley in the direction of Rory's home.

When I arrive, I park up the street and sit in the darkness to watch her apartment. The light is on, and I can see her moving about inside, but I need to take a moment. My head is spinning with chaos, and I'm still weighing up the consequences. But I know I need to get this done.

My past means I know how to survive in the shadows for hours, watching and anticipating, waiting for the right moment to pounce.

I know I should leave—for her sake *and* mine.

But I also know I won't.

Finally giving in to the need inside, I climb off my bike, walk to her front door, and knock.

When the door opens and her beautiful face appears, I feel an unfamiliar kick in my chest.

"You weren't at the fight tonight," is all I say.

She looks surprised to see me, but it disappears quickly. "You made it pretty clear that you couldn't help me."

"Is that the only reason you'd come to watch me fight?"

She tilts her head. "Would there be any other reason?"

Her seductive eyes and parted glossy lips tell me there is.

Fuck, I want her.

I don't wait for her reply.

Grabbing her by the nape of her neck, I drag her to my eager lips and kiss her fiercely, overpowering her completely and stealing her breath from her.

With a whimper, she melts into me, and fuck, her submission turns me on even more.

Devouring her mouth, I kick the door closed behind me and lead her backward into the living room.

This is what I've been aching to do since I left her apartment four days ago.

Four days of telling myself I'm not interested.

Four days of reliving the touch of her lips and the sweet taste of her pussy.

Four days of fucking my own hand as I recall the pleasure of sinking deep into her luscious body.

I don't like the distraction or the ache it builds in me.

Or the way I feel drawn to her.

So, tonight, I'm going to fuck it out of me.

Hard.

Bending her over the couch, I yank down her shorts and the tiny lace thong she's wearing and enter her with a desperate thrust. My body is exhausted from tonight's fight, but the adrenaline and excitement she stirs in me pounds through my veins and ignites a ferocious wildfire along the way.

I'm so fucking hard for her it makes me weak.

But I push the realization out of my mind and sink deeper into the pleasure of fucking her. Her pussy pulses around me, and in my head, the word *mine* flashes like a neon sign.

I push the thought away, frustrated, and grab her hips to start pounding harder.

But I don't come.

Despite her whimpers.

Despite the sight of her juicy ass bent over the couch.

Despite her tight pussy clenching around my cock.

Fuck.

Why can't I come?

The ache in my balls is about to kill me.

I thrust harder.

But it's not happening.

Don't get me wrong, it feels out of this world being inside her.

She's so wet and warm, and the way her pussy suckles my cock is knee-weakening.

The problem is me.

Fuck this need out of your body and leave.

Frustrated, I stop thrusting and drag my length out of her and turn her around. My cock is painfully heavy and slick with a mix of us both. Rory looks up at me, and I take her chin in my hand and pull her to my lips. Our kiss is a stark contrast to the hard fucking and frustrated need to come, and in that second, I know that this is why I am here. This is why I came here tonight. I will lie to myself about it later and tell myself whatever bullshit I usually tell myself.

But this here—this sensation of her tongue stroking against mine and what it does to me—this is why I came here tonight.

No.

I break off the kiss.

Fuck this need out of your body and leave.

Rory looks up at me with those big blue eyes. "What's wrong?"

She can feel my frustration.

I thrust open her legs ready to enter her again, but she stops me. "No."

Our eyes lock.

She reaches up and delicately brushes my face with her fingertips. "You're hurt."

Rory looks at my split eyebrow and the bruises.

"It's nothing. I'm fine."

"No, you're not. You're bleeding."

I catch her wrist. "I'm okay."

Her plush lips break into an amused smile. "Boy, he must've been something to do this to you. I've watched you fight for weeks, and you barely got a scratch on you. What happened tonight?"

"I was distracted."

"By what?"

Keen to avoid the question and aware of my hard cock standing at attention between us, I take a step closer and wrap my arms around her, my hands settling on her juicy ass and holding her to me. "Let's just say I had other things on my mind."

A small smile touches her lips. She slides to her feet and reaches up to guide my lips down to hers.

God, the way she kisses.

I wrap my hand around her throat.

We kiss, and it's warm and sweet. But that's not what I'm after. *Right?* Tonight is about ending this growing obsession so tomorrow I can go back to my normal self.

But the way she feels and smells and fucking kisses.

It's like I'm fucking hooked on the taste of her.

I push her up against the wall, determined to leave here with my common sense back intact. I pin her arms above her head and cage her in my arms.

She looks at me with dark, hooded eyes. "What do you want from me?"

I bury my face in her throat and growl out the word, "Everything."

Lifting her in my arms, she's as light as a feather. One arm holds her in place as I take my aching cock and rub it through her soaked pussy.

My breath leaves me in a ragged rasp. "*Fuck.*"

Despite my desperation to be inside her, I enter her slowly, ensuring she feels every hard inch sliding into her. But it's me who feels it most. Even though she cries out and arches her back, it's me who feels every sensation of light and pleasure as I sink in all the way to the hilt.

I let out a low moan and close my eyes, dropping my forehead to hers.

Her nails dig into my shoulder, and the shooting pain sets me off.

"Ares," she pants my name, her voice laced in pleasure, but I greedily kiss it from her lips. Plunging my tongue in, I take her breath as I give in and let the animal in me take over.

"Oh God, yes," she cries.

I thrust my free hand through her hair and grind harder into her. She arches her neck, and the sight of her pale throat does me in.

"Goddammit!" I growl as I'm rocked by a blinding light and mind-blowing pleasure that makes my knees go weak.

I drive harder into her as we both groan out our orgasms.

"Feel better," she pants as we come down.

Fuck.

It's like she can read my mind.

Like she knew why I came here tonight.

I press my forehead to hers. "I needed that."

Not that anything has changed.

I'm still hard.

"Something tells me you're not done yet," she whispers.

My cock twitches inside her. "You have good intuition."

Her kiss is deep and slow and sends a new wave of need through me.

Clearly, tonight's mission is still not accomplished.

If it ever existed in the first place.

CHAPTER 9

RORY

Ares kisses me awake at first light.

Outside, the sun hasn't even begun to breach the horizon, but I know he has MC business he needs to attend to. He doesn't say much about the Kings of Mayhem and what he does for them, but I know there's something going on today.

"Will I see you later?" I ask sleepily as he hovers over me.

He buries his face into my neck. "I'll call you."

When I hear the front door close behind him, I slip into a deep, uncomfortable sleep where my nightmares reign and my past haunts me. Splintered images of people long gone mix with bad feelings and unhappy memories until my skin breaks out in a sweat.

The buzz of my cell on the bedside table wakes me. But despite the nightmares, I'm not ready to wake up. It's still dark out, and after a night with Ares in my bed, my body needs the extra rest. But I'm not someone who can leave a message unopened. It'll scratch at the back of my mind until I look at it.

Blindly, I reach for it, wondering if it's Ares.

But it isn't.

Reading the message, my stomach drops, and a rush of nausea chases away any lingering thoughts of sleep.

In the shadows of my bedroom, I sit up and push my hair out of my face. Goosebumps pebble my skin as I stare at the words on the screen.

> **Unknown:** *Tick tock, Aurora. Your time is running out.*

A fresh zip of nausea tears through me, and I throw the cell phone onto my bed and stare at it like it just bit me.

An image of Donnie swings before my eyes, and I feel the haunting sensation of his fingers trailing along my skin and the stench of whisky and sweat in the air as he took and took and took from me. Then I think about my brother and the coffin, and a ghostly shiver travels down my spine. They're fractured memories tainted by time and pain but still as real as if they happened only yesterday.

Tick tock, Aurora. Your time is running out.

Reaching over to the bedside table, I open the drawer and pull out the Ruger lying beside a bottle of Advil and a tray of contraceptive pills. The gun is loaded, and I know how to use it.

The question is, when will I?

CHAPTER 10

ARES

"I'm not going to lie to you, boys. This is some of the craziest shit I've seen in twenty years of being in law enforcement."

Sheriff Pinkwater slides a stack of crime scene photographs across the table we use during Church. It's a long, rustic table made of red oak taken from one of the local forests. Usually, twenty-one patched members of the club sit around it. Today, there is only Jack, Paw, and Shooter, who is the club's VP and Jack's right hand, and me.

When Sheriff Pinkwater reached out and asked for help with a case he's investigating, Jack insisted we talk with him first before taking it to Church.

Pinkwater looks uneasy. "As you can see, what we're dealing with is mighty gruesome."

There are seven crime scene photographs.

The first one is of a young woman lying half-submerged on the riverbank, dead. Her eyes are half open, her skin pale, and her lips a ghostly blue.

"Her name is Kandy Kurtman. Twenty-two. She was a sex

worker from Fortune City. Used to be a bank teller but fell on hard times when the bank closed. Worked the streets to pay her rent."

I've known a few Kandy Kurtman's in my life. There is no shame in doing what you fucking got to do to put food on the table and keep a roof over your head.

"What happened to her?" Shooter asks.

"Got picked up by a John on a Monday night three weeks ago, was found in the river the following morning. Cause of death was strangulation." He reaches across the table to show us the image beneath it. "But this was done to her post-mortem."

In the second picture, Kandy is on her back, and across her naked stomach the word *lust* has been slashed into the soft, slippery flesh.

"Jesus Christ," Shooter mutters with a shake of his head.

"The medical examiner couldn't identify exactly what they used to carve the word, but she said it was a double-edged blade."

"Like a dagger," I say.

"Or a tactical knife. But yes, something like that."

The next photograph is of a man in a three-piece suit hanging from a rope in what looks like an expensive apartment in the city. His face is badly beaten and cut, and bloody dollar notes are stuffed into his mouth."

"This is Michael Merchant. A con artist and petty thief. He recently got himself involved with the Hermanns out by Green Holler way. You heard of the Hermanns?"

Everyone's heard of the Hermanns.

They're hillbilly mafia.

"The medical examiner removed seven one-dollar bills jammed into his mouth. Then, of course, there's this—" He points to the next photo where the word *greed* is carved into the victim's chest.

Paw shakes his head. "So, we're looking at someone who has a thing for the seven deadly sins?"

"Like that movie with Brad Pitt and Morgan Freeman where the serial killer picks off people and then leaves one of the seven deadly sins written somewhere nearby?" Shooter asks.

"It's called *Seven*," I tell him.

"That's it." He looks back to Pinkwater. "This guy got a hard-on for the seven deadly sins?"

"Not just that. It seems they have a thing for picking off people involved in organized crime. Kandi Kurtman was dating her pimp, a low-life called Jimmy Knuckles. He's tied to the Sullivan family, who are involved in everything from prostitution to money laundering. Merchant was involved with the Hermanns. These freaks are religious vigilantes, and they're not going to stop until they've made their point." Pinkwater pushes another two photos across the table. "These were taken at a crime scene yesterday."

The first photograph shows three men slumped around a kitchen table littered with empty beer cans and drug paraphernalia. They're sitting in a trailer that looks like it's never been clean, the stained singlets they all wear looking no better. Two of the men are upright, the third lays with his head pressed against the tabletop. All three of them are dead, each with a putrid foam oozing out of their mouths and a needle hanging out of their arm.

"You'd be forgiven to think it this was an overdose. But it's not. Someone forced those boys to sit down at that table before they filled them with a hotshot each. Their feet were bound to the chairs they sat on, and it's my guess someone held a gun on them to keep them there while they loaded pure, uncut heroin into their veins. That same someone then did this." He spins another photograph across the table showing the word *sloth* carved into the nape of each man's neck.

"You have an idea of who this *someone* is?" Jack asks.

Pinkwater adds another picture to the table. It's a surveillance image of three men dressed in suits but wearing Halloween masks. White faces with crosses for eyes and a maniacal grin on its lips.

"They call themselves The Three. Three psychos who go around doing…" he air quotes, "… God's work."

Jack's eyebrow shoots up. "Have they reached out and declared that?"

"Looks like they've declared it right across their victims' bodies," Shooter says.

"There was a letter found at yesterday's crime scene." Pinkwater opens his cell to show us a picture. "They placed the paper onto one of the victim's hands and stabbed a steak knife through it to hold it in place."

Jack takes the phone from Pinkwater and reads the letter out loud.

"We are The Three.
"Here to clean up the unholiness of man.
"Blood will be spilled for every sin.
"From start to finish.
"And we will re-begin."

"Re-begin?" Shooter questions.

"Shitty English," Paw says. "Tells us something, at least."

"That they're not very good poets?" Shooter raises an eyebrow.

"FBI linguistics should be able to pinpoint where they're from."

"No, there's just the one letter, and it's too short to tell us much," Pinkwater replies.

"Who are the men in the third photo?" I ask him.

"The Fallon brothers. Not the smartest tools in the barn, but they did manage to set up a lucrative heroin trade over in Copperville."

Heroin dealers.

I hate heroin.

I hate what it does to people.

And I hate the people who peddle it.

But these vigilantes are taking their disapproval to extremes.

A bullet to the back of the skull would have sufficed.

"We don't know who the men behind the mask are. The FBI is having trouble coming up with their identities. Truth be told, there's not a lot of resources to throw at this." He sighs. "To be more honest than I should, when three bad guys take out a sex worker, a con man, and three drug dealers, ain't no one from the top running to stop them. That's why the FBI reached out to local law enforcement and why I am reaching out to you. My gut tells me these assholes are just getting started, and if I'm right, then it's only a matter of time before the shitville train rolls through Appalachia and brings these psychopaths with it." He gives each of us a grave look. "They've got a taste for making people pay for their so-called sins, and they ain't gonna have any trouble finding a lot of so-called sinners around these parts."

"You think they're coming to Flintlock?" Jack asks.

"I can almost guarantee it." He pulls a folded map from his pocket and spreads it across the table. Using a red Sharpie, he marks a cross at the location of each murder. It shows a clear line heading toward Flintlock. "When the FBI reached out to the County Sheriff's Office, they said the Kings might be their next target because you're the biggest organized crime syndicate in the area."

"Actually, we're a club," Shooter starts but stops when Jack shakes his head at him. There's no point using that old chestnut on the sheriff. Pinkwater knows exactly who we are and what we do. He receives enough perks for turning a blind eye when it comes to our cannabis and moonshine trade.

My gaze drifts to the photographs on the table.

Kandy Kurtman's lifeless eyes stare up at me.

Twenty-two and already gone.

Poor fucking kid.

"We'll be ready for them if they do," I say.

I'm already killing them in a hundred different ways in my head.

I know people might see a comparison between me killing for hire and these freakshows killing in the name of the seven deadly sins. Because at the end day, we're all breaking the biggest commandment of all.

But I killed bad men who did bad shit.

And I mean, really bad shit.

Human traffickers. Rapists. Pimps who think it's okay to slap a woman around and get her hooked on drugs.

But these guys, they're just arrogant assholes who kill for fun.

Not only was Kandy Kurtman not in the same league as the assholes I killed, but she wasn't even in the same goddamn realm.

And carving a word into flesh postmortem? That smacks of evil bullshit to me.

God's work, my fucking ass.

My gut tells me these guys don't have a religious bone in their body. They merely need something polemic to justify their bloodlust.

"Just the three crime scenes so far?" Jack asks, standing over the photographs as he studies them, and Pinkwater nods. "So there's the potential for four more."

"Or countless, if you consider their *re-begin* threat," Paw adds.

Pinkwater looks serious. More serious than I've ever seen

him. "Three crime scenes, three ties to organized crime. Twice is a coincidence. Three times is a pattern." He leans forward. "I can't stress enough that it's my belief these clowns are going to come looking for you or someone related to the club."

When Pinkwater leaves, Jack calls Church and tells the rest of the club about The Three.

"Psycho fucks," mutters Dakota Joe. "Let them come for us, and I'll show them what wrath looks like. Any fuck who does that to a woman has got it coming."

"We don't wait for them to come looking," Jack says. "Paw and Shooter are already combing through the evidence Pinkwater gave us. Until then, it's business as usual. The crop harvest starts tomorrow, and we can't afford to get distracted by something that may or may not happen. Got it?"

In a lot of situations like this, organizations would retreat or lock down to protect their own. But we have a million-dollar crop to harvest. Besides, we're a motorcycle club, we're always ready for the unexpected.

When Church ends, Jack asks Shooter and me to hang back.

"I want you both to ride out to Fortune City with me. I want to visit Antoinette and the girls. See if they've heard anything unusual. And if these psycho freaks are roaming our territory looking for sinners, the House of Sin might as well have a neon sign pointing arrows inside."

Antoinette is the madam at the House of Sin. The girls are the women who work for her, women I have gotten to know extremely well over the last five years.

Jack must be taking The Three threat seriously if he's prepared to ride out to see the woman whose bed he used to warm before he was married. Especially when he's got a pregnant wife at home who will have his balls if she finds out.

But Antoinette is a good place to start for possible intel on these freaks. People talk. Men get loose lips, especially in the company of a woman who knows how to use her tongue. And because of its location deep in the Appalachian trail, a lot of criminals pass through the House of Sin, dropping secrets like breadcrumbs without realizing it.

I can't count on all my fingers the number of times Antoinette has called us with useful information about something.

In the parking lot, Shooter and I wait on our bikes while Jack calls Bronte. After what we just learned about The Three, he'll want to make sure she's aware of what's going on and to maybe lock all the damn doors until he gets home.

Not that the threat is immediate.

If it was, he'd already have Bronte wrapped in bubble wrap and surrounded by a hundred armed guards by now.

He'd also be doing everything to protect the men he considers his brothers.

But he's right. It's better to be alert than to halt everything for something that might not eventuate.

I look at Shooter. "You're not calling Beth?"

"Are you fucking kidding me? She'll have my balls if she finds out I'm spending the afternoon at a brothel."

"She'll have your balls if she finds out from someone else," Jack says, joining us.

"And who's crazy enough to tell her?"

"My sister is half demon, half psychic. She'll know. Try and hide this at your own peril."

Shooter thinks for a moment. "Fuck." He whips out his phone and walks away to call his girlfriend, the one who is wildly unpredictable, to tell her he is on his way to a brothel.

Jack laughs. Beth is his older sister. She has pure biker blood running through her veins. She is fiercely loyal to those she loves but volatile as fuck if you cross her. Jack wasn't lying when he said you'd cross her at your own peril. I've seen her reduce grown men to tears.

"How is Bronte?" I ask Jack.

"She was more concerned about me bringing home cucumber and balsamic vinegar than she was about me visiting Antoinette. She knows she has nothing to worry about."

"Cucumber and balsamic vinegar?"

"Cravings. Last week it was sliced apple and peanut butter. This week, it's cucumber and balsamic vinegar. And what my queen wants, my queen gets." He grins as Shooter rejoins us. "That was quick."

"Beth said of course she knows she has nothing to worry about. Apparently, your sister is also one-third bloodhound. Said she would be able to smell sex on me, and if she does, she'll make me a eunuch." He climbs on his bike with a grin on his face. "I fucking love that woman."

We take off into warm afternoon sunlight, and I relax into the ride, letting the meditative calm ease away any tension in my muscles.

But no matter how hard I try to avoid it, my thoughts turn to Rory. I tell myself I'm not going to see her again. That there's too much going on. That when I get back to the clubhouse tonight, I'll call her like I said I would, and when I do, I'll say goodbye.

But as the miles fly beneath my wheels and the Tennessee landscape merges into the beauty of Virginia, she's still on my mind.

During the night, I had reached out for her and held her to my chest, and she had settled against me like melted butter, a soft whimper falling from her parted lips. Our bodies had started communicating in the darkness before we were even aware. The language was subtle. A slight angle change of hips. The quiet whisper of fingers brushing against warm flesh. The soft sighs that fell from parted lips as our bodies shifted and moved against each other. All this culminating in the moment when we silently reached for each other, and I buried my face in her throat and sank deep into her.

I grit my teeth and begin to grind them, working my jaw as I push the Harley faster and the landscape whips past.

There's no point thinking about that shit.

Not the way I'm thinking about it anyway.

Like it's something I could get used to.

I focus on steering my bike through the winding roads leading us further into Virginia. Soon enough, the impressive Victorian building that is the House of Sin appears as we ride over the ridge.

It's a ride I've done many times before.

But it's the first time I've ever come here not looking for a woman for the night.

Because nothing inside here is going to quench the need I feel rising inside me.

"You think they're coming here?" Antoinette asks when we're sitting across her desk from her in the grand parlor she calls her office.

She is a gorgeous woman in her forties with thick, red-gold hair down to her tiny waist and fuck-me eyes that have tempted many men.

Today she's dressed for her part as the madam of the most popular brothel in Appalachia. She looks like she's stepped off the set of a western. Tight satin bodice. A long floaty skirt with a split up the side. Killer boots. She sits with one leg crossed over the other, exposing a firm thigh.

"It's too soon to tell," Jack says. "But I want you to be prepared. Take notice of any new clientele."

"I'll tell the girls to keep their ears to the ground. See what they can find out."

Jack stands. "Call me if you hear anything."

We walk for the door, but Antoinette stops us.

"Are you still happily married?"

Jack smiles. "Ecstatically so."

"Pity." She winks. "But I'm happy for you."

He winks back. "Me too."

We leave her office and descend the walnut staircase to the luxurious foyer below. But as we head for the door, a sweet voice calls out my name.

I turn around and see Ilsa. As petite as a pixie with a cute black bob and rosy red lips, she was the girl I always spent time with when I visited.

Her big eyes light up when she sees me. With a squeal, she comes running across the room and flings herself into my arms. "I didn't see your name in my diary," she says, wrapping her arms around my neck and crushing my hips with her firm thighs. "I'm so happy you're here."

I try to untangle her, but she's coiled tightly around me.

"Ilsa," Antoinette's voice floats down from the second-floor landing. "Ares is here on business, not pleasure."

Ilsa pulls back to look at me. "We're not hanging out?"

"Not today, sweetheart."

She looks crushed. Then she leans closer and whispers, "I get off at six if you want to hang around."

I set her on her feet. "That's a real sweet offer, but like Antoinette said, this visit is strictly business."

"I have my diary upstairs if you want to book in your next visit," she says softly, looking disappointed.

Ilsa is a sweet kid. Somewhere in her twenties, she's naturally nurturing and effervescent. She's seen me at my worst, and she still gets excited every time I visit.

"Not tonight, sweetheart." She looks crestfallen, so I lift her chin. "Hey, you apply to the colleges we talked about?"

"You remember that?"

"Of course. And I told you, if you needed help with any of it, you let me know."

She smiles, but it fades. "Ares, are you coming back to see me one day?"

"No, sweetheart."

"I didn't think so. You've got that look about you."

"Look?"

"Like you've gone and fallen in love."

Ilsa's words haunt me when I walk away.

But during the ride back to Flintlock, it's not Ilsa I'm thinking about. It's Rory.

Rory with hair the color of snow.

Rory with lips that taste like wine.

Rory who I can't get the fuck out of my head.

The ride home is a long one, and as the sun begins to sink below the horizon, she's all I can think about—the way she smells, the feel of her skin brushing against mine, and the sound of her soft breath as she falls asleep beside me.

I think about how tender her touch felt against my aching muscles last night, about the tender way she tended to my wounds, and how soothingly wrapped her soft body around mine as she slept.

My body aches and my shoulders feel tense, and my bed back at the clubhouse suddenly doesn't seem inviting.

"Fuck," I growl.

I wave off Shooter and Jack. They probably knew where I was going before I did, and giving in, I turn the Harley around and head in the direction of Rory's apartment.

CHAPTER 11

RORY

It's just gone dark when I leave the Spicy Crawdad. The parking lot is full of vehicles but empty of people. Coming from inside the strip club, I hear Kid Rock's "Cowboy" which signals the beginning of Brigette's routine.

Humming along, I walk to my car, but when I lean down to unlock it, I'm violently shoved from behind and pinned against the door.

"Don't fucking move, you slut bitch," growls a voice in my ear.

I smell the stench of whisky on his hot breath and feel the greasiness on his fingertips as they grip my arms.

Panic zips through me.

Donnie?

No, it can't be.

"Get off me," I demand through gritted teeth.

"What! You don't like this, slut? Isn't that why you shake that sweet ass of yours onstage? You want to get a man all worked up the way you do. Now give me your cash, you harlot, or I'm going to gut you like a deer. Then you and me are going to have some fun."

The man with the rank breath doesn't have a weapon in his hands because one of them is pressed into the small of my back while the other roams my thigh.

But he could have one in his pocket.

So I need to act before he can get his hands on it.

When you get raped repeatedly by a man who is supposed to protect and love you, you get good at defending yourself. You take self-defense classes so one day you can turn the tables on the asshole.

I catch him by surprise and slam my elbow into his ribs. Then I stomp on his foot and backhand my fist into his face. It's basic self-defense, and it works. With his head ringing and his nose gushing, my would-be mugger keels over.

Before he can straighten, I send my knee into his face, and he falls back. Hurt, he climbs onto all fours to steady himself while he fights the pain spreading through his gut and face.

But I'm not finished with him.

I kick an arm out from under him, and he collapses onto the pavement.

"Bitch!" He wheezes.

Pulling the Ruger out of my bag, I kneel on his spine and press the gun's barrel into the base of his skull. "Give me one good reason why I shouldn't blow your brains out all over this goddamn concrete."

"What the fuck?"

"Strike one. Your question is *not* an answer. Tell me why I shouldn't paint this parking lot with your gray matter."

"What the fuck? You're crazy!"

"Strike two… there you go again, answering a question with a question. You know how it goes… three strikes and you're out." I dig the gun in deeper. "So if I were you, I'd choose my next words very carefully. Now tell me, asshole, why shouldn't I end your miserable sorry ass life right here and now?"

"Because... because..."

I sigh and press my knee harder into his spine. "I'm getting bored. And just so you know, when I get bored, my finger gets itchy."

"Don't hurt me," he cries.

"But *you* were going to hurt *me*. I believe the term of endearment was 'now give me your cash, you harlot, or I'm going to gut you like a deer.' Help me out here. Am I right?"

He blubbers something inaudible. So I grab his hair, pull his head back, then slam his face into the concrete.

"Answer a lady when she speaks to you. I said, *am... I... right*?"

He's dazed for a moment, then starts screaming, "You're crazy! Help. Help me!" He begins wailing like he's the one who was pinned against the car and felt up by a whisky-soaked pervert demanding he hand over his hard-earned cash.

Fucking cry baby.

"Stop wailing, you pathetic ass. If you can't take it, don't fucking dish it." I lean down and whisper in his ear, making sure the tip of the barrel presses deeper into his skin, "You do anything like this again, I'm going to find you, and I'm going to use this here gun, and I'm going to pull the fucking trigger. Do you understand me, you fucking twerp? I've done it before, and I'm telling you now... nothing beats seeing the brains of your rapist spattered all over the ground."

This makes him holler some more.

Bennie and Lloyd, two of the bouncers from the Spicy Crawdad, come running across the parking lot. I put my gun back into my purse.

"You okay, Rory?" Bennie asks, panting.

I climb off the would-be-rapist-mugger man who just shit his pants and straighten my skirt. "You might want to take this man out the back and hose him off."

Mr. Shit His Pants looks up at Bennie and Lloyd. "Thank fuck, you're here. This bitch was about to kill me."

My nerves are still buzzing when I get home and find Ares waiting at the foot of the stairs leading up to my apartment.

I can't suppress my smile.

"This is becoming a habit," I say, walking by him to climb the stairs.

He follows. "A good or bad habit?"

"Bad," I say, stopping to unlock my front door. I glance at him over my shoulder. "But bad habits are my favorite kind."

When we're inside, he notices the red marks on my arms.

"That happen tonight?"

"Yes."

His temperature rises. "At the Crawdad?"

"Not exactly."

"What does that mean?"

"I was walking to my car, and a guy tried mugging me."

His nostrils flare. "Someone tried mugging you?"

"Yes, he *tried*. But he didn't count on my self-defense training or the three summers spent sparring with local boys in my uncle's gym."

"Are you okay?"

"I'm better than he is."

Ares' big hands curl into fists, and his breath leaves him with a ragged, harsh growl. "Where is he?"

"Changing his underwear. Put your hammer down, *Thor*, I took care of it."

The muscle in his jaw ticks. "He will pay for putting his hands on you."

"He already has?"

"What do you mean?"

"His face got up close and personal with the pavement."

"How?"

"I introduced them. Face meet concrete. The concrete won."

He looks surprised. "You did that?"

"Your tone implies I'm not capable of doing such a thing. Is that because I'm a woman?"

"It's because you're tiny."

"To you, everyone is tiny."

"You especially."

"I'm strong… I'm also slightly offended."

His temper eases. "I've seen you try to change a tire."

"That was different. Maybe I was trying to get your attention."

He raises an eyebrow. "Were you?"

I reach for his waistband, and my fingers walk across his warm ab muscles, making him flinch. "Did it work?"

He yanks me closer. "Oh, it worked."

"Then what does it matter?"

He gazes down at me. "I don't know if I should be scared or turned on."

"Oh, you're turned on. And maybe a little in love with me." I rise on my tiptoes to kiss him. "But that's because you're a very smart man."

I kiss him. A sweet, chaste kiss with a smile on my lips.

He takes hold of my chin, his tone serious. "You could've been hurt."

"Are you kidding? I'm infallible."

"No, you're a sexy woman walking alone at night." The back of his fingers whisper across my cheek. His gaze is warm, his expression less like he wants to burn down the world and more like I am the only thing he can see right now.

It makes me giddy and want to cry at the same time.

"I'm going to talk to Lacy… make sure you and the girls have escorts to their cars when they leave their shift."

"Fine, if that makes you happy."

I kiss him to stop him from talking.

And because of the way he's looking at me makes me nervous and happy all at once, and I'm not sure what to make of it.

It makes me kiss him rough and hard.

And he responds by groaning and kissing me just as rough and hard.

I pull back. "This is just sex, right?"

"Right."

I smile. "Good. Because for a moment there, I thought you were going to get all sweet and mushy on me."

His gaze is dark, and it smolders.

"I don't do sweet. Now get on your knees," he commands.

His voice is rough, a low growl that sends heat straight to my clit.

He unzips his jeans while I do as he says and sink to my knees so I am at eye level with his groin. He pulls out his cock. It's so big it curves up toward his deeply carved abs.

He grasps it at the base. "Now, suck it."

Again, I obey him, settling my lips over the wide, smooth head and gliding my tongue across the polished skin. I tease him and then draw him in deeper until he hits the back of my throat.

A tremor rolls through him, and he hisses in a rough breath. "That's it, baby, just like that."

I wrap my fingers around the thick girth and position myself so I can take him deeper. My tongue rims the sensitive skin beneath the hood, sending another shiver through him.

"Goddamn, you fuck good with your mouth."

His big hands drag through my hair and clutch the roots, sending a delicious sting across my scalp and over my body. I groan with wicked pleasure, loving the pain with the pleasure of his cock in my mouth.

"You like that? You like me hurting you when you're on your knees in front of me?" He grips tighter, and the sting intensifies, sending pebbles of pleasure rippling across my skin. "Is that what my little one wants?"

I groan in response, the throb between my thighs almost too much to bear.

I find the head of his cock again and rim it with my tongue, and he becomes putty in my hands. His knees weaken, his breath becomes ragged. It makes me feel in control, *powerful*, and it turns me on having him in my mouth. I can smell the intoxicating scent of his skin, and the ache tightens between my thighs. I'm so needy for his cock it would only take him touching me, and I would come.

He starts to fuck my mouth, his hips rocking, his balls tightening beneath my massaging hands.

"Goddammit, you feel good. That's it… fuck me with that pretty little mouth."

My grip on him tightens, and my hand increases speed with shallow, tight tugs, and he lets out an approving gasp. His head drops back, his lips part, and I know what's about to happen.

Sweet agony falls from his lips.

"You're going to make me come." He groans and grips my hair tighter. "*Rory—*"

I feel the head of his cock throb against the hollow of my mouth and warm saltiness as he starts to come. I keep massaging his length but pull back so he can see his cum spatter against my tongue and down my chin, his appreciative groans almost bringing me to my own orgasm.

Panting, he strokes himself until he's empty.

He steps away, the look on his face telling me this isn't over. Ares climbs onto the bed and lays down.

His cock hasn't softened. It's still rigid and ready.

I'm coming to learn he doesn't have a refractory period.

He takes the base of his cock in his hand. "Come and sit on my cock, baby."

I crawl over to him. "It's not too soon?"

He reaches up with his free hand and pushes a lock of hair behind my ear. "You fucking me with your mouth was mind-blowing, but I'm far from done with you, little one. I want you to ride me."

His words send an achy throb straight between my legs. So I slide my thighs on either side of him and shiver as he rubs the sensitive crown through my slippery folds.

He hisses in a rough breath. "Fuck, baby, you're so wet."

I'm throbbing hard now. He rubs against my clit, and I'm so turned on I can barely see straight.

I take his cock in my hand and slowly ease onto him, gasping as my body swallows the entire length of him.

"That's it, angel, take all of it," he breathes raggedly. "Take every fucking inch."

I pause, needing a moment for my body to adjust to his size. My small frame is no comparison to the bulk of him, but at this moment, I am in complete control, and I'm so aroused my pussy is saturated.

I slowly rock onto him, feeling stretched and completely full. Pleasure gathers inside me and between my legs.

Ares' hands grip my hips and drag me back and forward across his pelvis. The root of his cock rubs against my clit, the friction driving me closer and closer.

I teeter on the edge in that place where you know you're about to fall into a massive pool of pleasure, and the excitement makes your skin flush and your heart race even harder.

"Come on my cock," he begs, his face twisted in pleasure, his thick shaft pulsing inside me. "I need to feel that pretty pussy squeeze my cock."

I unravel on top of him and crash into my orgasm. "Oh... *fuck.*"

He follows, and our cries fill the room in a frenzy of pleasure.

Panting, we come back to ourselves, and he pulls me into his arms.

We're quiet for a moment as his fingers trail delicate caresses down my arm. His warm breath is even now and heats my shoulder.

Ares' finger lingers over the scar on my wrist.

His voice breaks the silence. "Looks like a bite mark."

Caught off guard, I quickly pull my hand free and hide it against my chest.

Behind me, Ares stiffens, and there's a pause before his voice cuts into the silence, "Did he do that?"

We both know who he means.

I hug my wrist closer and close my eyes.

I am not ready for this.

Ares leans closer, his voice soft and reassuring, his breath warm against the shell of my ear. "Don't be afraid of me, little one. You can trust me with your secrets."

The tenderness in his voice sends tears to my eyes, and my face tightens with emotion.

It's crazy because I don't even know him.

But it feels like I can tell him anything.

I hold up my wrist so he can see the puckered scar etched into my skin. It's a permanent reminder of my evil stepfather and how creative he could get with his teeth.

My voice is monotoned, almost alien, when I say, "The first time he raped me, I was fifteen. This was a warning to keep quiet."

I hear his rough exhale of breath behind me before he mutters, "Goddammit."

"After that, he visited me whenever my mom was bombed on vodka and pills, which was pretty much every night, and do whatever he wanted to do to me."

Ares

Ares curls his big hand over mine and brings my knuckles to his gentle lips. "You don't need to talk about it. If it hurts—"

"It does. But I want to share this with you."

I can't explain why. By rule, I don't tell anyone about what happened to me. About the horrible things Donnie did to me and how my mother let him.

But I feel safe in Ares' arms, and it makes me want to get it off my chest.

It feels *good* to get it off my chest.

He squeezes my hand. "Did you tell anyone?"

"I told my mom once, but she slapped me across the face and told me I was making it up because I didn't want to see her happy. The second time I told her, she slapped me harder and accused me of being an attention-seeker, so I packed a bag and ran away, only for the authorities to bring me back home. No one believed me."

Ares' voice is rough. "Why?"

My stepfather had enough cops on his payroll to start his own damn police department.

But I don't share that detail with Ares because it will only make him curious.

And I can't risk him wanting to know more and finding out the truth.

"My mom didn't want to face it. Or she didn't care. The jury is still out on that one."

It wasn't because she loved Donnie. She wasn't capable of love. *That* the jury is sure about. No, it was because she didn't want anything to upset the apple cart that was her life. My stepfather kept her in the life she was accustomed to, and every now and again, all she had to do was open her legs and fake like she enjoyed it.

And turn a blind eye to him messing with her daughter.

I swallow back the image of him creeping into my bedroom

at night.

"You mentioned once that you had a brother," Ares says.

I stiffen. "Yes."

"Did you tell him?"

"He was away at college on a football scholarship when my mom met Donnie. We weren't as close by then. When he left home, he stayed gone."

"And your uncle, the one who owned the gym?"

"He died of a massive heart attack the summer my mom married Donnie."

Ares gently rolls me onto my back and looks down at me. His face is strong and handsome, his expression dark and dangerous. But it's the darkness in his deep brown eyes that tells me how much he wants to take this pain from me.

"You don't ever have to hide from me," he says, his voice deep and strong. "Do you understand?"

"I thought this was just sex," I whisper.

"Doesn't mean I don't care."

I like that answer.

So I smile up at him and settle into the warmth of his shoulder.

He doesn't offer to kill my stepfather.

Which is good.

Because now I am here for entirely different reasons.

Even if I don't want to admit it.

CHAPTER 12

ARES

It's Family Day at the clubhouse, and the yard has been transformed into a giant kid's playground with an inflatable jumping castle and balloons everywhere you look.

The mood in the air is light. Tyler Childer's "Whitehouse Road" cuts into the sunny afternoon as I watch my club brothers dance with their old ladies on the makeshift dance floor. There's not a club girl in sight. When Bronte started this tradition a couple of years ago, she made it abundantly clear that the day was about family, not about dicks getting wet. It's G-rated, and our club girls come with a well-earned triple X rating, so they're not invited.

Not that our queen has anything against club girls. She'll party alongside them when the time is right. Hell, I've even seen her lick salt from the Tawny-Anne's double Ds while doing tequila slammers.

But today is about the old ladies and the kids.

And no one fucks with our president's old lady. She might look angelic, but she's equal parts angel *and* demon. Cross her, and she'll nail you with a look. And if that doesn't kill you, her fiercely protective husband will happily finish you off.

"Where's your girl?" Paw asks, sliding into the chair next to me.

I bring my beer to my lips and take a sip before I answer, "I don't have a girl."

He gives me a grin. "Just keep telling yourself that, buddy."

I decide to ignore him. Instead, I look around at the decorated compound. The sound of kids laughing and screaming in the jumping castle makes me smile. My gaze lands on Gambit having his face painted by a fairy in a pink tutu and glittery wings. Beside him, four little girls sit on tiny stools gazing up at him, transfixed as he lets the pretty makeup girl turn him into a fairy princess. He likes her, I can tell by the way he's turned to putty in her hands, and I don't doubt he'll get her number after this.

Across the yard, Merrick is gazing into the eyes of a pretty blonde girl he has his arms around.

At one of the tables, Bam is holding hands with a pretty brunette while his brother, Loki, has his arms around a stunning blonde.

When the hell did the twins get girlfriends?

Hell, is the whole world a couple now?

Or is Rory's presence in my life highlighting how lonely my life is?

I fight it.

Forming fucking feelings for someone is not on my radar.

But then life has a way of flipping the switch on you.

I would know.

Mine came out of the blue and turned my life on its ass.

Five years ago.

It was early morning, and the sun hadn't yet breached the horizon. Yellow light from the overhead lamp at the wharf entrance gleamed on the wet pavement as fog rose from the water to blanket the dawn in an ethereal veil. Seawater lapped at the barnacled skin of the jetty as sleepy seagulls squawked in the salty air. Somewhere out on the water, a fishing boat signaled its journey back to land.

I waited in the shadows. The invisible man. Ready to make my move as soon as the black Cadillac pulled into the empty alleyway.

I'd watched my mark for days, so I knew he'd be here at this time, in that car, waiting for the gates to open.

When I'm given a mark, I am told two things—their first name and the crime they committed against the De Kysa.

Anything else was left for me to work out.

So I stalk my marks, taking note of their patterns, habits. and where they would be at their most vulnerable. Then I execute the hit.

I only knew this guy as Graham. He used to be a bookkeeper for the De Kysa family until he decided to steal from them. The moment Vinnie De Kysa learned of his betrayal and where he was hiding, Graham's name was added to my hit list.

I knew this guy came here every Thursday to buy fresh snapper off the trawler for his wife. Tonight was date night. His wife liked seafood. Snapper was her favorite. I knew everything.

I also knew there was no CCTV or any kind of surveillance around this part of the wharf.

To be honest, I wasn't sure about this hit. Usually, the men I killed were involved in human trafficking or have murdered, hurt, or maimed an innocent person. But this guy was a white-collar criminal. He didn't hurt anyone. Just took what didn't belong to him, and it didn't sit well with me that I'd be ending his life over it.

But Vinnie did me a solid when he used his connections to find out the names of the three men who raped and murdered

Belle, so I owed him this.

When it was time, I strode up to the car and reefed open the door. I never worried if it was locked or unlocked. If it were locked, my Glock would have it open within seconds.

The mark was startled and froze as I slid into the passenger seat.

"Hi, Graham," I said calmly.

Because of my size, I'm a foreboding presence. But the black gloves and balaclava take me from intimidating to terrifying.

Graham looked like he was going to shit himself.

"Who are you?" His wide eyes dropped to the gun in my hand. "W-what do you w-want? W-why are you in my c-car?"

I pointed the gun at his head. "Guess."

"I-I don't k-know why."

"I can give you eight million reasons why."

That told him exactly who I was and why I was there.

If it's possible, his face grew paler.

"Let me guess, right about now you're wishing you didn't steal eight million dollars from Vinnie De Kysa."

He closed his eyes and started to sob.

"Come on, Graham, you must've realized Vinnie wasn't going to roll over and let you fuck him up the ass by stealing all that cash from him, did you?"

"I h-had to do it."

"No! What you had to do was not steal his money. That was legit your one job... protecting his assets."

"I m-made a mistake."

"You bet you did."

I pressed the gun barrel against his temple, and he winced.

"Please, not in front of my kid."

My eyes darted to the back seat, and all kinds of alarms went off inside my head when I saw a damn kid sitting in the car seat staring back at me with big doe eyes. He couldn't be more than *two years old.*

Dammit! Why didn't I look in the back seat before I climbed in?

Because in the two weeks I'd been watching him, he had never brought his kid with him.

Wait! Did he somehow know today was the day?

Is that what this is about?

Did he know I was coming, so he brought his kid with him as a shield?

I turned away from the kid to glare at my mark ready to drag him outside the car and off him right there on the wharf for putting his kid in harm's way.

But I don't.

Because after watching him for two weeks, I instinctively knew that wasn't the case. This schmuck might be an opportunistic thief, but he wasn't about to risk his kid's life.

This was just dumb luck.

Or bad luck.

Depended which side of the gun you were on.

"Please, let me get my kid home, and then I'll go anywhere you want."

I looked at the kid again.

Fuck.

Now the little guy was sucking in his lower lip. Any minute and he was going to start crying.

Double fuck.

I looked away to refocus and press the barrel of my gun to Graham's temple. He yelped, and it set the kid off. He started hollering in his car seat, and damn if I didn't feel an overwhelming urge to comfort the little guy.

Fuck. Fuck. Fuck.

I took in a frustrated breath. "How much of the money is left?"

"A-all of it."

Hating myself for what I was about to do because it meant I was going to have to smooth this shit over with Vinnie somehow, I said, "Then today is your lucky day, Graham, because I'm giving you a second chance. Do you understand? You're going to get that eight million dollars, and you're going to give it back to Vinnie De Kysa. Every last penny."

"H-how do I give it back?"

"I don't care how. FedEx it, Uber it, hell, send it via fucking carrier pigeon, I don't give a fuck, just fucking do it. You've got twenty-four hours."

"Okay, I-I will."

I looked at the kid. He'd stopped crying, but he was staring at me with those big eyes, and it was the strangest encounter I'd ever had during a hit. Because it wasn't fear I saw in his eyes, it was sadness. Hell, if I'm real honest, he looked more disappointed in me than anything.

Christ. I must be losing my mind because I felt that look right through to my bones.

Somewhere inside me a switch was flipped.

I turned back to Graham. "Twenty-four hours. Got it?"

"I u-understand."

"Good. Now, get in the back seat and comfort your kid."

We both climbed out, and he did as I instructed. He got his kid out of the car seat and hugged him tightly while I walked away without another glance and disappeared into the shadows.

As I walked, I cleaned my gun for prints, and when I reached the other side of the harbor where my rental car was parked, I threw it as far into the water as possible.

I was done.

I didn't want to be the bad guy anymore.

Less than twenty-four hours later, eight million dollars

stuffed into a leather sports bag landed on the front door of the De Kysa mansion, and I was officially unemployed.

The sound of kids' laughter brings me back to the present. Across the row of barbecue tables I see Jack with Bronte. He's rubbing her pregnant belly tenderly as they talk, and you can clearly tell she is the only thing he sees. His world starts and ends with her.

A knot forms in my chest.

Fuck it.

"Where you going?" Paw asks.

"To do what I should've done in the first place."

"What?"

"I'm going to call my girl."

Except I don't call her. Instead, I climb on my bike and ride over to her apartment. I won't lie, I spend most of the ride questioning if I'm doing the right thing. But the moment she opens the door, the violent kick in my heart tells me I am exactly where I want to be and who I want to be with.

I take her in my arms and kiss her long and deep, and she rewards me in all the best ways possible.

CHAPTER 13

RORY

"You never talk about your past," I say over the sea of bubbles.

When Ares arrived, I'd already drawn a bubble bath. The candles were lit. The bottle of red wine was open. But what was meant to be a solo affair turned into a twosome.

"Because that's where I like to leave it," he says.

He's bigger than big, so there isn't much room left for me in the bath, and even though we sit at opposite ends, I'm practically sitting on him. If I weren't basically a pixie, this wouldn't work.

"Anyway, I thought you liked it that way," he adds.

"I do, but at the same time, I'm nosy. I'm a Pisces, and we can be terribly fickle. We're two fish swimming in opposite directions, always changing our minds. What star sign are you?"

"A Scorpio."

"Oh, the dark, enigmatic sign in the zodiac. How fitting."

"You're teasing."

"Always. Do you believe in star signs?"

"I do."

That surprises me. "Really?"

"The moon can move tides. We're about sixty percent water, so it's not a stretch to think that other celestial entities could affect our personalities and moods if they can control something as big as our oceans."

"It sounds like you know a lot about it."

"There was a time in my life when all I did was read, and when you run out of crime thrillers and killer biographies, you have to move on to other stuff. Where I was, the choice was limited."

"Where was that."

"Prison."

His words bite into the air between us.

We stare at each other.

"Prison?" I whisper. "For what?"

He's very still as he replies, "For murder."

Despite the warm bath water, my skin pebbles.

"Does that frighten you?" His voice is low.

I don't move. "Yes."

His expression falters—almost as if it hurt him to hear me admit it.

"You don't have to be," he says. "I didn't do it."

I raise an eyebrow.

How many prisons are filled with people who *didn't do it*?

"Then how did you get sent away?"

His throat works as he thinks.

"I was an easy scapegoat. The town freak. The mutant everyone was afraid of, so it was easy to pin the crime on me."

I realize I've been holding my breath and let it go. "Do you want to talk about it?"

"Do you?"

His eyes are warm and dark as he gazes at me from the other end of the tub.

I nod slowly. "Yes."

He thinks. His stubble-covered jaw tenses. His black eyes distant.

"Hey, it's okay," I say softly. "You don't have to explain anything to me if it's hard for you."

"I want you to know. But I don't want you to be frightened of me. I would never hurt you." His brows draw together. "The person I was accused of murdering was my girlfriend."

The sharp inhale of breath rushes through my teeth.

His girlfriend.

My heart speeds up.

"Belle was the girl next door, and she was my first love."

There's clear pain in his voice.

Just as there's apprehension in mine.

"What happened?"

"Her parents didn't want her seeing me. Like the rest of the town, they were afraid of me. We used to meet in secret. I come from a small town where everyone thought I was some kind of genetic freak. Even my father hated me because my mother died giving birth to what he referred to as a monster, and everyone followed suit after that."

His words punch me in the heart.

"Belle was different. She was sweet and kind and could see past my size and awkwardness. One night when we were eighteen, we met at the old, abandoned theater in town. It was a safe place to meet without anyone seeing us. Afterward, we were attacked by three college kids out looking for fun." His voice becomes very low. "Once I was incapacitated, they raped and murdered her."

My hand shoots over my mouth. "Oh, Ares…"

"Despite my concussion, stitches, *and* the overwhelming evidence that I didn't do it, I was found guilty."

"How were you found guilty when they had evidence to say otherwise?"

"I didn't know they had the evidence at the time of my trial…" He takes in a deep breath. "It wasn't until years later when one of those innocent project-type people looked into it and unearthed all the suppressed evidence. Turned out the three overprivileged college kids had some big family connections. One was the son of a senator, the other a judge. The third one was an up-and-coming football star. Nobody wanted to see *their* lives ruined. It was easier to put away the mutant everyone was so afraid of. I did nine years before I was cleared."

I'm horrified.

Nine years.

His big arms rest on the side of the bath.

I reach for his hand and tangle my fingers in his. "I'm sorry, I didn't know."

His eyes soften, and he gives me a gentle closed-lip smile. "Now you do."

A tender look passes between us.

What he shared with me has pulled us closer together.

Whether we like it or not.

He clears his throat. "There's a party at the clubhouse next Saturday to celebrate the crop harvest."

I lift an eyebrow at him. "Didn't you just come from a party?"

"That was the family-friendly version. Next weekend will be a lot different. Less family, more boobs."

I can't help but giggle. "And?"

"And I'm thinking it'd be a good idea if you were there."

He looks so uncomfortable it's almost adorable.

I slide across the tub and curl my arms around his neck. "Are you asking me out on a date, Ares?"

Feeling my pussy rub against his cock, his expression turns downright carnal.

"If by date, you mean I take you to a party at the clubhouse and then get to fuck you into the early hours of the next day, then yes, it's a date."

He's downplaying the date, keeping it on a physical level. Reminding me that this is casual, that it's just sex, and we owe each other nothing.

But I like that he does.

Because at least one of us must keep a level head.

And, at the moment, it definitely isn't me.

Kissing him hard, I sink onto his cock and ride him all the way to nirvana.

***

A week later, I stand in the middle of my bedroom and start to panic.

Ares is due to pick me up in a few minutes, and I'm not even dressed.

It took me an hour to get my makeup right, but there's no saving my hair today. In the end, I pulled it into a messy bun on top of my head.

I sigh, staring at the small number of clothes left in my wardrobe.

When I arrived in town to find Ares, I never expected to be invited to the clubhouse for a party. *And I definitely didn't expect him to ask me out on a date.*

Now, there's a pile of discarded clothes on my bedroom floor as I stress about what to wear. I'm worried about how I look because it feels like I'm about to meet the family of a boy I really like.

And why does it matter so much to me that they like me?

This isn't me at all.

Hanging out with the man I asked to kill my rapist stepfather is beginning to fuck with me.

And that doesn't fit in with the plan at all.

CHAPTER 14

ARES

I feel like a fucking king walking into the clubhouse with Rory on my arm.

She looks gorgeous. Red lips. Short skirt and boots. Blonde hair pulled into a messy bun on top of her head with small pieces escaping around her beautiful face. *Seductive eyes that make promises of what she's going to do to my cock later.*

Rory grabs everyone's attention.

Even Jack does a double take, and he's so obsessed with his wife, he never looks at a woman more than once. Although Jack's double take is probably more to do with who is in his clubhouse than the girl on my arm being a perfect ten.

But still, it's a buzz.

"Wow! This place is incredible," she says, looking around in awe.

"It used to be a luxury hotel back in the thirties when Flintlock was a popular vacation town."

Almost a hundred years old, the old hotel has lost the glamor and luxury of its early years, but there are still echoes of it in the high ceilings, antique chandeliers, and the black and white checkered floor.

"If only these walls could talk," she says softly, still gazing around the grand ballroom that is now the clubhouse bar.

"Thank fuck they can't. I've seen things here that would make your eyes bleed."

"Oooh… like what?"

"Stick around, you'll see. My brothers are well-behaved now, but it's early."

"Now I'm intrigued."

"You might be sorry you said that."

I take her to the bar.

"Everyone is looking at me," she whispers.

"Do you blame them?" I lean down. "I don't know if you realize this, but you're fucking gorgeous."

She smiles, and I have an urge to kiss the red from her gorgeous lips.

TJ is tending bar, and when she sees Rory, she grins. "What can I get you, honey?"

"I'll have a whiskey on the rocks." She digs into her purse for money, but I stop her.

"You don't need to do that, it's free."

"Free?"

"For the Kings and their dates, yes. And if it weren't, I'd be paying, not you."

A wicked gleam enters her eyes. "So… this *is* a date?"

God, she's cute.

I can't help but smile. "Yeah, it's a date."

Rob Zombie is playing as we take our drinks and move away from the bar.

All eyes are still on us.

It's a weird sensation.

I like the way my brothers sweep their appreciative gazes up and down her perfect body, but I also want to kill them for doing it.

I wrap a possessive arm around her waist and lead her to a booth where we sit.

Paw appears beside me. "You're needed outside," he says. "It's Gabe."

I glance at my girl, but I don't want to leave her. "Is it urgent?"

"I don't know if I'd call a half-naked Gabe dry humping the fountain urgent. But Jack wants you to help get him down."

"Fuck."

"Yeah, wait till you have a visual."

I stand and take a quick look around the room. At one of the tables near the bar, Earl and Wyatt are locked in an arm wrestle. Farther down, on one of the couches, Loki is receiving a lap dance from the blonde girl I'd seen him with at Family Day.

Metallica's "Sad But True" plays as a dancer with hot pink hair works the pole on the small stage beneath a massive Kings of Mayhem sign.

And in the corner, club girls circle Bam and Merrick as they play pool with Dakota Joe and Shooter. Any minute now, Shooter's girlfriend, Beth, will walk in, and all the club girls will scatter. Beth isn't known for having a sunshiny personality, and none of them want to be on the receiving end of her razor-sharp tongue.

I lean toward Rory and ask quietly, "Will you be okay if I go handle this for a moment?"

She smiles. "Have you seen where I work? This is like daycare in comparison. Go look after your friend."

Her response makes me grin.

She fits in here. This could work. The thought hits me without warning, and I don't know how I feel about it.

I follow Paw out of the clubhouse.

"Gabe's losing it. Poor fuck," he says. "His head is totally screwed up over his divorce."

Gabe has climbed the old fountain and is straddling the cement mermaid. He's holding up a near-empty bottle of Tennessee whisky and singing Puddle of Mud's "She Fucking Hates Me."

Badly.

Jack is leaning against a fence railing pinching his nose.

I walk up to the fountain. "Get down, you crazy fuck."

But Gabe is too drunk to pay me any attention. Instead, he serenades me with another chorus of the song.

"I swear to God, Gabe, if you make me come up there and get you, I'm gonna kick your ass all the way back to Las Vegas."

"Las Vegas… where I left my heart," he slurs.

"And your pants, by the looks of it," I say because he's only wearing his boxers.

"They were wet—" He hiccups and drops the whisky bottle. "Oh fuck—" He loses his footing and crashes down to the three inches of water below. The fountain dried up years ago, but it's full of dirty rainwater and leaves.

"Get him out and help him to his room," Jack says. "Tomorrow, I'm going to sit the fucker down, and we're going to get his head straight."

"Fine! But if he pukes on me, I'm gonna throw him back in."

I haul Gabe out of the fountain and throw him over my shoulder.

"Take him through the back," Jack says. "No one else needs to see him like this."

There's an old service entry around the back of the clubhouse. Back in the hotel days, it's where the deliveries were received before they were taken inside to the kitchen. I carry Gabe in and down the corridors until we reach his room.

"Jesus Christ," Paw says when he flicks on the light. "It stinks like the inside of a garbage refuge in here."

Gabe's bed is covered in a sea of photographs.

Pictures of him and his wife.

Paw scoops them off the bed, and I drop Gabe onto the mattress.

He rolls onto his side and wraps his arm around his pillow.

"Come on, he needs to sleep it off," I say. I want to get back to the party. *Face it, buddy, you want to get back to your girl.* "Jack will sort him out tomorrow."

We return to the party and I see Merrick has joined Rory at the booth. The man looks like a male model and is never short of female company. So when I see him flirting with Rory, my blood pressure shoots through the roof.

"Calm down, big fella," Paw says. "He's just being friendly."

"Yeah, but his kind of friendly gets you pregnant," I mutter.

CHAPTER 15

RORY

For some reason, Ares can't get me away from the handsome biker with the bright blue eyes and dimples quick enough, and the death glare I see Ares give him makes me feel a little giddy.

"I want you to meet someone special," he says, leading me across the room to where an older woman stands at the bar. "Dolly kind of runs this place."

"I thought Jack was president."

"He is, and what he says goes. But when it comes to the clubhouse, Dolly rules the roost."

"Like a clubhouse mom?"

He smiles. "Yeah, like a clubhouse mom. But don't let her sweet face and kind eyes fool you. She can be frightening if you make her mad."

We walk over to a blonde bombshell with big hair and a dazzling smile. She's dressed in a pair of tight jeans, knee-high boots, and a denim jacket covered in sparkles.

When Ares introduces us, Dolly pulls me in for a warm hug. "It sure is lovely to meet you, sugar."

No sooner has the greeting left her glossy lips and she's rousing on the prospect for almost dropping a tray of freshly cleaned glassware.

"Lord help me… if you drop that tray, I'll tan your butt harder than a hide in a tannery."

The prospect looks worried. Like he'd rather face a hundred rival motorcycle gangs than have Dolly spank him.

"Sorry, Dolly," he says with a grimace.

She turns back to me, her eyes twinkling. "Don't mind me, honey. It's up to Jack to keep these boys in line, but it's up to me to house train them."

A beautiful blonde woman with wildflowers in her hair and a big pregnant belly appears beside Dolly. She has the sexiest lips on a woman I've ever seen.

Her eyes twinkle. "You must be Rory. I'm Bronte, Jack's wife."

Of course, the president is married to the most beautiful girl in the world.

"When Jack mentioned Ares had brought a date, I had to come and introduce myself."

She pulls me in for a hug.

God, she even smells perfect.

When she lets me go, she lets out a sudden gasp. She grabs my hand and places it on her belly so I can feel her baby kick. "Oh boy, this kid is itching for some attention. Feel that? He's definitely going to be a football player."

"When are you due?" I ask.

"Not for another four weeks. But that feels like a lifetime away." She looks at my whiskey with wishful eyes. "What I would give for one of those."

Dolly notices my glass is almost empty. "How about I get you another one?"

"Sure, that would be lovely, thanks."

She turns to Ares. "How about you, honey."

But Ares is already looking at me with a strange expression on his face. Not a bad one. It's more a look of contentment and happiness.

Dolly offering him a drink breaks him out of it. "Yeah, sure, that'd be good."

While Dolly fixes our drinks, I excuse myself to find the bathroom.

It's down a long hallway, past what I guess are bedrooms. Inside, I'm surprised by the condition. It's so clean and tidy. Then I think of Dolly, and it makes sense. She definitely runs a tight ship, and I can see her demanding nice facilities for the women.

While I'm peeing, the door opens, and someone enters. I hear high heels click-clack on the floor, then the door to the cubicle next to me closes. I finish up, but while I'm washing my hands, I hear a woman's voice in the cubicle.

"Oh, dang it," she says.

The next thing I know, the door opens and a cute, dimpled face appears in the crack.

"Hey, honey, you think you can get me a tampon from the dispenser on the wall?"

"Sure," I reply, walking over to the dispenser. "I don't see a coin slot."

"Oh, there isn't one. They're free, honey. Same with the condoms. Dolly says it ain't right to charge for them."

I like Dolly.

I offer the girl the tampon.

"Thanks," she says, taking it. "You must be Rory."

"You know my name?"

"Are you kidding me? The moment us girls heard Ares was bringing a date to the party, we all wanted to know who she was."

"Really, why?"

"Ares never brings dates to the clubhouse." She grins, and it's as wholesome as apple pie. Deep dimples and all. "Correction... he never dates, period. I've never seen him with a girl. And I've been here going on three years." She holds up the tampon. "Hold that thought."

The door closes, and I return to the mirror to apply a fresh coat of lipstick.

Apple Pie joins me a few minutes later. And it doesn't take me long to figure out that this girl is sweet. She screams pumpkin festivals and farmland.

Although, her tight denim skirt, bra top, and boots are more biker than bashful.

"So you're someone's old lady?" I ask.

It feels weird using the term, but while in Rome.

She looks at me in the mirror as she washes her hands. "I'm not a tie-me-down kind of girl. I'm more of a tie-me-up kind of babe." She giggles. "I don't want to be an old lady. I like my freedom."

"So you just hang out?"

She shrugs. "Hang out. Party. *Fuck.*"

An unfamiliar tingle takes up in the base of my spine.

"Anyone in particular?"

Please don't say Ares.

"I have a few boyfriends here." She giggles, then her eyes widen. "Oh, but not Ares. Oh, my goodness, not Ares."

She checks her image in the mirror, but then her eyes go round again. "Oh, dang it, I'm sorry. My name is Cinnamon." She offers me her hand. "Don't mind me, I ramble so much I sometimes forget my manners. You're real pretty, you know that? When I heard Ares was bringing a girl, I thought to myself, *Cinnamon, that girl is going to be somethin'*, and well, I was right." She rummages through her purse and pulls out a lip gloss. "And you know what, I'm so dang happy he's found someone.

You guys look real sweet together."

"Oh, we're not together."

She glances at me sideways. "Oh, honey, I've seen the way you two look at each other. You're together."

"We're just hanging out." I shrug to show her it's nothing serious. "I was surprised he even invited me along tonight."

She keeps glossing her lips but smiles to herself in the mirror. "Have you met everyone yet?" she asks.

"I've met a few but not everyone."

"Well, everyone wants to meet you. But they'll do it in their own way in their own time. And they're *real* nice. Jack, the president, now he can be *real* impatient and, oh my Lord, he can be scary, but really he's just a big ol' teddy bear underneath all that gruff exterior. And his wife, Bronte, have you seen the face on that one? She's so beautiful it's almost hard to look at her."

I think of the woman with the wildflowers in her hair, and I have to agree.

"There's a bit of an age gap there, but, girl, I'd happily call Jack *daddy* any day of the week. If he wasn't married, of course. I don't do married. A girl has to have her principles."

I can't help my smile.

This girl is Disney wearing biker fashion.

"Have you met Dolly and Earl?" When I nod, she continues, "They've been married forever. They're kind of like the club's Mom and Dad. Well, Earl really is Jack and Beth's daddy, and Dolly is their stepmomma, but they treat everyone else like their kids. Oooh… and have you met Doc and his wife, Lily? Now, there's a story. She used to be part of the Appalachian Inferno, so technically, she was the enemy."

"The enemy?"

"Yeah, it was kind of a forbidden love affair, but it worked out. Have you seen their kid, he's just the cutest thing? His name is CJ, and he's the best thing since sliced bread. I babysit for them.

Actually, I babysit for all of them." She sighs. "I might fuck like a whore, but I babysit like a momma."

She winks and gives me a dazzling, cute grin, and I think I fall in love with her a little bit.

"How long have you been hanging out with them?"

"I came up from Alabama three years ago for a vacation. Got invited to a clubhouse party on my second night in town and never left." She turns to face me and leans a hip against the basin. "And that's long enough for me to know that Ares the Giant has gone and done what we all didn't think he would ever do."

"Which is?"

She walks toward me. "He's gone and got himself a girlfriend."

When I open my mouth to protest, she places a finger across my lips.

"Come on, we've done enough jabbering. Let's go party."

She loops her arms through mine, and we leave the bathroom together.

When we return to the party, I see Ares leaning against the bar talking to Earl and Dolly. But there's a tall, leggy bombshell standing next to him. And she's standing *very close*. Her bare arms are pressed up against his, and her curvy hips tilt toward him seductively.

"And there's Tawny-Ann, trying to get Ares' attention again," Cinnamon says. But she doesn't say it bitchy. I'm starting to realize she doesn't have a bitchy bone in her body. "You watch, he'll untangle himself any minute."

To his credit, Ares seems unaware of Tawny-Ann's closeness. Or her attempts to gain his attention. Either that, or he's not interested. But then she reaches up and runs a palm down his back and starts rubbing his lower back, and he'd have to be dead not to notice.

When she looks up at him, she bats her lashes and digs her teeth into her lips as she gives him serious come-fuck-me eyes, and I hate the pang of jealousy that hits the amygdala region of my brain.

An urge to pull her off him via her extensions makes my fingers twitch.

But Ares straightens, turns away from her, and starts to walk our way. He's holding a glass of whiskey for me, his focus all on me.

And I can't suppress the smile.

Beside me, Cinnamon lets out a little squeal and whispers in my ear, "Yep, just like I said… that boy is smack bang all yours, darlin'."

Ares doesn't leave my side for the rest of the evening.

Much to Tawny-Ann's disgust.

Throughout the night, I notice her staring at him with a look of determination in her eyes I've seen before. Mom used to get it when she was scoping out her next meal ticket.

We're seated at a booth talking to Venom and Dakota Joe when she decides to make her next move.

"I'll Make You Love Me" by Kat Leon is playing as she walks over, looking like an Amazonian goddess with Ares clearly in her scope.

I take in the golden skin and legs for miles. Not to mention the big, beautiful boobs spilling out of the leather fringed crop top she's wearing.

I glance down at my chest.

I'm the Great Plains of Montana while she's the Rocky Mountains.

Completely different terrains.

"Hey, baby," she says to Ares, her tone dripping with seduction. She leans down, and her short skirt rides up to expose everything to everyone behind her. "How about you and I hit the bar for some tequila shots. I'll let you lick the salt off me."

My jaw hardens. *Is she actually making a move on him?*

She studies his face, her glazed eyes hooded, her tongue sweeping over her shiny lips. "Then maybe you could show me your room and lick me in other places."

Fire burns through me.

Hell, she's not just making *a* move, she's making *the* move.

Right in front of me.

Venom and Dakota Joe glance at each other.

Ares ignores the offer. Instead, he introduces me, "Tawny, I want you to meet Rory."

She doesn't bother looking in my direction. "Why?"

"Because I'm introducing you to my girl," he says gruffly. "Show her some respect."

She shifts her inebriated gaze to me. "They call me TA," she says with a smirk. "Because clearly, I have the best tits and ass in here."

I raise an eyebrow at her. "Or maybe because your name is Tawny-Ann?"

The look she gives me is pure frost.

She turns back to Ares. "Is she really your girlfriend?"

I answer for him, "Tonight, I am."

It's not enough for her to back away. She's drunk and horny, and she knows exactly who she wants to scratch that itch. Obviously, she doesn't think I'm any kind of threat to her when she runs a nail down his big arm and smirks. "When you get bored of her, you know where to find me."

Itching to wipe that smirk from her lips, I lean forward. "Hey, tits and ass girl, how about you back away from the table and go find another boyfriend for the night."

I ignore her gasp of indignation and turn to Ares. His eyebrows are raised, surprised by my aggressiveness. While I'm ready to pee on him to claim him as mine because this girl makes me feel all kinds of possessiveness, and I'm not sure how I feel about that.

I raise an eyebrow at Ares. "I think you'd better show *me* your room."

CHAPTER 16

ARES

I close my bedroom door behind me and the sounds from the party fade.

Rory sits on the end of the bed and leans back seductively.

And damn, she looks good on my bed.

She raises an eyebrow. "So this is where you make all those club girls moan your name?"

She's teasing, but I hear the jealousy in every word, even if she thinks she's hiding it.

And I'm not gonna lie, it turns me on.

The way she told Tawny-Ann to back off.

It got me hard.

Crossing the room, I drop to my knees in front of her. I part her legs, and the glimpse of her tiny underwear sends a wave of excitement straight to my cock.

"Does that make you jealous?" I ask, sliding my hands along the golden skin of her thighs until they meet the damp fabric of her panties. She trembles beneath my touch and bites down on her lip, her eyes heavy and hooded. "Thinking about me with the club girls in my bed, thinking about my cock being inside someone else?"

I don't give her a chance to reply, I yank her closer so I'm encased in her thighs.

She drapes her arms over my shoulders. Her face is stiff. Her eyebrow still raised.

"No, it doesn't."

She's lying.

She's jealous as hell.

But in a weird, warped way, it's turning her on.

She licks her lips, her eyes hooded. "Tell me what you do to them?"

I pull away to peel her panties down her legs, stopping to kiss the firm flesh of her inner thighs.

"Well, it depends whether they want it hard and fast…" I ease her panties off her legs and discard them, looking up at her as I add, "… or if they want it deep and slow."

Her lips part as I work my way back up her leg with my hands, followed closely by my tongue.

She shivers beneath me and arches her back.

When my face is between her thighs, I slide my tongue through her wet folds, and she moans, tangling her fingers through my hair. She tastes good, and I want to take my time eating her pussy, but I've been wanting her all night, and waiting any longer to be inside her might fucking kill me.

Standing, I pull off my t-shirt and shove off my jeans, then push her back on the bed and crawl over her.

My cock is heavy and hard and drags along her stomach.

"What I want to know is how *you* want me to fuck you."

She leans up. Her lips brush my ear. "I want you to fuck me like you fuck your club girls. Hard and fast, then deep and slow."

I turn to kiss her. "See, there's the problem," I say between kisses. "I don't fuck club girls."

She stalls, and her eyes narrow. "Bullshit."

I kiss her jaw, her throat, and the soft area behind her ear then back to her lips again. "I don't have any reason to lie to you."

"What about that blonde with big boobs and legs for miles? Tits and ass girl."

I grin against her lips. "Even Tits and Ass girl."

I try to kiss her again, but she's preoccupied.

"I don't know how good you are at reading women, but she looks at you like you're a tall glass of water and hasn't had a drink for days, and you're telling me you haven't gone there with her?"

My lips find her neck. "I didn't pay any attention."

"She propositioned you in front of me."

"Did she? I didn't notice. All I could think of was getting you in my room so you could have your way with me."

"Given the chance, she'd climb you like a tree."

"If you haven't noticed, the only person trying to climb anything is me. Have you seen what you do to me?"

We both look down at my cock grazing her belly.

I lift my head to kiss her again, but she puts a palm on my chest to stop me. "Admit she wants you."

I grin at her, loving this display of possessiveness. "Admit you're jealous," I tease.

"I will do *no such thing*!"

"Then I admit nothing."

"Fine." She snaps her lips closed.

Fuck, she's cute.

"You think you closing your mouth to me is going to stop me?" I glide my tongue over her wet lips. "You think that doesn't make me even more determined."

She turns her head, but I grip her chin and turn it back.

"Kiss me."

She can't help it. Her lips part, and with a groan, I slide my tongue in and seal my mouth over hers. I take possession, claiming it. *Claiming her.*

My cock flinches between us. "See what you do to me? How much I fucking want you."

I trail a finger over her stomach and across her bare pussy, loving how her mouth parts with a sigh and her face shimmers with the obvious pleasure she can't hide from me.

I find the slippery nub of nerves and begin to torture it with my finger, tormenting it with maddening circles until it's engorged and swollen, and she's stirring on the bed.

Beneath me, she fights the sensations coursing through her because she has a point to prove. But it's a losing battle, and she writhes restlessly, her body betraying her arousal, and when I slide one finger into her, a strangled gasp gets lost in her throat.

"I'm not going to come." She breathes heavily, fighting it.

"So you say." My finger finds the sensitive nerve endings once again, and she shudders. "But you forget one very important thing…"

She swallows back a gasp of pleasure. "W-what?"

I brush my lips to hers. "I'm very good at making you come."

I increase the pressure and pace of my finger and send her over the edge. She falls apart beneath me, her body succumbing to the ecstasy streaming through every limb, nerve, and fiber. I lean down to kiss her, and she cries out against my mouth, hating this and wanting it at the same time.

"What was that about not coming?" I rasp.

But it's hard to tease her when I'm so fucking hard. Because watching her come and feeling how wet she is, has my body screaming for satisfaction.

"Fuck you," she whispers against my lips.

I think about making her come again with my fingers, maybe add in some tongue, but there's no way I'd survive.

"With pleasure," I say, notching my cock to her and entering with one smooth thrust.

Her cry is husky and desperate as I rock my cock into her, and *fuck*, there is no fucking way I am going to last. Rory's possessiveness and jealousy, combined with the tightness of her pussy, has me wanting to come before I've even fucking begun.

"You're so fucking wet for me." I push in deeper, harder. "Just like I'm so fucking hard for you. Feel that, baby? Feel how fucking hard you make me?"

She whimpers and hearing her arousal makes my cock flinch. I'm aching to come. *Need to come.* Then she does the unthinkable. She tries to flip me and almost flies off the bed, but I roll with her so she doesn't hurt herself until I'm on my back and she is above me. She climbs on, reclaims my cock, and begins rocking against me.

My hands go to her hips. "What are you doing?"

"You always think you're in control."

"I *am* always in control."

"I mean self-control."

"That's what I mean."

"You don't get jealous?"

"Is this admitting you were jealous?" She glares at me, and I smile up at her. "Baby, I get jealous as hell. Seeing Merrick eye fucking you made me want to push all his teeth down his throat. But they were extenuating circumstances."

"Extenuating circumstances?"

"Have you seen how beautiful you are?"

"Don't try and sweet talk your way out of this."

"Out of what?"

"I'm taking control."

I grin at her, loving the way she's slowly riding me. "If this is you taking control, then feel free to take control anytime you want."

"I'm serious."

"I can tell by the serious look on your face. Look… if it makes you feel better, I relinquish control over to you."

"You couldn't handle it if I were in control."

"Is that a challenge? If so, then I accept. Do what you will to my body."

"Will you do what I tell you to do?"

"I am at your service."

"Okay, then prove this self-control of yours to me. Show me how you have sovereignty over everything you do."

"With pleasure. Do your worst to me."

"Fine. Don't come."

"Wait! What?"

"Don't come until I tell you to."

She starts to grind against me, and the slow build of heat ignites into a raging wildfire.

What the fuck have I agreed to?

"Are you trying to fucking kill me?"

"Not yet, not until I've won this challenge."

I bite back the urge to come.

"And what do I get when I win?" I rasp.

"You can do anything you like to *me*."

I arch an eyebrow. "Anything?"

"*Anything.*"

"Can I bend you over my Harley and fuck you?"

"I hope so."

"Can I tie you up… handcuffs *and* rope?"

"You'd better."

Jesus, this woman.

"You won't win," I rasp, trying desperately not to come.

Her grin is wicked. "You forget one thing."

"What?"

She leans down. "I'm very good at making *you* come."

Fuck.

How the tables have turned.

A warm flush spreads across my skin. My heart speeds up. My balls scream at me for a release. But I fight it.

I won't lose this challenge.

But what she's doing feels too good.

And the building tension is about to snap.

I grab her by the hips to stop her. "Don't move," I beg.

Christ, I'm so fucking turned on it feels like I'm going to die if I come. Like the sensation will shoot me so deep into outer space I might never find my way back to Earth.

Her dark gaze is seductive.

"What's the matter, Ares? Are you about to lose control?"

I'm too busy waging a war with my orgasm in my head to reply.

"Just... catching... my... breath..."

Oh God, she feels good.

I rasp, "Just... I beg you... don't... move."

A smirk tugs at her kiss-swollen lips, and I think she's going to do exactly what I've asked her not to do, just so I am at her mercy.

But she doesn't move.

No, what she does is so much worse.

While her hips remain stationary, she tightens her pussy around my cock and starts to milk it slowly with a series of torturous tight pulses and throbbing flutters that are *warm and wet and oh so good*, and there is nothing on this planet strong enough to stop me from coming.

My orgasm hits me like a shotgun blast.

My reality shatters.

I lose focus.

I lose control.

"Oh fuck..." I grab the sheet beside me as my mind splinters into a thousand pieces of bright light. My back arches, my eyes roll back, and I leave my body and skyrocket into a euphoric nothingness. I open my mouth to groan, but nothing comes out.

Finally, all the clenching gets too much for Rory.

"Oh God… Ares," she moans.

Her head drops back, and she drenches my cock as she comes.

But I am barely aware.

Barely breathing.

Barely existing.

My breath is gone.

Only my heartbeat remains.

I sink into the bed like it's a cloud.

Trembling with her orgasm, Rory falls onto me with a whimper.

I can't tell you how many times I've come in my lifetime.

Given there are not a hell of a lot of things to do in prison at night besides jerking it, it's safe to say it has been a lot.

But nothing has ever rocked me the way Rory just rocked me.

And I'm starting to think that nothing ever will.

She rolls over and looks at me, her eyes twinkling. "I win."

CHAPTER 17

RORY

As I wake, I have no idea where I am for a moment. Except that I'm warm and content, and my body is tired but completely relaxed and satisfied at the same time. I'm nestled against a rock-hard chest that is impossibly warm and encased by a pair of strong arms.

Ares.

I close my eyes again, lost in the comfort of his big body pressed against mine and the memories of what he did to me last night. He kept me up to the early hours of the morning, putting me in various positions and showing me exactly how good he can be with his cock.

I sigh, content. I'm so damn comfortable I don't ever want to leave. I want to wrap this moment up and tuck it away for safekeeping.

Unfortunately, I need to pee, so I reluctantly leave the comfort of Ares' bed and hit the bathroom. I glance around, taking in the intimate surroundings of the man I pretend I only want a physical relationship with. The bathroom is small, with a shower, basin, and toilet, and it's clean, the tiled floor so shiny I can almost see my reflection.

Washing my hands, I sneak a peek in his medicine cabinet above the basin. I want to know more about Ares, about the man, about the hidden side of him only he knows.

Which is dangerous, I know. But I am curious.

The medicine cabinet is full of typical male hygiene products—deodorant, hair gel, shaving products, toothpaste, and brush. But there is also a cherry ChapStick, which makes my heart swell in my chest. I don't know why. Perhaps it's because he is such a wall of testosterone and muscle that seeing something so sweet and girly is a glimpse into the tender side of him.

But then I wonder if a girl left it behind, and my skin tightens with jealousy, and the muscle in my jaw tightens. I gnaw at the inside of my mouth because thinking about him with another girl is as much fun as a lobotomy.

Slow down, Rory.

I close the cabinet and stare at my reflection in the mirror and mentally tell her off.

You could walk in on Ares fucking a hundred girls, and it shouldn't bother you.

But unfortunately, I know that's not the case.

When I leave the bathroom, Ares is still sound asleep. But he's rolled onto his back, putting his thick, muscular, and fully naked body on display. I pause and let my gaze slide over the thick slabs of muscle, the tight abs, the thick cock that rests against his thigh.

He's so virile I can almost smell the testosterone.

Immediately, my body responds with an appreciative throb. I could wake him up with my mouth, draw him down deep in my throat until he's hard and fully engorged, then ride him until we both fall apart. But he's in a deep sleep, and after last night's performance, he could do with the rest, so I decide to go in search of coffee instead. Dolly had said she'd have a pot on by eight, and it's almost eight o'clock now.

When I leave Ares' room, the clubhouse is still and quiet, but the heavy cloud of smoke and stale liquor still permeates the air. The bar is empty, but as I make my way toward the kitchen, I hear faint crying coming from down the hall. The noise becomes louder as I near a room with the door open. That's when I realize it isn't crying but moaning, and it's not one woman but two, and they're both on the bed with the biker called Ghoul. He's on his back while one girl rides his cock and the other sits on his face so he can fuck her with his tongue.

For a moment, I'm rooted to the spot, fascinated and unable to look away. Watching other people in this kind of intimacy has never been my thing, but I'm starting to realize that maybe I don't really know what my thing is. Ares is proof of that.

"If you're waiting for the money shot, you'll be waiting a while, Ghoul can fuck for hours," comes a voice from behind me.

I swing around and find a girl leaning against the wall further down the hallway. She must've been in the bathroom when I entered the hall because she wasn't there earlier.

Immediately, my cheeks flush.

"I thought I heard someone crying," I say, taking a few steps toward her.

She scoffs bitterly. "You probably did."

As I get closer, I notice her mascara has run down her tear-stained cheeks.

"Are you okay?" I ask.

The girl can't be any more than twenty-one.

"I'm fine." She tries to light a cigarette with shaking hands but gives up and stuffs it back into the packet. "Stupid, but fine."

Because I look puzzled, she holds up a pregnancy test, and clearly, the positive result is anything but positive.

I'm not a girlie girl and don't have many girlfriends, so I've never come across this before. But I immediately empathize with her because she looks like her whole world has crashed down around her.

"Do you want to talk about it?" I ask.

"Not a lot to talk about. I'm knocked up and an idiot because the father and I aren't together. I mean, I've always hoped it might turn into something…" She looks down the hallway. "Oh hell, who am I kidding… I've been in love with him since I first laid eyes on him."

"Does he know?"

"No." She looks horrified by the thought. "He'd run a mile if he knew how I felt about him. Let's just say he likes women. Lots of them."

Hell, what am I supposed to say to that?

"I'm sorry, you deserve better than that." I feel sorry for her. I've never been in love, but I can imagine it hurts like hell when it's unrequited.

Girl, you felt like you'd be hit in the gut when you saw that ChapStick.

She looks like she has thick skin, but she's emotionally worn out and lets her façade drop and her tears flow. She nods toward the bedroom, where the sound of two women orgasming floats down the hallway. "He's the father."

"Ghoul is the father of your baby?"

She hugs her arms and slowly, she slides down the wall. "Do yourself a favor and don't fall for Ares."

"Why?"

"Because falling for a King will ruin you for any man who follows him."

"What do you mean?"

"If you give him your heart, it'll never be whole again." She shakes her head. "You can also kiss goodbye your common sense. I mean, look at me, I'm sitting here in a hallway crying because I'm pregnant while my baby daddy is fucking two other women a mere two yards away."

I think about the first time with Ares. How all common sense left me, and we didn't use any protection. How I shouldn't think about him all day, but I do.

And how I shouldn't be here now, but I am.

"He doesn't know you're pregnant, and from what you've said, he doesn't know how you feel about him."

"Like that would make a difference."

"Why wouldn't it?"

"Are you kidding me, lady? If you didn't notice, he's down the hall with one girl bouncing up and down on his balls and another on his face. Where the hell do I fit into that equation?"

"Maybe if he knew how you felt about him, only you would be in that bed with him. But if you don't tell him, you won't know."

Dolly appears around the corner looking like a million bucks. Ares says no one really knows how old she is, that she's somewhere in her sixties, but she looks two decades younger.

"Good morning, ladies," she says with an effervescent smile, the rhinestones on her denim jacket winking under the hallway light. When she sees Roxy's tear-stained face, she frowns. "Baby girl, what's going on?"

Roxy holds up the pregnancy test and does her best to fight off another wave of tears.

Dolly crouches down. "Does Ghoul know?"

"He's a bit busy right now."

Roxy gives into her tears, and Dolly puts her arms around her shoulders and gives her a warm motherly hug which only makes Roxy cry more.

"I love him so much, Dolly. What am I going to do?"

"Well, first of all, you're going to pull yourself together, wash your face, and then you and I are going to figure out what comes next over some coffee." Dolly helps Roxy to her feet. "Come on, I just put a fresh pot of coffee on and some pastries in the oven."

Because Dolly's got this, I decide to leave them to it. "I'll leave you two alone."

"You don't want a cup of coffee?" Dolly asks.

Every cell in my body screams for one. But these two need to talk and going by Roxy's distrust toward me, it'll be better if I'm not there. Coffee will have to wait.

Besides, I have a sudden urge to slide my arms around Ares and hold him close.

"I should see where Ares is," I say.

As they begin to walk away, Roxy gives me a small, unsure smile. "Thanks."

Dolly looks over her shoulder and gives me a wink. "I think you're going to fit in well around here."

CHAPTER 18

ARES

Forensic floodlights illuminate the body. Half-submerged in water, it has been lying *in situ* for days. Animal and insect activity have had their way, and it isn't a pretty sight.

"The medical examiner is putting death at five days ago," Pinkwater tells us.

Twilight has settled over the river, and the crickets and frogs sing into the dying light. The foul odor of decomposition hangs heavily in the air.

"Do you have an ID?" Jack asks.

"We found his wallet in his back pocket. His license identifies him as Walter Hamilton of Redwood Town. His wife reported him missing two days ago."

Despite the loss of skin on the victim's face, I can make out the word WRATH carved into his forehead.

"He's been dead five days, but she only reported him missing two days ago?" I ask.

"Apparently, Walter doesn't mind a drink, and when he goes for one, it's not unusual for him to be gone a few days." He grimaces, the smell getting to him. "Apparently, Walter doesn't mind laying into his wife, either. He's got an ugly temper and a string of domestic assault charges."

"That explains the use of wrath," Jack says.

Mud sucks at our boots as we walk along the riverbank back to the parking lot.

"What is the organized crime connection," I ask.

"Walter is a bouncer and sometime bodyguard for the Sullivans."

"That's the second association of the Sullivans to be taken out by the Three. Are we sure the others aren't associated with them also, and this is the Sullivans cleaning house?"

"No, I had my deputies do thorough background checks on all the victims."

Walking toward our bikes, Jack glances back toward the body further up the river. "How many sins are we up to now?"

"So far they've used lust, greed, sloth, and now wrath," Pinkwater replies.

"That leaves gluttony, envy, and pride," I count.

"They're escalating."

"It also tells us something else," I add.

"What?"

"That they're here."

I ride away from the crime scene with a bad feeling in my gut. I don't return to the clubhouse with my club brothers. Instead, I keep riding through the golden dusk until I arrive at Rory's apartment. She hears my bike coming and is waiting for me at the door. When I climb the stairs and reach her, she jumps into my arms and kisses me.

And in that second, I know my heart is done for.

While Rory fixes us a drink, I shower to get the stench of death off me

Afterward, I join her on the terrace, and we sit under the stars.

"I've never seen your neighbors," I say as she hands me a whiskey.

"And you won't. According to the realtor, one of them spends the summer in Florida, and the other spends more time in his cabin. Julie, who lives across the hall, she's a nurse and works nights. I've been here a month, and I've only seen her twice. And whoever is in the apartment next to her is either a vampire or it's empty." She sips her drink and then puts it down. "Have you ever thought about moving out on your own?"

"Leave the clubhouse, you mean?"

"Yeah."

"Never thought about it. They're my family now."

She scoffs. "I couldn't wait to get away from my family. What happened to your Uncle Frankie?"

"He died when I was in prison. Throat cancer."

"I'm sorry," she says softly. "And your father?"

"He can rot in hell for all I care. He turned his back on me the day I was born and every day after. I don't know if he's alive or dead."

Sensing my mood change, she climbs onto my lap and slides her thighs on either side of my hips. My cock thickens in appreciation.

"Sometimes the people who are supposed to love us the most end up being the source of our greatest pain." She brushes a finger across the slight cleft in my chin. "I'm sorry he was cruel to you. You deserved better."

When I smile, she leans in and slides her tongue into my mouth. Reaching between us, she unzips me.

"You're a hungry little one tonight," I say with a chuckle.

"Are you complaining?" she asks, springing me free.

"Fucking never."

With a bit of adjustment, her hand wraps around the base of my cock, and I groan.

"I want you while I've got you,"

"What do you mean?" I rasp because now she's stroking me.

"Before we go our separate ways, I want you as many times as I can have you."

She sinks onto my cock and begins to rock her hips.

"I'm not going anywhere," I manage to say.

"Maybe not tonight." She licks her lips. Her luscious pussy is drenched as she grinds slowly against me. "And maybe not tomorrow, but eventually, you'll be gone."

"Don't be so sure." She clenches me tight, and my eyes roll into the back of my head. She's so fucking tight it's almost too good.

"It's just sex. It never lasts."

Her breath is ragged. Mine is too. I'm barely capable of carrying on this conversation because the pleasure is so intense.

Christ, she rides me so good she's got me ready to come.

My hands find her hips, and I gently guide her back and forth across my pelvis. She closes her eyes, and a look of euphoria ripples through her expression. Her pleasure is rising.

"Maybe we were too quick to label this," I say, fighting the urge to come.

"What are you saying?"

"I'm saying, I like this." I drop my head back. *I really like this.* "Let's take it one day at a time and see what happens."

Her hips grind to a halt as her heavy-lidded eyes search my face. After a moment, a slow smile spreads across her damp lips, and her wet pussy tightens around my cock, making me jerk beneath her.

She doesn't say anything, but her eyes sparkle with

agreement, and something passes between us.

When she starts to move again, she picks up her pace, and damn there isn't anything sexier than this woman riding my cock.

She begins to move wildly against me, then cries out as her orgasm hits. Her throat arches, and from out of nowhere, my climax smashes into me, and I pulse violently inside her.

I grab her hips, my moan long, low, and drawn out by the mind-blowing sensation of her tight pussy milking my cock of every last drop.

I've never come at the same time with a woman before. Usually, I take care of business first, making sure the woman I'm inside of comes before I chase my own release. But things are different with Rory, and wild horses couldn't have stopped that orgasm.

With a moan, she falls against me.

Before tonight, I couldn't get out of my own way to see what was happening between us. That there's something a little more than casual fucking involved, and instead of running from it, I feel myself being drawn toward it.

I tuck a lock of her hair behind her ear.

Maybe I want terrace and bath sex more often.

Maybe I like feeling the warmth of her body curled into mine as we fall asleep.

"You've gone really quiet," she says, running a cool hand over my shoulder and down my arm. A look of concern crosses her beautiful face. "What are you thinking about?"

I pull her closer. "That I really fucking like you."

CHAPTER 19

RORY

I really fucking like you.

Ares words echo in my head as I make my way through the busy departure lounge and board my flight to Boston. Walking down the aisle toward my seat, I force the image of him lying naked and hard in my bed out of my head and tell myself to get a grip.

Grateful for a window seat, I turn to look at the airport rolling by as we prepare to take off.

I need to see my father and my brother.

I need to regroup and get my head back on straight.

I knew it last night, the moment the words left Ares' lips.

I really fucking like you.

Those words are not part of the plan.

Him being in my bed is definitely not part of the plan.

Yet, somehow I've strayed off path, and last night had been a stark awakening.

His words scared me. They make me want to retreat.

But when he'd reached for me in the shadows of a new dawn

breaking into my bedroom, I had reached back. Even as he rolled onto me, I had opened my legs for him and searched for his mouth as he slid into me. And when he'd made love to me in the dull light, I had raised my hips to meet his as our soft moans fused together in the shadows.

I close my eyes. I can still taste his kiss on my lips and smell the soapy scent of his skin, and my chest aches with longing.

I really fucking like you.

Oh, how I wish you knew you shouldn't.

During the two-hour flight to Boston, I managed to sleep, which is good because I barely slept at all last night. I had tossed and turned restlessly in the heat of Ares' warm body, my dreams haunted by my stepfather and my brother, and the fucked-up situation I've landed myself in.

But despite the small amount of rest I get during the flight, when I land in Boston, I feel worse. Even the familiarity of my hometown doesn't help. Instead, I find myself missing the small-town feel of Flintlock and the people I work with at the Spicy Crawdad, wishing everything could be different.

Wishing I could fall in love with Ares.

Wishing there was something more for us.

I push the unwanted thought away because I've fucked everything up, and there is going to be a price to pay.

It's a given that I won't get away unscathed.

I accept that.

But I will do everything in my power to ensure it is as painless as possible for Ares.

Stepping into the rainy Boston day, I hail a cab and take it to the cemetery, immersing myself in the familiar landscape I've driven past a hundred times in the last twenty-two years.

My father's grave rests near the row of sugar maple and weeping hemlock trees on the far side of the cemetery. When he was alive, he was everything to me. My best friend. My protector.

The one person in this world I could count on.

Then he was gone.

Killed by a rival crime syndicate when I was only thirteen years old.

I had never known a pain like it and to a naïve daddy's girl, it felt like I was living in a nightmare.

Less than a year later, my mom married Donnie—one of my father's lieutenants—and a new nightmare began. Within twelve months, he was visiting my bedroom late at night.

As I kneel before my father's grave, I start pulling the weeds and dead flowers from around his headstone. My heart is a heavy weight in my chest as I wish for the billionth time he was still alive.

A few feet away, my brother rests in his own grave. His is a simple headstone with his name carved into the marble. There are no flowers. No trinkets. No sign that anyone has been there in weeks, *months even*, and they probably haven't been.

I'm the only one who visits his grave.

By the time Joey died, he didn't have many friends left. He'd pushed everyone away.

Including me.

When I heard he was missing, I hadn't seen him for four years.

Oh, I'd heard the rumors about him not being the same kid anymore. How the drugs had stolen his soul and turned him bad. But they were whispered by the very men who killed for our family or were involved in the seedy underworld and lived beneath a skin of lies, pretending they didn't do dark deeds in dark corners. So I took their word with a grain of salt.

Joey and I were born into crime. We were raised by the sword in a world where only the most vicious survived. He left for college when he got a football scholarship and never came home again.

I don't doubt he had changed. But in my head, he'll always be the seventeen-year-old boy who held my hand when our father's coffin passed us by and whispered, "Don't you worry, sis, I've got you."

A few feet away, a hooded warbler lands on a grand tombstone that towers above the rest. It's an ostentatious structure of black Italian marble and crystal, and it's so ridiculously over the top, it's almost out of place.

The name blazoned in gold leaf across the marble is hard to miss...

Donnie Hatzakorian

My stepfather.

The man I told Ares I wanted killed.

Yeah, he's already dead.

His life was snuffed out by three bullets. One to the head, another to his heart, and one point-blank ranged shot to the balls.

That was where I shot him first. His balls. It didn't kill him. It just hurt like a motherfucker, and watching him suffer was payback for all the evil things he did to me when I was young, all because he could.

By rule, I don't even look at it when I visit the cemetery. Because the less amount of time I spend acknowledging his regretful existence, the better.

The truth is...

I didn't hunt down Ares to kill anyone.

I hunted him down because I want revenge for my brother's death, and I know it was Ares who ended Joey's life.

I don't know why.

It was the one question I was going to ask him right before I put a bullet in his head.

No one could ever tell me why.

Not the police.

Not my family.

No one.

For some reason, Joey's disappearance and death is shrouded in secrecy.

I know he wasn't a saint. We were raised by the sword, and my brother often let that lifestyle seduce him.

But my mother says Ares killed Joey in cold blood.

And it's up to me to take revenge.

I'm not visiting Flintlock to fuck Ares and develop feelings for him.

I'm there to kill him.

My mother lives in a narrow, two-story house in Dorchester with her fiancé, Connor. He claims to be a wealthy entrepreneur, but really, he's just a local gangster who spends more time taking other people's money than making his own.

He's nothing like my father, but thankfully, he's also nothing like my dead stepfather. The only thing the three men have in common is their lack of respect for the law and a complete disbelief in earning an honest buck.

Clearly, my mother has a type.

As the cab pulls up out in front, I brace myself for what's coming because there's a good reason why I don't visit much—my mom is a cold-hearted bitch.

There isn't a degree of warmth in her ice-cold demeanor, and she definitely has no maternal instincts. She only gave birth to Joey and me because my father wanted babies, and she wanted my father. But she made it perfectly clear from the beginning we were an unwanted interruption to her life.

When she opens the door, she's hardly excited to see me.

"Well, look at what the cat dragged in." She turns and walks away so I have to follow her into the living room. The house used to be nice back when my father was alive, but now it's shabby and dimly lit, except for a ribbon of dusty sunlight breaking in through the curtains.

"You come to tell me it's done?" she asks. Despite the early hour, she's already sipping from a can of White Rascal.

Mom hasn't changed much over the years, so her big hair, hooped earrings, and tight jeans are no surprise. She's never gone easy with her makeup, and today is no different. She's gone heavy with the black eyeliner and pink lip gloss, although the smoky-eye eyeshadow is new.

She looks like she's stepped out of the 1980s.

When my father was alive, he put a lot of diamonds and gold on my mom. He also gave her all the money she wanted. But money can't buy you class, and Ariana still doesn't have a shred of it.

"No, it's not done," I say.

"Why not? You said you were going to do it." She shakes her head as if I'm the biggest disappointment in the world, then lights a cigarette. "I should've known we couldn't trust you to get it done."

"It's under control."

"If that asshole is still breathing, then it isn't under control."

"Yeah, well, sending me stupid text messages isn't going to make it happen any faster. Seriously, *Tick tock, Aurora?*" I gesture to the can in her hand. "You need to lay off the alcohol."

"And you need to do what you said you were going to do."

Frustrated, I challenge her, raising my voice. "Why should I?"

"Because if you want to continue suckling at the teat of your father's wealth, you will do what I tell you to do."

My father left me a small inheritance when he died. Money he made from shady dealings and his life in the crime that kept food on the table and hundred dollar notes stuffed into the wall cavities of our house. For some reason, he put my mom in charge of Joey and my trusts until we turned thirty, which, for me, is only a year away.

Not that his money has ever been motivation for me to do anything. I've always been fiercely independent. And this *suckling* that my mom so eloquently refers to was actually me attending college.

"You know what, keep the damn money. I don't need it."

"Oh, that's right, you dance now." My mother scoffs, waving her can of liquor at me. "Shaking that ass for pennies."

My skin heats under the weight of her patronizing tone and smug gaze.

Dancing might not pay as well as a trust fund or the crimes her various husbands commit to keep her in a certain comfort, but it's been way more enjoyable hanging out with the staff at the Spicy Crawdad than the people my family associates with.

And I'd like to see her spin one hundred and twenty pounds around an aluminum pole using only her core muscles.

"Laugh all you like, but at least it's honest work."

"Says the woman who agreed to kill the man who murdered her brother." She takes a drag on her cigarette and raises a skeptical eyebrow at me. "Tell me, how does that fit in with this newfound righteousness of yours?"

I lift my chin defiantly. "That's why I'm here. I've come to tell you I've changed my mind."

The amusement vanishes from my mother's face. "What the fuck do you mean *you've changed your mind*?"

"Exactly what it sounds like, I've… changed… my… mind. I'm not doing it."

Her lips tighten. "You told me you'd take care of it."

When my brother went missing five years ago, I knew something bad had happened. Then last year when his rotted corpse was pulled from the watery grave in a Florida swamp, my worst fears were realized.

Following Joey's funeral, my mother and I had shared a rare moment of affection. She had dramatically cried in my arms and pleaded with me to ease her pain. At the time, I didn't know how. I couldn't bring Joey back. I couldn't change what happened. *No, but you could avenge his death. Just like you took care of Donnie.* We bonded in our grief, finally united by something, and it was all I'd ever wanted from my mother. *Love.*

But standing here now, it all makes sense. This was never about retaliation for Joey's death but about my mother manipulating me into doing her bidding.

Another one of her games.

How could I be so stupid in not realizing this sooner?

Oh God, how I hate her.

She let Donnie rape me.

She didn't believe me when I confided in her.

But in a moment of weakness following Joey's death, I'd pushed it all aside when she'd dangled the affection I craved in front of me, and like a junkie, I'd sold my soul for a hit.

"Ares is a decent guy, he didn't do this," I say adamantly. "And I won't be responsible for taking an innocent man's life."

Before she can say anything else, Connor, *fiancé extraordinaire*, walks into the room. He's wearing suit pants and a button-up that's too tight. Gold gleams on his fingers, and his oily ginger hair is slicked back off his forehead, exposing his receding hairline.

I don't like Connor. He thinks he's Mr. All That, but he's so not.

There is something a little slimy about him.

But he's a perfect fit for my mother. They're both as delusional and classless as the other.

In a perfect world, they'd fall into a big well of their hatefulness and disappear.

"You're just in time, Connor," she says. "Rory says she's changed her mind."

"About what?" He takes mom's cigarette from her hand and sits on the couch. He spreads his arms along the back, parts his legs like he's king of the house, and gives me a smug look that gives you goosebumps.

Mom lights herself a new cigarette. "Apparently, she's changed her mind about taking care of that Ares prick."

He pauses the cigarette at his lips. "Are you fucking kidding? You know what I had to do to get that information, and now you're telling me you're backing out?"

"I think your information is wrong."

Connor stands, turning red with sudden fury. He doesn't appreciate being told he's wrong.

He points the burning cigarette at me. "You listen to me, kid. I'm a big fucking deal around here, and I've got connections coming out of my asshole, so when I tell you something, you had better believe that it is *one hundred percent* fact. This Ares asshole was the hitman of choice for the De Kysa family. You remember them? They're the biggest mafia in these parts, and they spill blood all over these streets for whatever goddamn reason they want. They ordered the hit, and Ares completed the job. My contacts say so. So don't you fucking dare doubt it. That cunt killed our Joey. You can take that to the fucking bank."

Our Joey.

That's rich.

He didn't even know Joey, and the only reason he is being so adamant about this is to win favor with my mother.

My mother's beauty does the most stupid things to men.

"Why would they want Joey dead? It doesn't make sense," I say.

In the corner of my eye, I see mom shift restlessly and turn away to stare out the window.

I look at her, a strange sensation creeping up my spine. "What aren't you telling me?"

But she refuses to answer. Instead, she bites on a long, fake nail.

I turn to Connor. "Why the fuck did the De Kysas order a hit on Joey, and why is this the first I'm hearing about it?"

I was simply told who killed him and then handed a photograph with a name and address scrawled on the back. I was told not to ask questions and get it done.

"Why is there so much secrecy surrounding his death?"

Connor sucks on his cigarette. "Because there are bigger things at play, and you don't need to know about them."

"Does it really matter why they killed him?" My mom snaps. "Your brother is dead, and someone has to pay."

"And you said you'd take care of it," Connor reminds me, smoke puffing out of his mouth as he talks. "And either you take care of it, or we send someone else to do it."

If they send someone else to do it, Ares will be dead by the time I get back to Tennessee this afternoon.

"That won't be necessary," I reply quickly.

Connor knows a lot of thugs who'll do it for one of the rolls of money stashed in the freezer. And it won't be quick. It'll be messy and bloody.

I need some time to figure this out.

Find out what the fuck really happened.

"Good, then I expect it done by the end of the week." He reaches down to stub out his cigarette in the glass ashtray on the coffee table. When he straightens, he tries to unnerve me with a menacing look. "No more fucking around... you hear me? You get it done, or I will."

He strides out of the room, and I barely restrain from rolling my eyes. It was meant to be a dramatic exit, I'm sure, but he tries too hard to be intimidating to *actually be* intimidating.

"Well, this has been charming," I say, deciding it's time to leave.

I've absorbed enough toxicity for one day. And I'd be lying if I said the information about Joey didn't unnerve me. Someone has gotten something wrong somewhere.

"No, please stay," my mother says with heavy sarcasm. "Stay for some tea, cake, and a tête-à-tête. You can tell me all about how you dance naked in front of fat old men for crumpled dollar notes."

I ignore her and walk toward the door but pause to look at the woman over my shoulder. "You didn't even care about Joey in the end. Why do you care now?"

Her eyes sparkle with malice and too much alcohol.

She shrugs. "Because I can."

I stare at her in disbelief.

She isn't just cold-blooded. She's a cold-blooded *sociopath*. She doesn't care about Joey being dead. This woman only cares that someone took something from her.

It's always about *her.*

Without giving Mom another look, I walk away and close the door behind me.

I won't come back here again.

I'm done.

I hope for a clean getaway, but I have to walk past the kitchen to get to the front door, and Connor is standing at the counter looking at something on his phone.

"A word of warning, Aurora." His voice cuts into the silence. "I won't tolerate your petulance like your mother does."

He's trying to intimidate me... *again.*

But he fails... *again.*

Instead of fleeing the house like I want to, I walk straight into the lion's den to face the lion. Or in this case, an over-dressed sixty-year-old with whisky flush and a receding hairline.

I cross my arms to show him that his intimidation tactics won't work on me. "And I won't tolerate being threatened. Make your point."

I don't just dislike Connor, I loathe him.

And by the look on his face, the feeling is mutual.

"You know, I met your father once," he says out of nowhere.

"Congratulations." I raise an eyebrow at him.

"He was a right prick, and I see the apple doesn't fall far from the tree."

The hair on the back of my neck stands on end, and my blood boils.

But I don't react.

I won't give him the satisfaction of knowing that his words have an effect on me.

"But he had balls, your father did. Big fucking balls. And he was a loyal sonofabitch, if ever there was one. How do you think he'd feel about his only daughter not giving a damn about his only son being murdered? He'd be rolling in his fucking grave with disappointment at you, girlie."

I have to hand it to Connor, he certainly knows where to land a blow—right in the middle of my weak spot. *My father.*

To make things worse, he's right. My father *would* be disappointed that Joey's murder hasn't been avenged, and the idea that I'm letting him down is too painful to bear.

But again, I won't let Connor see that.

"With all due respect..." I murder him with cold eyes. "Go fuck yourself."

The asshole smiles, clearly enjoying my pain.

"I'm only saying what you already know." He lights another cigarette. "If you won't do it for your mother, then think about your father."

I think about him every damn day.

Pain twists in my chest.

And I know he would be disappointed in me if I don't do this.

Feeling the pain of what I have to do, I look my stepfather right in the eye. I hate him with every ounce of my being, and I hate it more that it is him who has made me realize I have to do this.

I glare at him. "You should be careful, Connor. My mother's men have a habit of dying."

And turning my back on him, I show him *how* to walk out of a room.

CHAPTER 20

ARES

I spend most of the day helping the prospects and Dakota Joe fixing the storm damage on the grow barn. A month ago, mother nature battered Flintlock with a summer storm and left a trail of uprooted trees, broken buildings, and debris scattered across the county.

Our grow barn—where we grow our out-of-season cannabis crop—was hit hard. Not structural, but the cosmetic repairs were significant enough to take up most of the day.

Thankfully, none of the soon-to-be harvest plants were damaged in the storm.

By late afternoon, Dakota Joe, Shooter, and I grab a drink at the clubhouse bar while the prospects finish off the repairs.

We're playing poker and drinking beer when the roar of motorcycles fills the clubhouse. Jack, Shooter, and I jump to our feet. The bikes riding into the parking lot don't belong to our brothers, and we're not expecting guests.

"Who's on the fucking gate?" Jack growls.

Before anyone can answer, three bikers wearing Devil's Steed cuts walk in, led by a tall man with long gray hair and an equally gray beard.

"Don't fucking blame your prospect," he declares. "We was coming in one way or another. But we're coming in peace."

Jack's face is murderous. He's already murdered our prospect in his head for letting these guys past our gates, and by the way he's looking at this gray-haired leviathan, he's murdering him too.

"You must have some balls on you to come into my club uninvited."

The leviathan holds up his hands. "I apologize. But when it comes to family, you make stupid-ass decisions and risk getting your ass kicked. This is me taking that chance."

"What do you want?"

The leviathan drops his tough-guy guard. "Those pricks got my daughter, and I need your help to find them."

Turns out, the leviathan is Jethro, President of the Devil's Steed, a club based near Fortune City.

Jack and Jethro sit down at a booth while Shooter and I stand, our eyes pinned on the two bikers Jethro has with him.

"This ain't no pissing contest, boys. You can relax. My boys ain't looking for trouble," Jethro says. "We're here looking for help. Not to cause trouble."

"Riding into a man's club uninvited is one way to start trouble. Next time use a phone."

"Let's make sure we swap numbers then. Next time, I'll call."

Jack's frown smooths. *Point taken.* "What's this about?"

Jack gestures for Shooter and me to join him and Jethro while Jethro nods at his boys to sit in the next booth.

"You heard of The Three?" Jethro asks.

"The name has been mentioned a few times. What of them?"

Jethro lets out a rough breath. "Those bastards roughed up my daughter. Got her when she was driving home from a dinner date. Dragged her out of the car and tied her to a fucking tree and did this to her."

Jethro shows us a picture on his cell. In it, a young woman is lying in a hospital bed, her face completely covered in bandages and a breathing tube coming out of her mouth. He swipes again, and a beautiful blonde girl with big blue eyes and a smile like fucking sunshine appears on the screen.

"That's what my baby used to look like before they got to her. This is what those fucking lunatics did to her." He swipes again to show us a crime scene photo. In it, she is barely recognizable. Her face is black and bloody, so swollen you can't even tell it's human. Carved into her forehead is the word PRIDE. "She was on life support for two days. The swelling on her brain almost killed her."

"The cops confirm it was The Three?"

"Before she was put into an induced coma, she told them a few things." His throat bobs. "As the pricks were cutting into her, they told her she could thank her daddy and her love of social media for what was about to happen to her."

"She's on social media?" Jack asks.

"She's one of those... what the fuck do you call them? An influencer? Has some account on Instagram with a few hundred thousand people who follow her. I don't get the whole social media thing. Don't understand why people care what someone else ate for breakfast. But she was a beautiful girl, and strangers cared what she did."

It's clear that the psychos calling themselves The Three not only prey on people associated with organized crime, but they study them before they take aim and attack.

Hurting and disfiguring the daughter of a motorcycle club

president, who makes a living as an Instagram star made her the perfect candidate to drive home the point of *pride*. In their fucked-up minds anyway.

Jack shows very little emotion. His only reaction is the subtle coil of his hands in front of him on the table. But I know him. Inside, he's thinking what he'd do to these psychos if he comes across them. If this had happened to his daughter, Hope, he'd rain down fire and brimstone until everything was burned to the fucking ground.

"How old is she?" he growls.

"Nineteen. She's been visiting from college."

"Is she going to recover?"

"The girl she was…" he sighs, "… she's gone for good, Jack. She's going to need surgery, but they have to wait until she can breathe on her own and for the swelling to go down before they'll do anything. She'll survive, but she's going to be disfigured." Jethro's wide chest lifts with a deep breath. "Can you fucking imagine what that's going to be like for her?"

The leviathan suddenly looks small. The thought of what his daughter will have to face is too much to bear.

"Can she talk? Or does she still have the breathing tube in?"

"It came out today."

"Has she said anything?"

Jethro lets go of a rough breath. "She asked me to let her die."

Jack's fists tighten on the table. "I have a daughter. What do you want from the Kings?"

"I want you to help me find those fuckers. And I want you to bring hell with you."

Jack calls Church, and within the hour, all the Kings who aren't at the crop harvest are gathered in the war room.

While Jack brings them up to speed, I sit in the bar with Earl and Dolly and keep the Devil's Steed occupied with some King's Pride.

Jethro toys with his shot glass. His brow furrowed.

"Your girl… what's her name?" Dolly asks, refilling the glass.

"Katey."

"That's a real pretty name." Dolly smiles warmly. "And what are Katey's favorite flowers?"

Jethro thinks for a minute. "Daisies. She's always taking photos with daisies."

"Well, when she wakes up tomorrow, there'll be fresh daisies in her room, I'll make sure of it." She gives Jethro a wink. "Let her know the Kings are thinking about her."

He raises his shot in appreciation and then throws it back.

Jack reappears.

Church is over.

"Let's ride."

Jethro's daughter is barely conscious when we get to the hospital.

Not a lot triggers me but seeing the young girl hooked up to machines and trussed up like a fucking mummy kicks me in the gut.

Only her lips and eyes are visible. Her gaze is hooded and sleepy, but her eyes are open enough for me to see the trauma in them.

I've seen that look before.

They broke her.

Jethro sits and takes her hand in his. "It's okay, baby. I'm here. I brought some people with me, men who are going to help us. Squeeze my hand if that's okay with you, honey, squeeze my hand."

Her fingers tighten around his beefy digits. Beside her, the beeping on the heart monitor speeds up when Jack moves closer to the bed.

"It's okay, sweetheart," Jethro reassures his daughter. "He just needs some information. Anything you can remember."

"I'm sorry this happened to you, darlin'," Jack says in a voice I've never heard him use before. It's gentle. *Soothing.* "We're going to find the people responsible, okay? But I need your help. Do you feel up to talking to me about it?"

Big blue eyes bounce between Jack and Jethro before she nods.

"The scum who did this to you, did they say who they were?"

She nods. "The... Three." Her voice is raspy from the breathing tube she had in.

"That's what they called themselves?"

She nods.

"The doctors tell you what they cut into your forehead?"

Again, she nods.

"They say anything while they were doing that to you?"

"They said they won't stop..." She struggles to speak. "Until they've made an example of all the... sinners."

Jack asks, "Can you remember anything about them that might help us identify them. Any jewelry? Distinctive marks? Tattoos?"

"One had a tattoo on the top of his hand. It looked like a clock face... but instead of numbers, there was the letter H in the center and... the number two." Her throat works as she struggles to swallow, her breath gurgled and hoarse. "And the number eight."

"Sounds like a symbol," Jack says.

I open Google on my phone. "It is."

I bring up an image and show Katey. "Is this the tattoo?"

She sobs. "Yes."

I show Jack and Jethro. "It's the symbol for Azrael. The angel of death."

"How'd you know that?" Jethro asks.

"Prison. It gave me a lot of reading time."

Katey turns to look at Jack. "They're... fucking... evil. Someone has to... stop them."

"Darlin', that's exactly what we plan to do."

Her breathing is rough. "Why are you helping me?"

Jack crouches down. "I have a daughter your age, so when your daddy came to us and said he's going to find who did this, I agreed to get the Kings involved. I don't want you to worry, okay, darlin', because the psychos who did this aren't going to be wasting oxygen for too much longer. Now, I ain't gonna lie to you, you've got some journey ahead of you, that's for real. But you're gonna get through it, one day at a time. You got me?" He looks at Jethro. "Anything she needs, and you can't get it, you come see me."

Respect passes between the two presidents.

Jack stands, but Katey reaches for his hand. "I'm the only one who has survived one of their attacks."

"That's right."

"Are they going to... come after me again?"

"You're safe. Your daddy ain't gonna let anyone hurt you. And if you get scared, I want you to know that it's not just your daddy's club behind you, but you've got the entire Kings of Mayhem Motorcycle Club behind you too. You got that, kid?"

It's late when we leave, but I don't want to head back to the clubhouse. I feel restless. Worked up. Seeing that kid beat up and broken on the hospital bed makes me want to punch something. I need to hit the gym, pound the bag for an hour or two to work off some of this restless energy. But as I ride toward Oscar's Gym, I suddenly veer off and pull up to Rory's apartment.

I fucking need to touch her.

Taste her.

Get fucking lost in her.

She opens the door, and just the sight of her beautiful face fuels the need in me. Without a word, I step inside and take her in my arms and kiss her fiercely because her lips are like wine, and I am the addict who needs them. And after the shit I saw tonight, I need her to soothe the panic in my heart.

If anything fucking happens to her.

I hoist her up into my arms. I can't get close enough to her.

"I need you so fucking much right now."

I kick the door closed behind me and carry her across the room.

Once in her bedroom, I shred her clothes from her tiny frame and spend the next hour getting lost in her luscious body.

CHAPTER 21

RORY

"Is she going to survive?" I ask, horrified by the gruesome details Ares shared about Katey. We're lying in bed, the sheet pulled up to our naked waists. Ares' thumb grazes my shoulder as he stares up at the ceiling.

"Physically. But the scarring will be a mental hurdle."

His warm brown eyes fill with empathy but also fury. The mix is a turn-on.

"Seeing her like that..." His voice is hoarse. "Things won't ever be the same for her."

I didn't plan on seeing Ares tonight because my visit to Boston was still fucking with me. Hell, seeing my mother and her fiancé was still fucking with me when I got home and unlocked my front door. All I wanted was a shower, to crawl into bed, and slip into a long, dreamless sleep.

But Ares knocking on my door changed everything, and ironically, it was the very man who I am meant to kill, who pulled me out of my funk and made me feel better with two mind-blowing orgasms and Chinese takeout.

Now, I lay tangled in his arms, my body content and relaxed in the afterglow of what his giant cock did to me.

While a war rages in my head.

I lean up on my elbow. "She's so young. When this kind of thing happens, sometimes it makes me think there isn't any justice in this world."

"Sometimes you gotta make your own justice," he says, his jaw ticking.

"Do you really believe that?"

"I live by it."

I look up at him. "Is that what you used to do when you worked for the De Kysa?"

His eyes dart to mine, and he searches my face.

He frowns. "I never mentioned the De Kysa to you."

Fuck.

Imprisoned by this questioning look, I race into damage control. "In passing, you mentioned working for the De Kysa." I shrug as if it's nothing. "Boston is my hometown. I know who the De Kysa are and what they do. I figured you worked for them in a similar role as the Kings."

His gaze is scorching, but I don't look away. I play it cool as if I hadn't just put a giant foot in my mouth.

He has never mentioned the De Kysa to me, and he knows it. But he is silently questioning it, and I hope it's enough for us to move past this slip-up.

Finally, he asks, "Does that bother you?"

Inwardly, I breathe a sigh of relief.

"I guess that depends on what you did for them."

He pauses and then surprises the hell out of me when he says, "I took care of bad people."

My blood runs cold. My throat tightens.

A tornado spins wildly through my emotions.

"Took care of them?"

"Whatever needed to be done."

I struggle to swallow past the cold ache.

He killed our Joey in cold blood.

Connor wasn't lying. It was true. Ares worked for the De Kysa and killed Joey for them.

My voice is small. "Why are you telling me this?"

"Because I wasn't lying when I said I fucking like you. I think there is something between us that is more than sex, right?"

After a pause, I nod. It's all I can manage because inside, I am being torn in two.

My heart agrees with him while my head is screaming bloody murder.

He killed your brother.

He reaches up and tenderly brushes my hair from in front of my eyes. "So I need you to know who I am. Who you're in bed with. Who's inside you. And I want you to trust him and know he is never going to hurt you. I'm fucking falling for you, Rory, and I don't want you to find out who I am and run away from me later. So, this is me. I've got blood on my hands from working for the De Kysa and blood on my hands working for the Kings. It's who I am." His face is an emotionless mask, but the emotion burns bright in his eyes. "My question... am I the kind of man you could fall in love with?"

My heart pounds wildly.

Yes, she cries.

But I can't say the words because my throat is too tight with emotion.

All I can do is nod.

He crushes his lips to mine, and I kiss him back with a hunger I've never known. His hands roam everywhere, his tongue and lips kissing me into a dizzying high.

Ares doesn't fuck me with the urgency he brought over with him tonight. This is different. Another wall has crumbled, and when he makes love to me, I can feel more walls dropping around us, and it makes it easier to get lost in him. To forget what is happening outside of our bubble.

Afterward, we listen to the rain against the windows, and when Ares falls asleep, I lay in tortured silence and listen to his gentle breath.

Tick tock, Aurora.

Surrounded by his infinite warmth, I fall into a deep sleep where nothing good resides, and all my dreams are nightmares.

We were at the beach. The little cove where my father used to take us on the weekends if he wasn't busy with work. There were no waves, and I was standing at the shoreline, trying to skim rocks, but so far, none of them had danced across the water, they simply sank a few feet away.

I picked up another rock. But it sank too, and I hung my head with a sob.

"Oh, for heaven's sake, Rory, stop being such a crybaby," my mother snapped behind me. I looked over my shoulder to where she was sitting in a beach chair, a cigarette in one hand and a half-empty glass of wine in the other. Her blonde hair was wrapped in a scarf Daddy brought back for her from one of his business trips, and she was wearing a sparkly top that glittered with a thousand silver stars in the sunlight. "And look at that bathing suit. You're going to have to lay off the waffles and gelato if you want to wear things like that, Aurora."

"Ariana, she's nine years old," my father said, refilling her wine glass. "She doesn't need to hear shit talk like that... let her be a child." He turned away from her and winked at me, his warm smile keeping the chill of my mother's meanness at bay.

My father was a scary-looking man. His eyes burned with green flames, and bad words often fell from his thin lips, but they'd only ever said nice things to me. I knew men were afraid of him. But not me. He'd only ever been kind and loving to me. I was his princess.

But my mother wasn't done with me.

"She'll be two hundred pounds by then," my mother scoffed, crossing her legs and taking a puff on her cigarette. "If she keeps eating the way she does, it will be like stuffing a piglet into a bikini come next summer."

I turned away from her cruel comments. I didn't want to look like a piglet in a bikini or whatever that meant. Anyway, what did she know? She was the one wearing a full face of makeup to the beach and enough gold she'd sink right to the bottom of the ocean if she fell in.

I decided to ignore her. It wasn't my fault Mom didn't like our days at the beach, but I was usually the one who ultimately paid for it.

Joey joined me at the water's edge. "You know, if you want it to skip, you're going to have to hold it the right way."

He picked up a stone and showed me how to hold it, flat between the thumb and forefinger. I watched as he bent down and sent it skimming across the top of the still sea water. It bounced at least four times.

"See, it's all in the angle." He grinned proudly. A gentle wind came off the water and played in his floppy sun-kissed hair as he picked up another rock and handed it to me. "Now you try."

I looked down at the water lapping at our feet and then at the rock in my hand, but when I looked back at Joey, he wasn't the sweet boy with the dimpled smile anymore. He was a grown man with facial hair and sweaty armpits. He looked strung out and impatient. Drugs had taken their toll, and his skin was pale and his cheeks hollow, his eyes yellow and sickly.

But it's what I saw in them that really sent a shiver rolling through me.

Menace.

There was something not right with him. Something frightening and cruel that I'd never seen before.

I glanced over to my mom and dad, but they were gone.

So had the sun.

Gray clouds gathered at the horizon, and an oppressive heaviness hung in the air.

"This is what you wanted, wasn't it?" he said angrily.

"What do you mean?"

"You wanted me to be dead."

I took a step away from him. "How can you say that?"

"Because you know."

"Know what?" He wasn't making any sense. "Joey, I don't know what you're talking about."

And suddenly, we weren't at the beach anymore. We were in the garage of our family home in Dorchester, standing in a tiny ribbon of light beaming into the room from inside the house.

"Why are you looking so frightened of me, sister?"

The darkness in his voice sent a shiver up my spine.

"I'm not frightened," I lied.

"You believe what they say about me, don't you... sister?"

"No, I don't," I snapped out.

"Then why haven't you done it yet?"

"Done what?"

"You know." He circled me like a predator stalking his prey. "It."

"I... I don't know." I hugged my arms around my waist. I didn't feel safe, and I wanted to leave this garage. I wanted to get far away from my brother, and I didn't know why. I'd never seen him like that before, and I didn't like it.

"It's because you're in love with him." He stopped moving, but his stillness was just as creepy. "And you love him more than you ever loved me."

I met his gaze and saw the madness there.

"That's not true," I whispered.

He disappeared into the darkness, and I turned around, searching the blackness for him. I couldn't see him, but I could hear him, and he began to taunt me from the shadows, singing like a child.

"Rory and Ares sitting in a tree..."

"Stop it," I said.

"K.I.S.S.I.N.G."

"I said, stop it."

"First comes love, then comes marriage..."

I slammed my palms to my ears. "I'm not listening."

A stillness settled over the garage.

"You love him, don't you, sister?"

My arms fell to my sides. "No."

"Yes, you do, and you love him more than you ever loved me."

"That's not true."

"Yes, it is. Because if you loved me half as much as you love him..." He rushed at me from out of the darkness, his face twisted into a snarl and blood gushing a gaping wound in his throat. *"You would've put a bullet in his head!"*

I wake up in a rush, my heart pounding.

It takes me a moment to catch my breath, and as I do, the images and emotions of my dream begin to rapidly recede. When they're gone, a wave of emotion washes over me, and I have to fight back the surge of tears behind my eyes.

I sag against the pillow and glance over at Ares. He's sound asleep, his powerful body heavy with slumber, his beautiful face softened as he dreams. This man really is the most breathtaking man, and I have to stop myself from reaching out and touching the sharp contours of his beautiful face.

He's an oxymoron.

A vicious killer with the strength of a giant and the body of a god.

But he also has the beauty of an angel, right down to the long soft eyelashes that delicately rest against his smooth cheek as he rests.

Frustrated and confused, I shove off the sheet and leave the comfort of my bed, carefully padding across the floorboards so I don't wake Ares. In the kitchen, I pour myself a glass of water and gulp down a couple of cold mouthfuls, then lean my elbows against the counter and drop my head into my hands.

Behind the sugar and coffee canisters is a Ruger SR1911 handgun.

Fully loaded.

I reach for it, my palm closing over the cool metal shell, my fingers resting against the trigger.

Ares took my brother from me.

And it's my job to make him pay for it.

I know that.

I agreed to that.

My father would want that.

"Everything okay?"

I look up to see him standing in the doorway of the bedroom, looking sleepy and disheveled as he palms his eyes and yawns, and a familiar kick thumps in my heart.

Even crumpled from sleep, he still looks like he could carry the world on his broad shoulders. He smiles sleepily, and a knot of desire tightens in my gut. My hand remains on the gun, but as I watch the Adonis in tight trunks walk toward me, his golden body ripples with muscle and power, a new need takes over my body, and a tiny pulse flutters between my thighs.

I remove my hand from the gun. "I had a bad dream, but I'm okay now."

He comes around to my side of the counter and towers over me, engulfing me in the warmth of his body. I'm not worried about him seeing the gun because I'll say it's for protection. But it's hidden, and he doesn't see it.

"You want to talk about it?" He reaches out to touch my face, his fingertips feather-like against my throat. I close my eyes against the sensation, and without thinking, I lean into them. "Sometimes it helps."

"No," I whisper, seduced by his touch.

When I open my eyes, I'm met with a gentle warmth in his and a tenderness I'm not expecting. It tugs on my heart, and I have to push the feeling away and remind myself of why I am here and who he is. I can't forget that no matter how intoxicating his touch feels against my skin or how mind-blowing it is when he covers me with his muscular body and grinds into me to make me come...

... this man murdered my brother.

I take a step away from him, but he catches my wrist, and the warmth of his gaze sears into mine as he takes my face in his big hands and leans down to kiss me.

His kiss is comforting, his mouth warm and inviting. As it moves over mine, I think about the gun behind the canisters. I think about reaching for it. I think about raising it and pressing the tip of the barrel to his jaw and completing what I came here to do. But then he takes the kiss deeper, and a growl falls between us, and those thoughts fall away as small pleasurable fires ignite throughout my body.

"Don't be afraid, little one. Our dreams can't hurt us." He wraps his arms around me. "And I'm here to chase any of the monsters away."

Tears prick at my eyes. *This man.* He's so damn protective.

I have to hold back a whimper when I grip onto his big arms and kiss him fiercely.

"Fuck me," I beg against his lips. "Make me forget."

With an aroused growl, he spins me around and bends me

over the counter, where he pushes me down. He nudges my ankles apart, and his hands glide over my hips and down my legs as he removes my underwear. "What my girl wants, my girl gets."

My girl.

I can't hold back my tears, and they spill down my cheeks onto the counter.

Standing behind me, he cups my ass and moans. "So good. So perfect."

He shoves down his sweatpants and sinks into me, his low groan rippling in the air around us.

My pussy throbs.

But so does the hole in my chest.

I'm so damn confused.

My hand slides across the marble counter and through the space between the sugar and coffee canister until my fingertips brush against the gun.

When we were kids, Joey was my best friend. Our father was dead, murdered because he was a crime boss in an unstable time when families were at war over power, money, and turf, and our new stepfather was a cold-hearted deviant who believed he could take what he wanted, when he wanted, and from whom he wanted.

There was a time when Joey protected me against the harsh realities of being raised in a crime family. But as he grew older, he became more distant and less interested in protecting me.

But I still loved him because he was my brother.

We had a bond.

But the man sliding his cock into me ended it when he killed him.

Yet the more I get to know Ares...

Oh God, a delicious sensation takes up in every nerve ending of my drenched pussy, and I can't stop the desperate groan that falls from my parted lips.

A war rages inside me.

And as I come on Ares' cock, I still don't know which side is going to win.

Afterward, we fall into bed, and he pulls me into his strong arms.

I feel safe in his embrace.

"Do you believe in destiny, Ares?"

"Yes."

I murmur into his big bicep. "Do you believe in God?"

"I believe in something. Do you believe in God?"

"I didn't think I did, but sometimes I find myself talking to him."

Ares leans down and tenderly kisses the crown of my head. "I know what you mean. Every fucking day I thank him for sending you to me."

CHAPTER 22

ARES

With the harvest in full production, I spend most of the day overseeing the transportation of the day's yield to the packing house.

When I'm done, I leave and stop by Rory's apartment to take her for a ride.

She's dressed in a yellow summer dress, cowboy boots, and a sunny smile, and the moment I see her I feel that familiar kick in my heart.

"Why are you looking at me like that?" she says self-consciously. "Have I got something on my face?"

I slide my hands around her waist. "No, you're fucking perfect."

We set off in the late afternoon light with the cloudless blue sky stretching above us and the warm golden sun on our backs.

I sigh and settle into the ride. There's nothing like the feel of my girl's arms around me and her lush curves pressed against my back as we ride through the magnificent landscape of Eastern Tennessee. Farms give way to winding mountain roads and breathtaking panoramic views of treetops and rocky mountain passes.

I feel free and happy.

Hell, I'm so fucking content I can't get this stupid goofy grin off my face.

Life is near perfect.

I push the Harley harder and enjoy the whip of the wind in my hair and the sting of fresh air on my face. It takes us almost an hour to get to the lookout. When we do, I pull off the road and carefully navigate the Harley down the dry, beaten track through the trees and come to a stop on the rocky lookout.

This is my thinking place, where I go when I need to decompress all the thoughts and feelings that twist chaotically through my mind. Here, I feel at peace as I look out over the sea of trees and deep valleys below.

I don't bring people here.

It always felt too sacred to share with anyone else.

But I want to share it with Rory.

"What's this place called?"

"Deadman's Pass." When she frowns, I ask, "You don't like the name?"

"Oh no, I do. I think it's perfect." She turns to look back at the sweeping view, and sunlight glints in her beautiful eyes. "Because standing here is like looking into the face of paradise. Kind of like you've died and gone to heaven."

I like her take on the name.

"Unfortunately, the story isn't as nice as that."

"No?"

"According to legend, the name comes from a curse. They say when the leader of a local village discovered his only daughter, a striking beauty called Aiyana, was sneaking around with a warrior from a rival village, he was going to kill this young warrior, but his daughter pleaded for her father to let him prove his worth. Her father agreed and said to the warrior boy that if he set off into the wilderness and survived three moons in the mountains and snow, then he would step aside and allow their union."

As I speak, Rory watches me with big eyes.

"So the warrior boy confidently did as he was asked because he knew the mountains and the valleys, and he knew how to survive the harsh weather. But what no one knew was that Aiyana's father had also sent his most trusted warrior to follow the boy and kill him, telling him not to return until his blood stained the snow. Three days later, he came back and silently nodded that it was done. For months, Aiyana waited for her love to come back, but when he didn't return, she fell weak and soon enough, it was obvious she was dying."

Tears well in Rory's eyes. "Did she find out what happened to her love?"

"In his grief of seeing her on her death bed, her father admitted what he had done and begged for her forgiveness. But Aiyana could not forgive him. Instead, she cursed him and anyone who dared pass this part of the mountain after a certain time of year."

I turn to find Rory looking up at me with sad eyes.

"Now it is said that if you come past this point at a certain time of year, the likelihood of you coming back again is slim to none, not because the wind and the snow and the bone-biting cold were sure to get you, but Aiyana's curse. Since then, the pass has claimed many lives, and so it was named Deadman's Pass."

Rory looks sad.

I reach for her face, cupping it in my hand, and it reminds me of how tiny she is in comparison to me. "It's just a legend. It probably never happened."

"Legend's usually start with something."

The tale seems to have struck a nerve with her which intrigues me because there is so much I don't know about her. So much that *I want to know* about her.

"I didn't take you for a romantic at heart," I say, stroking her cheek with my thumb.

"Oh, I am. I've just never been in love."

I lean down and brush my lips against hers. "Never?"

"Never."

My tongue sweeps into her mouth, and she whimpers, sending a bolt of lust right to my cock.

"Does that mean you're opposed to it?" I ask against her lips.

"It means… I've never met anyone worth the sacrifice."

"It doesn't need to be a sacrifice."

"In my experience, there is always someone who has to give up something. But then, I suppose it will be worth it for the right person."

I meet her eyes. "I think so too."

Her smile is gentle. Her eyes are shining.

"This is a special place," she whispers, turning to stare out at the view. Her words make me happy. As if she can really feel it, she entwines our fingers and looks back at me. "Thank you for bringing me here."

I squeeze her fingers. Suddenly, I feel the urge to show her everything that means something to me, and the idea of sharing more of my life with her gets me excited.

"Will you bring me back here again?" she asks.

"Anytime, baby. Just tell me when, and I'll make it happen."

"Thank you." She wraps her arms around my waist and then whispers as an afterthought, "You're so good to me."

"Given the chance, I'll give you whatever you want, little one."

She rises on her tiptoes, and her words tickle the shell of my ear. "Good, because right now I want you to fuck me up against your bike."

Her words go straight to my cock and get me so damn hard, I'm about to bust open my zipper.

"Your every wish is my command."

I take her against my bike, sinking deep into her with a growl. And when she comes on my cock and sags against my Harley, I join her.

I drop my head back and let my orgasm crash through me, and my growl of pleasure echoes across the valley as I pump and pump until I'm empty and we're both shaking. But when I've finished coming, I remain inside her. I'm not done yet. I want this moment to last because chances are I'll never see another moment like it in this lifetime. Not like this. Not as perfect as now. The view. The golden light. The sight of my girl bent over my bike. Her luscious pussy milking me and keeping me hard.

And as I start to fuck my girl slowly again, I watch the sun sink deeper into the hills and realize I'm not falling for her anymore.

I'm already crazy in love with her.

It's dark by the time we get back to her apartment. We shower together, and when she's pressed against the tiles, I make her come with my tongue until her knees buckle and she can't stand. Then afterward, we cook dinner in her tiny kitchen, and I get struck by how much I enjoy domesticated life and how easy it would be for me to leave the old life behind.

I've never pictured myself doing any of this—cooking dinner, talking into the night, falling asleep every night in a pair of warm, comforting arms.

But I'm here for all of it.

After dinner, we take our drinks onto the terrace and sit under a star-scattered sky. The night is warm and peaceful, and I'm fighting with the words on the tip of my tongue.

I want to tell her I love her.

But something is holding me back, and the words never come.

Even later in bed, when I pull her into my arms and she wraps her luscious curves around me, I'm still hesitant. Instead, I fall into a heavy sleep where I dream about a future with my girl and forget about the gnawing feeling I have growing in my gut.

A gnawing feeling that tells me something isn't quite right.

Sometime in the middle of the night, I get up for a glass of water.

In the kitchen, something hidden behind the coffee canister catches my eye.

It's a gun—specifically, a Ruger SR1911 handgun.

I don't touch it. When DNA gets you wrongfully imprisoned once, you get shy about leaving your fingerprints and skin cells in the wrong place at the wrong time. And something about this gun being carefully concealed on the kitchen counter tells me this is one of those situations.

My gut churns with unease.

Why does Rory need a gun hidden behind her kitchenware?

I know she's afraid of her stepfather finding her, and I get that she wants to protect herself if he does, but it's not the presence of the gun that disturbs me. It's the placement of it that gives me concern.

It screams unusual.

Too specific.

Like something I'd do. I push back on the thought.

Rory is as much a killer as I'm the Pope.

Still, something doesn't feel right.

I don't say anything when I return to bed.

Instead, I try to convince my instinct I'm wrong. That there's no reason for Rory not to have a gun, given the circumstances.

The next day, Jack wants me to ride out to the grow barn.

The grow barn is a massive brick and timber structure that used to be a canning factory back in the 1930s. Flanked by two cornfields, it looks empty and abandoned, nothing like the growing facility where we nurture thousands and thousands of marijuana plants from seedlings to mature adults.

Most of our plants are grown throughout Appalachia amongst the outdoor crops of Christmas trees and tall pines on farmland we lease from farmers. But those crops are seasonal, and quality can depend on the elements. Our grow barn allows us to churn out a new harvest every three months, and the quality is never by chance. Alchemy, our expert moonshiner, also knows how to cultivate the perfect high.

Today, Jack and I are visiting to oversee the transport of the product to the drying facility a few miles away. Hired patrols help us keep the area secure. As we pull in, Gambit is standing with two men dressed in black. Everyone is wearing Kevlar and armed with heavy-duty rifles.

They wave us through, and we park next to a refrigeration truck where local workers load crates of freshly harvested buds into the back. Once loaded, they'll head over to the packing facility we have at a farmhouse a few miles down the road.

Inside the grow barn, a sophisticated airflow system keeps the temperature where we want it, while protecting workers from getting high. But today, the aroma of freshly cut buds hangs heavy in the air. Sweet and sticky.

"Are we still on schedule?" Jack asks Alchemy, who is in charge of production.

"So far, we've harvested seventy-five percent of the crop," Alchemy explains as he leads us through the barn. "We expect to have the other twenty-five done by tomorrow."

Jack pats him on the back. "Good work, Al."

Alchemy remembers something he forgot to tell the men loading the trucks and disappears outside while Jack and I walk through the sea of marijuana plants.

"So your girl, is that something serious?" he asks, inspecting the buds on one of the plants.

"It's getting to be."

He looks at me and nods. "Bronte liked her. Said she had a good feeling about her in her waters, whatever the fuck that means."

That makes me smile.

"I have a pretty good feeling about her too."

Neither Jack nor I are into talking about our feelings.

But part of Jack's role as president is to check in with his men.

Make sure they've got their heads on right.

It's why he's keeping a strong eye on Gabe.

"You think she's someone who might hang around?"

"I hope so."

He smiles. "Sounds like it might be a good thing. She's made friends quickly. Cinnamon was around to babysit Rhett and wouldn't stop talking about how much she likes her. And Dolly thinks she's sweeter than... *what did she fucking say...* stolen honey or some shit like that." He shakes his head. Dolly's never short of a metaphor. "Sounds like she's a good fit."

"I was thinking the same thing."

Jack pauses. His grin fades. Something has triggered his sixth sense. He looks around.

"Do you hear that?"

"I don't hear anything."

"Exactly. It's too quiet outside."

He's right, there is an eerie silence. There are no voices. No movement.

Jack looks at me, and my hand slides to my gun.

Just as his slides to his.

We turn around to leave the barn but come face to face with three men in suits wearing Halloween masks.

And one of them is holding a motherfucking flamethrower.

CHAPTER 23

RORY

"Well, here's a sight for sore eyes," Dolly says as I walk into the clubhouse bar. She gives me a friendly wink and leans against the polished counter.

I slide onto one of the bar stools, my stomach in knots because of what I'm about to do.

I've come to tell Ares everything.

And I mean everything.

Planned assassination and all.

I mean, after last night, how can I not?

This morning, I woke up alone, but Ares' warmth still lingered in the sheets, and in that moment, I realized I couldn't continue with the lie.

Not after last night.

Not after those words.

I'm fucking falling for you.

Killing a man for being evil is one thing. Stringing along a man with a good heart is another.

Ares isn't the monster I thought he was, and somehow, I've

become the villain in this story. Now I'm here, ready to tell him everything, despite knowing I'll probably lose the best thing that's ever happened to me, and at the same time, break his heart in the process.

But it's the right thing to do.

I'm nervous, and Dolly can tell. "Everything okay, honey?"

No, everything sucks.

"Of course, I'm just a little tired." I force a smile. Dolly is the mom I never had, and it kills me to know I'll be letting her down too.

I'm going to lose the family I've always wanted.

"You here to see that gorgeous man of yours?"

Yep, but I'm about to destroy him.

I press two fingers into my temples. "Is he here?"

"He and Jack rode out to the grow shed, but they'll be back soon. Can I get you a drink while you wait?"

Yes, a tall glass of cyanide because I'm a terrible person.

I lean my elbows on the bar and push my hands through my hair. "Is it too soon for tequila?"

"I'm sure it's five o'clock somewhere." She grabs a bottle and two shot glasses, lining them up in front of me. "Everything okay with you and Ares?"

You mean, besides me being here to kill him?

"Yeah, of course," I say, but my face says otherwise.

"You know, it's been a long while since I've seen that boy smile, and now, he's smiling every day. Come to think of it, I don't think I've ever seen him so happy. Didn't used to be the word I'd use to describe him, but since you've come along, he's happier than a pig in mud."

I feel the heat of her gaze on me.

Oh boy, she's going to hate me when she finds out the reason I walked into all their lives.

The weight of it settles on my chest.

And Dolly can tell.

She leans against the countertop. "You know that boy has a sad past. He doesn't talk about it, not to me, not to Jack, not to anyone but Paw, and that was only because a night of heavy drinking loosened his lips. But I know his past haunts him. He has a deep wound in that big heart of his, a wound that keeps bleeding with every day that passes." She tilts her head. "You look like you're here to add to that bloodletting. But I hope I'm wrong."

I buckle under the weight of her knowing look, and my hands go to my face. "Oh, Dolly, I've fucked-up. I've fucked-up real bad."

"So bad that you have to hurt him?"

I drop my hands so I can make eye contact. "I don't want to hurt him."

"Then don't."

"I have a secret," I whisper, tears welling in my eyes. "A terrible secret."

She pours another shot and hands it to me. "Oh, baby girl, we all have our secrets. There ain't no crime in that."

"But what if that secret can hurt the one you love?"

"That's why they're called secrets. You don't tell, he won't know, and he won't get hurt. Unless he's in danger, of course..." She pauses, then straightens and raises an eyebrow, a sharp edge enters her tone. "Is that it, Rory? Is Ares in danger?"

"You wouldn't believe me if I told you."

"Try me."

I drink my shot, stalling.

Dolly's tone is still sharp. "Honey, you tell me what the hell is going on. If that boy is in danger, you need to start hollering."

Before I can reply, Dakota Joe, Bam, Loki, and Merrick walk into the club, stirring up the atmosphere in the room with the frenzied energy of a tornado. Too busy giving Merrick a hard time for the three hickeys on his neck, they don't notice the tension that crackles in the air between Dolly and me.

It feels like the walls are closing in on me.

She knows I'm a terrible person.

Suddenly, everyone's cells start to ring.

Everyone's except mine.

Dolly answers hers, "What the hell? Slow down, Earl. I can't understand what you're saying."

I feel a shiver run down my spine.

Something is wrong.

Very wrong.

And everyone is talking at once, and I can't make out what is being said to who, about what.

Just then, Venom runs into the clubhouse from one of the bedrooms, throwing on his cut as he races for the door. "Someone set fire to the grow shed."

Fear prickles along my skin.

Ares is at the grow shed.

I turn to Dakota Joe. "I'm coming with you."

"Like hell, you are, lady. Jack would fucking kill me. And that's not even half of what Ares would do."

"But—"

"Stay here," he growls.

I turn to Dolly for help, but she clearly agrees with them, and I watch them all walk out of the clubhouse.

Clearly, there are rules when you belong to a motorcycle club.

But right now I don't give a damn about their rules.

Not when Ares' life is in danger.

I grab my car keys off the bar and race out of the clubhouse. By the time I peel out of the parking lot, I can only just see Dakota Joe's taillight up ahead.

It's a perfect summer evening. The stars are out, and there's a warm breeze in the air. But as I near the part of town where they keep the cannabis fields, the sweet tang of burning marijuana hangs heavy in the air.

In the distance, an orange glow cuts into the fading light. As it gets closer, a new wave of fear washes through me when I see the bellowing smoke and ferocious fire. The barn is completely engulfed. Flames flare into the evening sky, and a rain of glowing embers falls onto the field below, catching trees and plants alight.

Dakota Joe pulls up next to Venom and Ghoul. They're off their bikes by the time I come to a skid beside them.

Doc is already on the scene and treating Gambit who is bleeding from bullet wounds. Further along, two men who I have never seen before lie still in the grass.

My stomach rolls and I can't breathe.

"Is there anyone still inside?" Dakota Joe asks Venom and Ghoul.

"Jack and Ares," Venom replies.

Just as he says it, the barn roof collapses, sending ferocious flames high into the sky.

Ares.

My heart screams his name.

There is no way anyone can survive a fire like this.

"Fuck this," Ghoul growls.

He tries to run toward the barn, but Dakota Joe thrusts out an arm, and Ghoul slams into it. "You go in there, and it's suicide."

"Our sergeant-at-arms and our president are in there."

"You've got an old lady now and a kid on the way. You stay out here."

"I'll go," Venom says.

"No one goes," Dakota Joe growls.

As the fire rages, the embers rain onto the cornfields, and they catch alight too. Within seconds, the dry crop is fully ablaze.

I watch on helplessly.

I want to be sick.

The sound of approaching fire trucks wail in the distance, but they're too far away.

I can't watch this happen and not do anything.

Without thinking, I take off toward the burning barn. Dakota Joe reaches out to stop me, but all he manages to grab onto is my shirt which I leave behind in my wake as I run through the scrub. I don't have a plan. At this stage, I'm running on pure adrenaline. All I know is the man I love is inside that burning barn, and I can't stand around and watch it consume him.

The heat of the fire licks at my skin as I get closer, and I can hear the groan of timber as it succumbs to the intense temperature and collapses into the raging inferno. My lungs burn. My heart aches. But I have to do something.

God, if you let him live, I promise I will do better. I'll become a nun. I'll repent my sins. I'll do whatever you want me to. Just please don't let him die.

And then they appear out of nowhere. Two men silhouetted against the flames as they run out of the burning cornfields.

My heart jumps to my throat—it's Ares and Jack.

I run toward them, not stopping until I collapse into Ares' arms. "Oh, thank God, you're safe." I don't even realize it, but I'm crying. "Are you okay?"

Jack keeps walking. But I'm barely aware of him or the burning barn and the glowing embers floating in the air around us. All that matters is that Ares is alive.

I reach up to touch his face, desperate to feel him.

"Little one..." he whispers.

I gasp out a ragged cry. "Are you hurt?"

He drags my hands to his lips. "I'm not hurt."

A sheen of sweat and ash coats his skin, but he doesn't appear to be burned.

"I saw the roof collapse..."

"I kicked a hole in the wall, and we escaped into the cornfields before the ceiling caved in."

I drag his face to mine and press my forehead against his. "Please tell me you're okay."

"I'm okay. But you shouldn't have come. What were you going to do, run into the burning barn and save me?"

"If that's what it took."

He looks furious but amused at the same time.

"You're pissed at me," I say.

"You put yourself in harm's way. Of course, I'm pissed at you." He clutches my hands. "Baby, if anything happened to you—"

"I feel the same way. That's why I'm here."

He shakes his head.

"You and your fucking logic," he mutters.

He wraps his arms around me.

"Who did this?" I ask.

"The Three."

"Are you sure?"

"Yeah, I'm sure."

Doc interrupts us, "I'm gonna need to check Ares out."

"I'm fine," Ares says gruffly, not willing to let me go. He grasps me tighter to his powerful body. Not because he needs me close but because he knows *I* need him close. "I said I'm fine."

"Get her home," Jack calls out to him.

He's pissed I'm here too.

I've broken their rules by coming here, but I'm not sorry. I'd be dying a slow torturous death waiting for news if I hadn't.

A sudden screaming cuts into the chaos.

Both Ares and I turn in time to see a figure covered in flames come running out from the cornfields toward us. His screams are terrifying, but I can't look away. He only gets so far before he drops to his knees.

"Who is that?" I can't believe what I'm seeing.

"One of *them*." Ares' voice is low and dangerous.

"Where are the other two?"

"One is inside the barn, but he won't be causing any more problems."

Meaning either the fire got him or Ares did.

"And the third one?"

"Probably burning to a crisp in the cornfield."

I watch as Jack and Shooter stride over to where the man dropped to the ground. He's still on fire. Still screaming.

"Look away, baby," Ares rasps.

He buries my face in his shoulder but not before I see Shooter take out his gun. I hear a shot, and the screaming stops.

Suddenly, I'm trembling and cold, almost as if I'm going into shock. Ares keeps a protective arm around my shoulder as he walks me away from the scene. "Come on, I gotta get you home."

At his bike, I stop and turn to look over my shoulder. A ghostly finger runs down my spine. It's like someone is watching this scene unfold from the silhouetted tree line in the distance, and I feel their furious gaze narrow in on me. "He's out there," I whisper.

"There's always going to be someone out there. But I won't let anything happen to you." He swings his leg over his bike. "Just stop making it so damn hard to keep you safe."

I wrap my arm around his waist, and we take off into the evening, leaving the carnage behind us.

That's when I realize my new reality.

I'm in love with Ares.

And losing him is going to hurt.

CHAPTER 24

ARES

After arriving back at Rory's, I shower and take my time under the stream of water to get the smell of smoke out of my senses and to ease the tension in my shoulders.

Tonight was a close call, and we were lucky to make it out alive. If we hadn't busted a hole in the wall of the barn and escaped into the cornfields, I'm not sure I'd be standing here now.

Pressing my hands against the wet tiles, I duck my head so the water rushes over the nape of my neck and down my back.

At first, no one said anything. It was a standoff. Five men staring at each other.

Then it happened quickly.

The psycho with the flamethrower ignited his weapon and sent a burst of fire toward us. Jack and I dived for cover, the space between us lit up by a roaring arc of orange flame.

Smoke filled the air as plants caught alight. Still lying on the floor where I landed, I shot blindly in the direction of The Three hoping like hell to hit one of them. Through the smoke, I saw one of the men stalking toward me. Head bowed. Shoulders squared. A big fucking hunting knife in his hand.

I shot him three times in the chest, but he kept coming at me. The fuckers were wearing body armor.

He lunged for me, but I rolled to the side, narrowly escaping his knife.

There was no time to get to my feet.

When he lunged at me again, I kicked his legs out from under him, and he hit the floor.

"You're not wearing body armor on your head, asshole."

I put two bullets into his masked forehead, and he went limp.

I jumped to my feet. The shed was fully alight. Plants glowed with green and gold embers. The heavy stench of smoldering cannabis filled the room, stinging my eyes and filling my lungs.

Any minute now, the whole place was going to erupt.

More gunfire chips into the heavy smoke-filled barn. Pop! Pop! Pop! But through the smoke, I caught a glimpse of the two vigilantes retreating to the front of the barn. There's a glimpse of evening light through the darkness and then the sound of the doors slamming shut and the deadbolt closing.

They'd locked us inside.

Through the heavy smoke, I found Jack.

"This whole place is going to go," he said, coughing. The smoke was thick, the heat searing. Only a few feet away, a smoldering pile of weed erupted into bigger flames. "If the fire reaches the fertilizer, this barn will go off like a bomb."

"They've locked us in. The only way out is to bust our way out." I scanned the burning building for a weak point. Flames crawled up the walls and across the tall ceiling. Another flare of fire shot into the air as the seedling nook ignited. We only had minutes before the smoke would overpower us. "There!" I point to where I patched the damage caused by the storm. It's

our only route out of the building.

We ran through a rain of flames dripping from the ceiling.

Behind us, the fertilizer drums caught alight.

The Grim Reaper stormed toward us through the flames.

I kicked the wall boards. Jack joined me, the smoke getting thicker and thicker, the flames coming closer.

The timber boards finally gave way, and we broke into the fresh air and ran for the cornfields just as the barn erupted into a fireball.

I turn off the faucet and step out of the shower.

Wrapping the towel around my hips, I leave the bedroom and find Rory curled up on the bed, lost in thought. Moonlight streams in through the window and seems to hold her in a trance, her beautiful face as smooth as porcelain in the silvery light.

"Are you okay?" I ask, breaking the stillness.

She turns her face toward me, and I see she's been crying. Tears slide down her flawless cheeks.

"Angel," I say, sitting on the edge of the bed and taking her in my arms. "Don't cry."

"I'm sorry," she says. "I don't know why I'm crying. I'm not normally a crier, I swear."

I can't help but smile. She's adorable. "Tonight was frightening." I bring her to my chest and smooth down her hair. "Even for me."

She smiles against my bicep. "Liar. You didn't look frightened."

I smile, but it fades. I'm used to hiding the chaos taking place inside.

Cradling her in my arms, I slide in behind her and sink my head into the pillow, my inner turmoil soothed by the sweet song of her breath.

We lay there in complete silence, each lost in our own thoughts.

I wasn't lying when I said I was frightened. For one terrifying moment when the flames were chasing me and the smoke was too thick to find my way out of the burning field, I honestly thought I was going to die. The reaper was chomping at my heel, ready to bring down his sickle and drag me down to Hades, and I was frightened. Not because I'm afraid to die, I accepted death a long time ago. Hell, I've prayed for it, and one time I even searched for it with a homemade shiv in my prison cell.

But not tonight. For the first time in my life, I feel the need to put distance between myself and death.

Because I'm in love with Rory.

And the thought of not making it out of the flames to see her again terrified me.

She rests in my arms, and a wave of contentment settles along my body. I don't want to just protect how this feels, I want to protect *her* from everything.

"I'll do it," I finally say, breaking the silence.

Rory stirs in my arms.

"Do what?" she murmurs.

"Kill your stepfather."

Her body tenses.

"I'll take care of it," I say.

She rolls onto her back and stares up at me. In the pale light of the moon, her eyes are wide shiny orbs, her skin as pale as a porcelain doll.

I cup her face. "I'll make him pay for what he did to you and make sure he can't ever hurt you again."

Her brows pull in as her gaze searches my face. "Why now? Because we sleep together?"

"No." My thumb grazes her cheek. "Because I'm in love with you."

She quickly untangles herself from my hold and sits up. "You don't want to love me."

Her words catch me off guard.

"I don't?"

"No, because love doesn't lead to anything but heartache."

"Now you're beginning to sound like me."

"I'm serious, Ares. I've never been in love, and I don't ever want to be because the people I love die, and it hurts."

Her words sting.

Hearing the woman you've fallen for tell you that she doesn't want you to love her is like a searing hot poker to your balls. But I know it's because she's scared.

She loves me.

I can feel it in the way she touches me.

It's in the way she kisses me.

And it's there in her urgent whimpers when she sinks onto my cock and rides me.

I don't blame her for being scared.

Being in love with her fucking terrifies me.

She gives me a grave look, her skin pale in the moonlight, her hair cascading over her naked shoulders and down to her breasts.

I reach up to cup her face. "The only person I ever loved died, and for a long time, I didn't think I'd ever feel this way about someone else. For two decades, I ran from it. But then you came crashing into my world, and things haven't been the same since. I'm in love with you, little one, and there isn't a goddamn thing I can do about it."

A tear slides down her cheek, and I wipe it away with my thumb. "It's why I want to do this. I want to make him pay for laying his hands on you."

More tears spill down her cheeks. "You would do that for me?"

"Angel, there isn't a goddamn thing in this world I wouldn't do for you."

Her face breaks, and she starts to cry.

Sitting up, I gather her into my arms, and she softens against me and sobs into my chest. She feels so tiny and soft and so infinitely perfect. My heart twists with longing to protect her from everything and anything, even her own tears. I smooth down her hair. "It's okay," I whisper.

"When I saw the barn collapse..." She lifts her head, and her cheeks glitter with the trail left by her tears. "When I thought I had lost you... in those minutes, it didn't feel like the world would ever be right again. And then you were there, and you were alive, and the relief made me weak all over I could barely breathe."

"So why are you crying?"

Her face breaks again. "Because that's when I knew I had fallen in love with you."

My heart soars, and I can't stop the smile playing on my lips. "You say that like it's a bad thing."

"It is," she sobs. "Because I wasn't supposed to fall in love with you."

"Says who?"

She stops sobbing, and with a sharp hitch of breath, she becomes very still, and it's almost like darkness enters her big almond-shaped eyes. Her expression changes, her eyebrow lifts, and she seems to get lost in thought.

"Hey?" I tuck a lock of her hair behind her ear. "It's okay, you don't have anything to be frightened of."

Her gaze comes back to me, and she looks frightened. "Ares, there is something I need to tell you."

The coolness in her voice is unsettling as well as the fear in her expression.

"You can tell me anything," I say, not liking the sudden mood change.

I don't like the way she looks uncomfortable as she tries to find her next words, either.

"There are things you need to know."

"Then tell me."

She draws in a deep breath. "I'm not who you think I am."

"People very rarely are, baby."

"Who I was when I came here isn't who I am now."

I cup her jaw. "I don't care who you were or what you've done, what matters is now."

"You couldn't possibly mean that."

"I can, and I do."

The sharp shrill of my cell cuts into the tension and makes her jump.

It's Jack.

I answer it, but I don't take my eyes off Rory. "Yeah."

Jack doesn't waste time with pleasantries. "I need you back at the clubhouse. I've called Church. We need to clean up this mess." He hangs up.

It's the worst timing in the world because I have a feeling Rory is about to pull the rug out from under me, and I need to hear her say it. But I'm sergeant-at-arms, I have to be where my president tells me to be, and he will kick my ass if I don't get there as soon as possible.

"I have to go, but we'll talk when I get back…"

I pause. I feel so in love with her right now, but there's a shadow looming in the distance. Her body language has changed. She's closed off.

"Don't be afraid, baby. Do you love me?"

"Yes," she whispers.

"Then that's *all* that matters."

I dress quickly, not liking leaving her like this. The sooner I get this club business done the better. But something tells me it's going to be a long night.

"I'll be back later," I say, throwing on my cut.

I turn to leave, but her voice stops me.

"Don't take this the wrong way but don't come back tonight."

Alarm bells go off in my head, but I don't show it. On the outside I remain perfectly composed. "Why?" I ask calmly.

"Because I need time to think."

"About what?" My tone is sharp.

"This is happening very quickly."

"I'm aware, but so what?"

"It's a lot for me to take in right now. I'm just asking for some time."

I hate that she's asking for time. *That she has doubts.* But I'll give her what she's asking. Reluctantly.

In the doorway, I pause. "I'll call you tomorrow."

She nods and pulls the sheet higher around her. I don't want to leave, but she doesn't want me here and I need to get back to the clubhouse. Without another word, I walk out and close the door behind me.

Walking to my bike, I feel a heavy weight around my heart.

She's not telling me something.

And whatever it is, it's got her frightened.

CHAPTER 25

ARES

"We have to get rid of the bodies," Jack says.

We're in Church. It's late.

"We could take them over the border, stick them in a boat, set it alight, and send them downstream somewhere." Ghoul has a talent for creative body disposal. "I'm up for it."

"No, they get turned to dust tonight." Jack turns to me. "You, Shooter, and Dakota Joe take the bodies to Seamus at the crematorium. He's expecting you."

"Where are they?"

Dakota Joe pulls a face. "Stinking up the back of my truck."

"What about the fucker who got away?" Venom asks.

A thorough search of the now smoldering cornfields and a mile radius surrounding the grow barn didn't turn up any sign of the third vigilante.

"He'll be hurting," Jack says.

"And he'll be mad as fuck," Shooter adds.

Jack drums his fingers against the table. "He doesn't have his buddies anymore, and it will take him some time to regroup. By then, we'll have more intel, so it'll be easier to track him down."

"How is Gambit?" Banks asks.

"Doc is at the hospital with him. He's going to be okay," Jack says.

When The Three broke through our security with silencers attached to their guns, Gambit was shot once. The security guards multiple times. Gambit was still alive and conscious when I last saw him. The guards weren't so lucky.

"The Three must've been watching us and took advantage of a vulnerable point in our security line to attack," Shooter says.

"What about the locals who were loading the truck?" Merrick asks him.

"They pulled out of the parking lot minutes before it happened. Alchemy was with them."

"Out of curiosity, do we know what deadly sin they were planning on using?" Earl asks.

"No way of knowing. The only two sins left were gluttony or envy. Maybe in their twisted brains they thought our crops fed the marijuana-smoking gluttony of the people who use it? I don't fucking know. It's hard to untwist the twisted." Jack leans forward in his chair. "Now, everyone get home and get some shut-eye. Tomorrow, we clean up the rest of this mess. I want to see all eyes back here by seven."

When Jack calls an end to Church, Shooter and I join Dakota Joe in his truck and drive out to see Seamus at the crematorium.

Seamus is a sixth-generation crematorium technician. His family has been turning the dead residents of Flintlock to ash for more than a hundred years.

Wearing a sleeveless T-shirt and a greasy trucker's cap, he grins as he hits the buttons on the panel next to the retort, where one of the psychopaths lies in a cremation capsule.

"Want to tell me who's in my chamber today?" Years of tobacco chewing has turned his teeth brown. "Ain't nobody famous, are they?"

"Ain't nobody who is going to be missed," I say.

"Fair enough." He shrugs. "Two bodies is going to take me around eight hours. You want to pick up the cremains in the morning?"

"We'll send the prospect over to collect them."

"Cool. Before I forget..." he passes me a folded piece of paper, "... it's the fingerprints Jack requested."

Jack wants the fingerprints of the deceased so Pinkwater or one of Paw's contacts at the FBI can run them through the national database.

Dakota Joe hands Seamus an envelope stuffed with cash. "As always, the Kings of Mayhem are appreciative of your assistance *and* your discretion."

"Hey, no problem." He grins again. "You turn 'em, and I'll burn 'em."

It's late by the time I get back to the clubhouse. In a couple of hours, the sun will be up, and we'll be back to cleaning up this mess.

In my room, I pull off my cut and fall onto my bed. I'm bone tired. All I want is to sleep and stop the chaos in my head.

And to put the thought of losing Rory out of my mind.

My alarm goes off at six. I get up, shower, and pretend my chest doesn't ache with longing and fear. I focus on the day ahead. We're still in damage control, thanks to those psychos and their fucking flamethrower.

I check my cell for any messages, my heart quietly hoping there is one from Rory. But just like the million times I checked it in the last eight hours, there isn't any.

I throw on my cut and try to push it out of my mind, but the feeling I might be losing her hangs over me all morning.

During Church, I'm preoccupied and even quieter than usual when we visit the smoldering ruins of the grow barn.

By the time we break for lunch back at the clubhouse, I'm crawling the walls because I need to see her.

"You wanna tell me what's got your panties in a twist?" Paw asks, biting into a burger dripping with hot sauce and cheese.

"It's nothing," I reply, pushing my food away.

I can't eat.

Rory asking me not to come back last night and her radio silence ever since has got me twisted up inside.

I don't doubt she loves me.

What I do doubt is whether I'm enough to stop her from running away from what's got her frightened.

"Brother, I've known you four years, and in all that time, I've never seen you push food away. You sick?"

I stand up so fast I knock over my chair. "I said it's nothing."

I walk away and hit the clubhouse gym for the next two hours because I'm about ready to ping off the walls with restless energy.

I beat the bag until I'm breathless. I yank the battle ropes until my arms are burning with fire and flip the tractor tire until my shoulders beg me to stop.

When I finally give in and stop punishing my body, I see Paw leaning up against the wall, looking at me.

"Want to tell me what's going on?" he asks calmly.

"Like I said, there's nothing to tell."

"You've been training for two hours on as much sleep. What's happening in that head of yours?"

Chaos. That's what's happening.

"I need to work off some energy, is all."

"Yeah, well, I'm sure punching bag doesn't agree. I think I saw it sigh with relief when you walked away." I go to walk past him, but he stops me. "Is this about Rory? Has something happened with your girl?"

I hesitate long enough for him to decide he's right.

"You guys have a fight? You know, I've never seen you like this over some girl before."

I glare at him. She's not just *some girl*.

"Don't give me your fight face," he says calmly. "I'm simply pointing out that you're distracted, and maybe now is not a good time to be."

"Don't worry. I'll be right to fight Raptor on Friday night."

"Hey, I don't give a fuck about that. We might not be blood brothers, but you are my brother. If you're not okay, talk to me. Don't carry it alone. Let me help you. It might ease some of the pressure banging about in that skull of yours."

I don't want to talk about it.

Don't want to face it.

But Paw is right.

Talking about it might help, even if sharing things isn't in my nature.

"There's something she's not telling me, and whatever it is, it's got her running scared. She tells me she loves me and then tells me not to come around for a while. That she needs space."

He grimaces. "She say how long she needs space for?"

"Told me not to come back last night."

"You hear from her today?"

I shake my head. I've checked my phone a million times. Even gave in and called her, but it went to voice message.

"Could be nothing," he says.

"Or it could be everything."

"There's a lot going on right now."

"No, shit."

"You need to get your head back on straight. Go see your girl. Do whatever you got to do, just fix it."

"She's keeping something from me, and every time she tries to bring it up, she gets scared and pulls away. She tried telling me something last night. But then she got scared again and told me not to come back. Whatever is going on with her, it's big enough to make her want to run away."

"Then you need to find out what it is."

I walk away.

In the quiet of my shower, I stand under the warm stream of water and brace myself against the tiles. My shoulders ache. Hell, everything does.

Drying off, I dress and check my cell again, but the screen is still empty.

It's been almost twenty-four hours since I left her apartment.

"Fuck this," I growl, shoving my cell into my cut and grabbing my keys off the bedside table.

But before I can leave, Paw appears in the doorway.

The look on his face sets off warning bells in my head. "What?"

He has a laptop in his hands, and he holds it up. "You need to see this."

On the screen is the software he uses for facial recognition.

"You ran a check on Rory? Why the fuck would you do that?"

"She's not who she says she is, Ares."

"Fuck you."

"You know it's protocol."

I want to throat punch him for looking into my girl's past. But he's right. Anyone who gets close to the Kings is subject to a background check.

Ares, there is something I need to tell you.

My stomach tightens with unease.

And I take it out on Paw.

"I don't give a fuck what you found out. I know who she is."

"No, you don't."

I brush past him, but he stops me and shoves the laptop into my chest. "Read it."

I glance down, and immediately something catches my eye.

Her name isn't Rory Jones.

It's Aurora Murphy.

My stomach knots as I read on.

It also tells me that her stepfather, a seedy sonofabitch called Donnie Hatzakorian, is very, very dead.

He was murdered a year ago.

So why the fuck did she come all the way to Tennessee and ask me to kill a dead man?

CHAPTER 26

ARES

She opens the door, and my stomach drops when I see her face.

She's been crying. It also looks like she hasn't slept at all.

My instinct is to reach for her, but I don't.

"What are you doing here?" Her voice is soft.

Over her shoulder, I see two packed suitcases, and the knot in my chest tightens. I look back at her, but she's looking down, a frown pressed into her forehead.

"Don't," she whispers.

I brush past her to enter her apartment. "You're leaving me?" I can't hide the desperation in my voice.

"I have to go, Ares."

"Where?" I bite out through gritted teeth.

"Back to Boston."

The chaos in my head spins wildly, and it's hard to contain my emotions. My fists clench, my face tightens.

She's fucking leaving me.

I storm over to her. "I tell you I'm in love with you, and you pack your fucking bags?"

"Yes."

"Tell me why."

"Because I didn't come here to fall in love." She lifts her gaze. "I came here to kill you."

What.

The.

Ever.

Loving.

Fuck?

Her words echo around the room and then hit me right in the goddamn heart like a bullet.

I don't move as my head scrambles to work it out.

She's here to kill me?

None of this makes sense.

My pulse races in my neck, my heart a time bomb ticking wildly toward detonation.

She doesn't love me.

For a split second, my knees falter.

Then my emotions roar out of me.

I see the Ruger that had been hidden behind the sugar canister sitting on the countertop. I grab it and slap it into her hand.

"Then do it," I demand.

Because at that moment, I can't stand the pain.

I'll welcome death with open fucking arms.

When she doesn't move, I grab the barrel and press the tip to my forehead.

"Do it!" I growl.

I see the war take place inside her. See the confusion. The pain. The havoc. She came looking for me so she could put a bullet in my skull. *Well, here's your damn chance.*

"What are you waiting for?" I growl, pieces of my heart still splintering through my body.

"Stop it," she growls back.

"You want me dead, then fucking do it."

She lifts her chin, searching the corners of her mind for her next move. *To pull the trigger or not.* She doesn't fight me. Instead, she clicks the magazine release on the Ruger, and the clip falls to the floor between us. She knows the gun won't fire without the magazine attached.

Frustrated, I throw the inoperable firearm across the room. For a moment, we're both silent. Yet inside, I'm anarchy. So I grab her by the jaw and force her backward until her back hits the wall. I squeeze her chin, my agony getting the better of me. But she isn't afraid. Her haunted eyes don't leave me, they're tear-filled and sad. But I don't scare her, not as much as what is taking place inside her does. A lone tear escapes and slides down her cheek.

"Why?" It's all I can manage. It's the only word screaming inside my head, a tornado of chaos turning circles in my brain.

Her chin quivers and another tear falls. "Because you killed my brother."

CHAPTER 27

RORY

Immediately, he lets me go, and I slump against the wall, exhaling sharply.

"Your brother?"

I look at him for the first time since he released me. "Joey Murphy."

The moment the name registers in Ares' brain, his expression morphs into complete surprise. But it's quickly replaced with fury, his eyes the darkest I've ever seen.

"Fuck." He turns away and runs his hand over his head, then swings back to me. "Joey Murphy was your brother?"

When I nod, his brows draw in tight.

Time stretches out before us.

"And you came here looking for revenge?"

"Yes."

"You were going to kill me?"

"Yes."

The weight of my confession crashes around us.

His hands fist at his sides, and I see the anger simmering

beneath a dark expression.

"All that shit about your stepfather—"

"Was true. He did do those things to me."

"But he didn't kill your mom like you said. She's alive."

"Yes, she's alive. But everything else I told you… the rapes, the abuse, he did all of that and that is why I put three bullets in him."

"*You* killed him?"

"I couldn't let him get away with what he did. I thought you, of all people, would understand that."

His angry gaze burns across at me. "And then you came looking for me to make me pay for Joey's death."

"Yes."

The muscle in his jaw ticks. "Then why didn't you?"

I can barely breathe. "Ares—"

"Why didn't you follow through with your plan? Why start a relationship with me?"

"Because I wasn't expecting—"

"You weren't expecting what?"

"I wasn't expecting *you*."

A wild, tortured growl escapes him, and he stalks toward me, stopping only inches away. "What does that even mean?"

I look up into his beautiful, tormented face and feel the pain tighten in my chest when I take in the blazing eyes and handsome features. His hair hangs loose and falls in wild waves down past his shoulders. He's never looked so beautiful, and it kills me to be so in love and so enraptured by the very man I should hate.

Tears well in my eyes.

"Before I came here, you were just a monster in a photograph. Then I saw you at one of your fights, and suddenly you weren't that monster anymore. I kept coming back to watch you. I didn't know why. It didn't make sense to me that I hadn't done what I was sent to do. All I knew was the need to know more about you, and I thought if I got close to you, I would understand it all better. Why you did what you did. Why I felt so drawn to you. But when I met you, I couldn't stay away." I sob. "Then I fell in love with you."

He pushes me away. As if my words hurt him.

"Don't talk to me about love," he says, his voice thick.

"It's true."

He turns away but quickly swings back. "Do you even know who your brother was?"

"Of course, I do."

"I don't think you do. He did sick, bad things, Rory. Depraved and vile things that hurt people."

I glare at him.

"Don't say that."

He's wrong. Joey wasn't depraved. Or sick.

That was Donnie's style, not his.

"Why do you think I killed him?"

"It was a De Kysa hit."

His expression smolders with unspent fury. "It wasn't a De Kysa hit."

He's lying.

"I know he wasn't a saint, but he didn't have a depraved bone in his body, and you killed him. You were a hit man for the De Kysa. They paid you to kill him."

"They didn't pay me to kill him."

"There were rumors that he did something to one of their family members—"

His dark, low voice cuts me off. "I said... it *wasn't* a De Kysa hit."

"Are you saying you didn't kill him?"

"No, I killed him."

My emotions explode out of me. "Then if it wasn't a De Kysa

hit, why did you take my brother from me?"

"Because he raped and murdered my girlfriend," he yells.

I stare at him in stunned silence as his words spin around me.

He went to prison for his girlfriend's death. He told me he was wrongfully accused. Now, he's saying Joey was responsible for her death.

It doesn't make any sense.

"No," I say.

"He was a rapist and a killer, Rory. And Belle wasn't the only one. There were others."

I think about the boy who taught me to skim stones and how to tie my shoelaces and my anger erupts out of me like lava.

"Don't you say that to me." I point an angry finger at him. "Don't you dare speak about him like that."

"It's the truth."

I shove him in his chest, and because I don't know what else to do, I start to pummel him with my fists. Not that it does anything but shoot pain up my forearms.

He grabs me by the wrists to stop me. Which, of course, I struggle against. But it's no use, he is too big and too strong, and I'm no match for his strength.

"Listen to me..." His grasp tightens, and he speaks rapidly. "In the last couple of years of his life, Joey was involved with some pretty fucked up people. Real mean sons of bitches who did vile and depraved things. Joey trafficked young women for them... some of them who he raped and murdered. But before that, he and his over-privileged college buddies raped and murdered Belle. You might not want to hear it, but goddammit, it's the truth."

I struggle against his hold on me. "Stop it."

"I did nine years because of him, Rory. Nine years. Do you know what that does to a man? It makes him mad. It makes him seethe and simmer, and the need for revenge festers. So when I took a job for the De Kysa, and Vinnie De Kysa got the names of the three men who were responsible for what happened that night, I went looking for them, and I made them pay. Do you hear me, Rory? I made them pay for what they did."

"I said stop it!" I cry. "You're lying. It was a hit. You killed men for the De Kysa. Joey would never do those things. They got the wrong man."

He slams against the wall beside me. "You want honesty? Yeah, I dedicated a good portion of my freedom to ridding this world of stains like your fucking brother. I killed them all, and I don't regret a single damn one of them, including your brother."

"Fuck you."

"Fuck me? Fuck him for what he did to those women. For what he did to my Belle."

"Get away from me."

Instead of giving me space, he inches even closer.

"If I hadn't ended his life, think of all the women he would've killed. All those families are missing someone around the dinner table. All those lives were snuffed out because he couldn't keep his psychopathic hands to himself. There is only one way to look at this, Rory, and it's my way. The world is better off without him."

I cry out. A knife couldn't have cut me as much as his words.

"I hate you."

"Hate me all you want… I don't give a fuck anymore. You've already taken everything with your lies." He lets go of me and removes his cell from his back pocket. "You want fucking proof of what a psycho your brother was?" He scrolls through it, then hands it over. "Then here's the damn proof."

On the screen is a black and white video. It's hazy, but I can clearly see a girl cowering in the corner of a room. By the look of her, she couldn't be any more than twenty-one. She's sobbing, and when an unseen presence enters the room, she shrinks back. A man enters the frame. He smiles over at the camera and then unleashes a violent backhand to the woman.

It's Joey.

There is no mistaking it.

My throat goes dry.

This can't be.

I watch on in horror as Joey continues to abuse the girl, nausea unfurling in my gut. He's violent. A monster. She begs for him to let her go. Pleads that if he frees her, she won't tell anyone. But he toys with her. Pretends she has a chance for escape. But even I can tell by his intimidating body language that this is not going to end well. And it doesn't. He lunges for her.

The girl cries out at his brutality but goes silent when he viciously enters her.

"No, this can't be true," I whisper.

Joey laughs as he continues his assault.

My hands shake violently. "Oh, Joey, what happened to you?"

I want to look away, but I won't because it is proof that I am wrong. *So wrong.* My brother, the boy who used to hold my hand when I was too afraid to walk up to my knees in the ocean, the boy who put his arm around me and told me we were going to be okay when our father's coffin passed by us, the boy who saved all his allowance to buy me a Barbie doll when I was six, and he was just twelve, spent his adult life as a monster. A sick, twisted monster.

The old image of him seeps from the wound in my chest that is my broken heart. My happy memories of him are replaced by the reality that Ares is right. He was vile and depraved.

"I didn't know," I whisper, bile rising in the back of my throat. On the screen, Joey continues to force himself on the girl. I close my eyes, but they snap open when I hear the girl begin to beg for her life, and I watch with a broken heart as Joey squeezes his hands around her throat.

Fighting the need to puke, I watch the life drain from her eyes and her body go limp.

Pleased with himself, Joey smiles up at the camera like a sick fuck and reaches up to turn it off.

I push Ares' cell into his hand and begin to pace.

"It can't be real. Someone must've edited it." My brain races to make sense of what I just watched, of what happened to my brother, desperately clinging on to a fading morsel of hope. Fraught, I turn to Ares. "Maybe they were role-playing. Maybe they were acting out a fantasy…"

For the girl's sake, I prayed none of it was real.

And for me too.

"It was all real, Rory."

"Someone could've set him up." But even as I say it, I know what I saw and heard in that video were the cries of a terrified young woman.

"It was found on his cell. The video is real."

I start to pace again, wringing my hands frantically.

I hadn't seen Joey in four years before he disappeared. His drug use had created a huge rift between us.

When I had tried to talk to him about my concerns, he'd made it abundantly clear he didn't want my opinion.

The Joey I knew died a long time before Ares got to him.

But I didn't know he'd become something so dark.

Then it hits me like a truck.

Feeling a rush of horror, I turn to Ares. "How many were there?"

His shoulders stiffen, and he takes a tentative step toward me.

"Don't do this—"

I grit my teeth. "How many women did he hurt?"

"Rory—"

"Tell me, goddammit!"

"That my employer knew of... five."

Five.

"No..." I gasp, but the word gets lodged in my throat like a lump of fiery coal and kicks the air out of my lungs.

He hurt four more women.

I want to puke.

"You think there were more?" I barely manage to talk.

"There were five videos, Rory. I don't think he saved all his depraved acts for the camera."

Meaning there could be many more women who suffered at the hands of Joey.

I'm breathless.

My shoulders slump, and I break, and I don't even care that I am falling apart in front of Ares. I have no strength left because I am broken. Straight up split in two. And it doesn't matter that he might kill me in revenge for my betrayal.

I sag against the wall and begin to sob.

Everything I've held on to since the day I found out he was murdered was a lie.

Joey was a fiend.

Across the room, Ares' anger seems to dissolve.

He walks over to me and crouches down so we're at eye level.

He touches my chin, so I'll look at him. The anger is gone from his eyes, but the hurt is still there, and I can't stand it.

"I'm so sorry," I whisper.

He rakes his gaze over my face but says nothing. Then he gathers me up in his arms and carries me over to the bed. I wind my arms around his neck, sobbing as I press my face into his neck. "I'm so sorry."

He lays me down and climbs onto the bed behind me, securing me in the heat and strength of his arms as they hold me to his broad chest.

And in the silence, he lets me fall apart until I eventually fall asleep.

When I wake, the sun is dying, and long shadows fill my bedroom. In the distance, storm clouds bruise the sky. There's a blanket over my legs and a glass of water on the bedside table.

I'm alone.

My apartment is still.

He's gone.

My heart drops to my stomach.

Has he left for good?

I sit up. "Ares?"

He appears in the doorway, and a wave of relief washes through me.

"I thought you had gone," I say softly.

In the dusky light, he looks big and powerful, but he's stiff and quiet, his jaw tight.

As he moves toward the bed I can feel his pain.

Guilt washes over me.

Oh God, what have I done?

He sits on the edge of the bed, and I ache to touch him. But he sits far enough away to tell me he doesn't want that.

"How are you feeling?" he asks.

He's talking about Joey.

"Like my world has crashed around my ankles, and I only just realized."

It's a bitter pill to swallow to realize you've been played by your mom.

There was no hit.

She knew why Ares did what he did.

She just didn't want to admit what her son had done all those years ago, and because of the cover-up, she would never have to. But by God, she was going to have her vengeance for her son being taken from her.

And I was her perfect little pawn.

She never got over what I did to Donnie. She never forgave me for taking her husband from her. Just like she couldn't forgive Ares for taking her son from her. So she set me up. She used my emotions against me and rolled the dice in her new game by begging me to take vengeance on the man responsible. And what better time to draw me into her web than after watching my brother's coffin lower into the ground. Emotional, I was ripe for the picking and stood no chance against her manipulations.

"I didn't know he had become something dark before he died." I lift my gaze to his. "Was it quick? Did he know?"

His jaw clenches. "It wasn't quick."

"Was he scared?"

"Yes." His voice is cold and clipped. *Detached.* "I told him why, and then I killed him."

Despite knowing what Joey had become its still fresh and Ares' words hurt.

His lifts his gaze to me. "Was any of it real? The things we did?"

"What do you mean?"

"Us? All of it. Was it all part of the plan to make me fall in love with you and then break my heart before you killed me?"

I gasp, my eyes wide. The idea that he thinks I faked my feelings makes me want to cry again.

"I love you," I whisper. "That's *not* a lie."

He doesn't believe me. His eyes tell me he wants to, but I can see on his face that his common sense tells him I'm a big fat faker.

"Everything was real." I reach for him, but he pulls away.

He's not ready.

"Will you ever be able to forgive me?" I ask softly.

"Will you?"

"I need some time to process it all. Who Joey became. What he did. But I love you, and..." My emotions break, and I sob. "I understand now."

Ares stands and walks to the window. The storm clouds have swallowed the remaining rays of sunlight and cast the afternoon in an eerie gloom.

"This isn't going to work." Ares voice is rough. "You and me."

"Don't say that," I plead softly.

He turns back to me. "Staying together only ever means hurting you day after day. I'd rather die than do that to you."

Oh God, he's ending this.

I shake my head, knowing where this is going. "You don't love me?"

His nostrils flare. "I fucking love you like I've never loved anyone else."

"Even when I share the same blood as the monster who did those things to those women... to Belle?"

"You're nothing like him," he growls. "Do you hear me? Nothing. You're everything that is good and right in this world. But whatever this is between us, it's been built with lies, deceit, and darkness. You'll never forgive me because, at the end of the day, I took your brother's life, and I know that won't ever stop hurting you. And I can't do that, Rory. I can't wake up next to you every day knowing I'm hurting you."

I start to cry. "But I forgive you."

"You say that now—"

"Please don't do this," I whisper.

He looks toward the door.

My heart breaks.

My body goes cold.

My voice is small. "Are you breaking up with me?"
I see the pain on his face as he replies, "Yes."

CHAPTER 28

ARES

I don't know where I get the strength to walk away.

I'm numb.

Fucking numb.

When she was asleep, I made the decision to leave because it wouldn't be fair to her if I stayed.

This is never going to work.

Those words killed me to say. Because I'm fucking crazy for her, and the idea of her being gone from my life is destroying me from the inside out.

But I need time to think.

It starts to rain as I leave her apartment, and thunder rolls through the clouds as I descend the stairs and walk toward my bike.

I wasn't expecting you. Her words echo in my head.

Just like I hadn't expected the kid in the back seat all those years ago. But he was there, and he changed the direction of my life.

I get it. I'm the kid in the back seat. The unexpected change in her life.

But feelings die, especially when they're built on lies.

"Wait." Her voice cuts into the gloomy light.

I pause, but I don't turn around.

"Don't leave," she cries out.

If I thought for one second she could forgive me, I'd turn back.

If I believed it wouldn't hurt her to see me every day, I'd go running to her.

But I took what was dear to her, and I sent it straight to Hell, and she doesn't need to be reminded of that when she rolls over every morning and sees me lying there.

"Ares, please don't walk away. I know you probably hate me, but I love you."

I don't hate her.

I fucking love her.

With every sorry beat of my cold black heart.

"Please tell me there's a chance for us," she pleads.

I can't help myself. I turn around.

Standing in the rain, she looks so small and sad, and a knot forms in my chest. I want to take her in my arms. Instead, my fists clench.

"You'll never forgive me," I say, the rain coming down harder and soaking me, my T-shirt clinging to my body, water dripping down my face.

"It's not you who needs forgiveness. It's me. I need your forgiveness. But if you need to hear me tell you that I forgive you, then I will. I forgive you, Ares, with all my heart, you have my word. I know why it had to happen, and it's all I need to move forward." She walks down the stairs but stops at the bottom. "But can you forgive me? Can you understand why I did what I did and forgive me for it?"

I want to tell her yes.

That she's right.

But before I get the chance, the shadows behind her move, and in a flash, something grabs her from behind and drags her into the darkness and out of view.

I've never moved as fast in my life.

I run to where she was standing only seconds earlier, but she's gone, swallowed by the shadows.

One of those psychos is still out there. Jack's words flash through my mind.

Fuck. *Fuck. FUCK.*

I run after her, around the apartment block, and in the distance, I see her struggling as a man drags her across the neighboring parking lot. To subdue her, he slams her face into the side of a van, knocking her out.

I see red.

Every neuron ignites with murderous rage.

I run toward them, but he shoves an unconscious Rory into the van and starts firing his gun at me. A bullet whistles past my head, then another hits the row of mailboxes beside me.

In seconds, he's inside the van and skidding away.

I run back to my bike. I leap on and roar out of the parking lot, riding through the rain like a man possessed.

Wind whips around me, and the hard summer rain stings my face as I follow the ruby taillights through the gloom. I don't have time to call anyone. The precious seconds I'd lose calling for help would mean I'd lose sight of them.

Lightning passes through the clouds as we leave the town behind us and head toward the county line. Houses and barns become fewer and fewer, and the landscape opens up to wide fields.

I'm gaining on him but he shoots at me, almost knocking me

off my bike, making me lose seconds as I struggle to regain control.

The van flies over railway tracks way too fast, sending dust and debris into the air as it recovers and speeds off. In my peripheral, I see the light from the train. In a few seconds, it's going to cut me off if I don't get over the tracks.

I will beat it.

I have to.

In the final second, I screech on the brakes and almost come off my bike as it skids and slides beneath me.

Fuck.

The seconds pass in agonizing slowness as I wait for the train to pass.

Every rumble of the train wheels is torture, and when the final carriage passes, and I can see ahead of me again, they're gone.

I've lost them.

I take off over the tracks and into the darkness. There isn't a lot out here. No homes. No buildings. Just the abandoned marina a few miles beyond the woods. It's the only place this road leads to, and unless The Three have somewhere hidden in the hardwood forest, that's going to be my best shot at finding Rory.

I slow my pace, my eyes razor sharp as I search the dark woods for any sign of life as I pass by.

This is my fault.

If I hadn't walked away from Rory, then this would never have happened.

My grip tightens around my handlebars. *If he hurts her I will kill him slowly and painfully.*

As the marina comes into view, I approach it slowly.

A few summers back, three EF3 tornadoes touched down in the area and decimated it. Wooden logs from the broken docks and boat slips stick out of the water like gray bones. Abandoned boats covered in mud and weathered by neglect list on their sides in the black water. It's eerily quiet and dark, except for the single light coming from a boat floating quietly at the end of the dock.

It has to be them.

I reach for my gun but come up empty.

Fuck.

When I left the clubhouse this afternoon, I only had one thing on my mind and that was confronting Rory, and I forgot to grab my piece off my bedside table.

But I can't worry about that now.

Before I leave my bike, I fire off a quick message to Jack, then I scan every direction, looking for movement. Thankfully, it's not raining here, and I can see better. Behind a weathered boat shed, the tail end of the van sticks out.

Left a little too conveniently in plain sight.

I sneak along the dock toward the boat, knowing what's in play here.

The psycho who took Rory wasn't trying to escape.

He wanted me to follow.

CHAPTER 29

RORY

I wake with a pounding headache.

What the fuck happened?

Opening my eyes, my vision is blurred, and I feel sick. I'm in a chair with my hands tied behind my back and my feet bound to the legs. Blood drips down my face and seeps into my mouth.

Wait, did someone hit me?

My head spins with mental confusion.

Did Connor send someone to kidnap me?

The floor rocks from side to side, and a wave of wooziness washes over me. Either the knock to my head gave me vertigo, or I'm on a boat. I squeeze my eyes open and shut to shake off the fog, and slowly, my surroundings come into focus. I'm definitely on a boat.

I fight the ropes binding my wrists together and try to move my feet. But it's no use, they're tied up tight.

Through the open door, I see a man standing on the deck with his back to me. He's not moving. He's just standing in the dark like a creeper.

He's watching. Waiting. Staring into the shadows as if he's expecting someone he knows. His stiff shoulders and straight back tell me he's ready to inflict pain.

Even with a possible head injury, it's not hard to work out he's waiting for Ares.

I'm not the target.

I'm the damn bait.

And Ares is walking into a trap.

"Hey!" I call out.

The psychopath jerks his head to look at me but doesn't move.

Of course, he doesn't. Because me calling out only serves his purpose more. It's a beacon that will attract Ares to the boat. But Ares is already out there. *I can feel him.* And he needs to know what he is walking into.

"Hey, freakazoid, you standing on the boat deck waiting for someone to step out of the shadows?"

He turns to face me this time, and I finally get a good look at my kidnapper.

My stomach drops. He's not one of Connor's thugs.

I take in the suit and the mask.

Oh fuck, the mask.

He's one of those psycho freaks who burned down the grow barn.

One of The Three.

I think back to what Ares told me about the vigilante group and what they did to their victims.

What they did to Katey.

The silent psychopath stalks toward me. His knife gleams in the dull light.

I shrink back.

He's going to kill me.

And he's going to make sure it hurts.

"You should probably move away from my girlfriend," says the booming voice out of nowhere.

Standing right in front of me, the psychopath looks me in the eye, and I see him smile behind his mask.

He's been waiting for this.

Over his shoulder, Ares fills the doorframe. "Put down the fucking knife and step back from her before I break every bone in your sorry ass."

The crazy man with the mask doesn't turn around. Instead, he uses the hand not holding the knife to remove a gun from his suit pocket.

My eyes widen. "Gun—"

The psychopath spins around and fires at Ares. Bullets splinter the wooden doorframe and walls, and Ares falls to the floor, the thump vibrating through the little cabin.

I scream.

He's not moving.

The psychopath stalks over to him and takes aim, ready to finish him off, but my window-shattering scream momentarily distracts him.

I'm not sure what the plan is, all I know is I need to stop him from shooting Ares again.

As it turns out, it's all Ares needs.

He rises from the floor, his face a mask of pure wrath, and the room explodes with his fury.

He storms toward the mask-wearing-crazy-man and swings a powerful arm at him, catching him in the head and sending him to his knees. Psycho-man drops the gun and it spins on the floor.

"You think you can hurt my girl and get away with it?" Ares grabs the gun and takes aim. "See you in Hell, motherfucker."

He pulls the trigger and the psychopath crumples to the floor. He fires again but the clip is empty. In a rage, he discards the weapon and kneels to finish the psycho off with his fists, his face wild with anger as he breaks bone and cartilage and sends blood splattering across the linoleum. Satisfied the limp psycho is done, Ares hauls him off the floor and drags him outside to the deck, where he tosses him overboard.

I hear the splash of water and the stomp of boots before he reappears.

Kneeling, he quickly unties me, and I can feel the rage coming off him because it burns like wildfire.

"Are you okay? Can you walk?" he asks.

I nod frantically, but the sudden movement sends waves of pain to my face. "I think the bastard broke my nose."

Ares' nostrils flare and his teeth are gritted, but his hand is impossibly gentle as he cups my jaw. "I'm so sorry, baby."

"Don't be sorry. Just get me out of here."

When I stand, a wave of nausea makes me falter, and I stumble. Ares doesn't hesitate. He lifts me up and carries me out of the cabin and off the boat, then strides along the dock with me in his arms.

"It's okay, you can let me down," I say.

"Darlin', I ain't letting go of you. Not ever again."

"Does this mean you're not breaking up with me?"

He sets me down. "What?"

"The breakup. Have you come to your senses and decided to forgive and forget?"

He looks bewildered. "You really want to talk about this here? Now?"

"Yes! So answer the damn question."

I must have concussion because now is not the place to have this discussion. But I'm determined to have it.

A rough breath leaves his lips. "I don't want to say goodbye. I never did."

"Then fucking don't."

He gives me one of his rare smiles as he shakes his head. "You're impossible."

"I know, but it's one of the reasons why you love me." My smile fades. "You do still love me, right?"

To respond, he steps closer, takes my face in his big hands, and kisses me. His tongue slides into my mouth, and I moan. His answer is loud and clear.

He takes my hand. "You sure you can walk?"

"Yes, now get me home."

"First, let me call Jack."

As he reaches inside his cut for his cell, something catches in the corner of my eye.

A shadow rises out of the dark water like a swamp creature and takes aim at Ares.

"No," I cry.

As it fires, I step in front of Ares, and everything turns black.

CHAPTER 30

ARES

"There's nothing you can do for her," the doctor says as he ushers me out of the room. He's British, his words clipped and fancy.

"Is she going to die?" I can barely talk around the lump in my throat.

Inside, I'm a fucking mess.

Since getting Rory to the hospital, I keep reliving the horror when she stepped in front of me and took the bullet to her chest and fell to the ground.

"It's too soon to tell, I'm afraid. We've done what we can, it's up to her now." The doctor tries to give me a sympathetic look but looks awkward instead. Either the cut I'm wearing scares him, or it excites him. It's hard to tell. "In the meantime, let's get you fixed up. That shoulder has got to be hurting."

"I don't need anything," I say gruffly.

"But you've been shot."

The moment Rory fell, I charged at the psycho. He shot me in the shoulder, but it wasn't enough to stop me. Through the pain and threat of death, I took his gun from him and shot him.

A lot.

Now, I'm bleeding. But I'm too wired on adrenaline to feel the pain.

"I'm not leaving her."

"I get it, you're worried about her. But you need to be strong for her and that gaping hole in your shoulder isn't going to help matters. May I suggest you look after yourself so you can look after her?"

"Fine, do what you gotta do, but then I'm coming back here, and I'm not leaving until she wakes up and walks out with me."

He nods. "Well, it's a start, I suppose."

In one of the emergency room cubicles, he removes the bullet. My insistence on no painkillers sparks that fear versus fascination in him again.

"You've got a strong pain threshold," he says, impressed. "But then, you certainly fight like you do."

"You watch me fight?"

"Oh, Ares, my boy, you won me fifty dollars against the Scorpion."

I grunt, but my mind automatically switches back to Rory, and it brings a new wave of fear with it. My hands curl into fists. If she dies, I don't know how I will survive this.

"Look, if I can offer you some advice. You seem like a lovely fellow, and you obviously love Aurora. But torturing yourself over what has happened isn't going to help her. It's not going to help anyone." This doctor likes to talk when all I want to do is quietly torture myself. "Honestly, the best thing you can do for her now is to make sure everything is taken care of, so when she wakes up, all she has to focus on is getting well again."

After he sews me up, I convince the doctor to let me see Rory again. But we're stopped on the way to her room by Sheriff Pinkwater and Jack.

"You found him?" I ask.

"Right where you said we would. Full of holes and floating in the lake." Pinkwater's gaze slides to the doctor, then back to me. "He had so many holes in him, we're lucky he didn't sink."

"Forensics is at the boat now," Jack adds. "So are the FBI."

"FBI? They didn't know about it two weeks ago."

"Now they do." Pinkwater shakes his head. "Just in time to take all the fucking credit."

"Let them. We don't want the exposure," Jack says.

He's right. With exposure comes interest. With interest, comes trouble. Especially when you make good money from a thriving marijuana and bootlegging business.

I don't linger, I need to see Rory again.

But as we pass, Jack stops the doctor. "Anything she needs, she gets."

He knows how much Rory means to me. He also knows why she was in town. When she was in surgery, I filled him in on the details. I was hesitant about telling him, but I've never hidden the truth from Jack. It's why he counts on me so much.

I thought he'd be pissed.

Call me a dumbass for falling for the wrong girl.

But he thought about it and then nodded. "If Bronte had come to town looking to put a bullet in my ass, I would have loaded the gun and handed it to her."

The doctor takes me to see Rory.

And again, the sight of her unconscious and connected to machines kills me.

Standing by her bed, my knees go weak. *I love her so damn much.*

I reach for her and touch her face, wanting to soothe her but at the same time needing to feel her.

"Maybe touching isn't such a good—"

I throw the doctor a murderous look.

He shrinks back. "But, of course, studies do suggest it might help. Some even suggest it encourages them out of comas. But there's no—"

I turn back to Rory but direct my words at him. "Stop talking."

"Of course, I'll be as quiet as a mouse. In fact, how about I give you both a moment of privacy."

"That would be a very good idea," I say.

He leaves, and I kneel beside the hospital bed. Rory looks so small and vulnerable, and Christ, it fucking hurts to know it's my fault. If I had only checked the psychopath for a second gun before I threw him overboard, she wouldn't be in this bed.

I take her hand in mine and press my lips to her cool skin. "Don't leave me, baby. Don't you do that to me. I didn't know what fucking love was until I met you, and if you don't wake up and tell me to take a chill pill and lighten the fuck up, I don't know how I'm going to fucking survive it."

Another wave of fear rolls through me, and I drop my head.

This is pure fucking hell.

But I have to do something to make it right.

The doctor said the best thing I can do for Rory is make sure things are in order when she wakes up so she doesn't have anything but her recuperation to think about.

I think about everything that's happened in the last five weeks since she walked into my life and stole my heart. About the hit. About the lies. About the mess we've made. And it makes me fight the tears forming behind my eyes. My jaw hurts from gritting my teeth, and there's an iceberg in my throat.

"Wake up, little one, and I promise I'll make things right."

I stand and lean down to kiss her forehead before I leave.

Then I storm out of the room to find Jack.

An hour later, we're on our way to the airport.

Ares

By the time we land, Paw has gotten us all the information we need to know.

We take a hire car to Dorchester. Rory's mom, who according to Paw's information, is called Ariana, opens the door. Dressed in a satin jumpsuit and enough gold to sink a ship, she's smoking a cigarette and smells like beer.

Her eyes light up when she sees Jack.

But when she sees me, her appreciation turns to horror.

She doesn't slam the door in our face, she's too busy running for the hills.

No doubt, going for a gun.

Which would be good since Jack and I are unarmed. Airports don't like you carrying a couple of handguns stashed on your body, and we didn't have time to sort an alternative. If she gets a gun, I'll take it from her.

As soon as we enter the house, a fat man with a receding hairline steps out from the kitchen to the left, blocking our path. He's wearing nothing but a white tank top and pants. He gleams with gold jewelry, a gold watch, gold bracelets, and a thick gold chain around his neck sitting on a bed of wiry white and ginger chest hair.

"What the fuck are you doing here?" he asks me.

Ariana runs at us, yelling and pointing a gun like she's Ma Baker.

But it's nothing for me to take it off her.

One second, she's holding it, the next it's in my hand, and she's staring at me like I've performed a magic trick.

"Do your worst, you motherfucking murderer. You killed our Joey. You're a cocksucker, a goddamn motherfucking cocksucker."

Jack glares at her. "Shut up."

But she ignores him and lunges at me. I sidestep, and she loses her balance, and I have to grab her arm to stop her from falling.

"Fuck you." She has mean eyes. "Get your motherfucking hands off me."

"Your daughter is in hospital," I say.

She gives me a blank look. "So?"

I grit my teeth.

I should've let her fall on her face.

"You don't want to know? Or you don't care?" I ask.

"I lost that kid years ago. She was a daddy's girl. She didn't like me, and I didn't much like her. Last I heard, she was shaking her moneymaker for men in some seedy club. Girl is probably better off dead."

I hate this woman.

Her words set off a violent storm in my head, and I struggle to contain it.

She goes to say something more, but Jack sears her mouth shut with a threatening look.

He holds up the gun. "You'll put your goddamn manners back in and show us some respect. Let's talk in the living room." He points to Ariana. "You, Calamity Jane, lead the way."

The house looks like it used to be nice, but years of neglect have made it shabby. Yellow nicotine stains crawl up the walls, and dust motes dance in the hazy light.

Jack points at the faded couch for them to sit while I look around. The house stinks of cigarette smoke and stale beer. Behind me, bone China knickknacks clutter the alabaster mantelpiece.

"What the fuck do you want?" The fat ginger asks.

Jack gives him a searing look. "I'm here to offer you a warning. Now, I don't offer warnings, usually I just shoot people. But Rory means something to the Kings of Mayhem, so out of respect for her, I'm here offering you a get-out-of-jail card, so you both keep your trap holes closed until I say you can open them again. Got it?"

The two pieces of shit glance at each other and then nod.

"The hit you put on Ares, it ends right now. No more talk about revenge. No more crying about past deeds, and I don't know… all the shit you two like to stir up. It stops right now. I'm a busy man, and I have bigger fish to fucking fry than having to deal with two deadbeat wannabe gangsters, so don't make me come back here and kick your damn asses. Because I will. And I promise you, I won't be as friendly as I am being now."

Fat Ginger looks like he's about to burst.

"Speak," Jack drawls.

"You think you can come in here and make demands?"

"I'm doing it, aren't I?"

"Who the hell do you think you are?"

"Okay, I'm getting bored." Jack sighs wearily. "So here it is, loud and clear for all the dumb fucks in the room. Stay away from Tennessee, call off any assassination attempts, and I won't burn your fucking world to the ground." He issues his warning with a coldness that could freeze a raging inferno. "I don't care who you *think* you are or what you *think* you can do. Whatever it is, we'll do it bigger and better than you."

Despite looking like he's about to shit his pants, Connor scoffs. "So you say."

Jack doesn't flinch. Doesn't move. Just keeps his blazing stare on the frightened man. "Do you really want to find out?" He pauses, his eyes sharp. By the look on Connor's face, he doesn't. "You make a move on any of my brothers or me, and it will be considered an act of war."

I remove an envelope from my cut and throw it onto the cluttered coffee table. Inside is the money from every one of my fights.

Ariana stares at it like it's lost treasure. Her mean eyes light up, and she licks her thin lips. "What is that?"

"Ten thousand dollars."

"We don't want your blood money," the fat ginger says.

But Ariana looks at him like he's just told her perms are no longer in fashion. "Shut up, Connor."

I hate both of these people.

"This isn't blood money," I say. "This is a one-time offer. A generous one. You stay out of Rory's life, and you stay out of mine."

"Why the hell would you hand over all this cash for that little—" She stops, her eyes blinking a few times. "Wait, you mean to tell me you and Rory..." Ariana laughs coldly and starts slow clapping. "That little slut."

With one swipe of my arm, I clear the mantelpiece behind me of all the bone China knickknacks. They crash to the floor and smash to smithereens. Ariana screams, and I have to resist screaming back.

"Call her a slut again, and I'll do that to the rest of this cesspit," I growl.

Ariana glares at me, her mouth gaping while the fat ginger seethes on the couch. "You asshole. You and that slut deserve one another."

I kick over a porcelain statue of Aphrodite that was holding a dead plant.

If I had to live in this shit hole, I'd shrivel up and die too.

Porcelain scatters across the floor.

"So far, you're not very good at obeying the rules."

Ariana snaps her cruel cold lips shut.

"Well, I guess that's our cue to leave. Thanks for the hospitality." Jack gives them a cold smile and holds up the gun. "And for my new Glock."

We walk away without another word and once outside I suck in a deep breath of fresh air. No wonder Rory came looking for me. Those people are vile fucking creatures.

Before we head to the airport, we stop at the harbor, and Jack throws the gun into the water.

"Feel better?" he asks as we climb back in the car.

"We should've just killed them," I say.

He smiles as he starts the engine. "Now you fucking tell me."

It would've been easy for me to put bullets in their skulls, especially knowing how Ariana turned a blind eye to her husband raping Rory. But logistically, it would be a nightmare and more trouble than it was worth.

Do I trust their word that they'll stay away? No fucking way.

But do I trust their lust for money and their desire to keep breathing? Absolutely.

They don't want to risk waging a war against the Kings of Mayhem, and they know it.

They're getting away with everything lightly. Initiating a hit against a King is not only a declaration of war but also plain stupid.

Jack gave them a free pass.

They'd be wise not to poke the bear again.

After dropping off the rental car, we walk over to the airport.

Just before we're about to board our flight, my cell rings. It's Paw.

"Rory just woke up."

CHAPTER 31

RORY

Damn, my chest feels like I've been run over by a military convoy.

I reach for the cup of water on the tray and suck it down like I'm drinking for Olympic gold.

For the last two days, I've lingered in and out of an opiate haze. I've snatched rare moments of wakefulness between fractured dreams and nothingness, but not enough to ask any questions. Although, I was lucid enough to know that every time I opened my eyes, Ares was sitting beside me with a tortured look on his face and red eyes that pleaded with me not to die.

We haven't spoken. I couldn't have formed words in my medicated brain if I'd tried.

Today, they're starting me on new meds. I'm not sure why.

When Ares appears in the doorway, my stomach knots. My warrior king looks like he's about to fall apart, and it makes my chest ache.

I smile up at him and watch the relief cross his face.

"You're awake," he says, sitting beside me and taking my

hand. To my complete surprise, tears well in his beautiful warm eyes, and he has to fight them off.

I reach up to cup his face. "Hey, it's okay. Turns out *I am* infallible after all, maybe even a superhero."

"You took a bullet for me. Are you crazy? You could've died."

"I think a simple thank you would suffice here."

"You're seriously quoting me right now." He presses a kiss to the back of my hand. "Baby, promise me you won't *ever* do something like that again."

"You mean I might have to?"

"Don't be cute."

"Don't be so tightly wound."

His eyes are impossibly warm.

I can see how much he loves me.

"I'm sorry," I say.

"Don't you apologize to me. It's me who needs to apologize. Fuck, Rory. I should never have walked away from you."

"We didn't know this was going to happen."

"But it did."

I squeeze his hand. "And now it's over so we can move forward, right?"

"Can we?"

"If you can forgive me for coming to Flintlock to kill you. Or do I need to take a few more bullets first?" I raise an eyebrow at him to let him know I'm joking, but he only looks more tortured. "Sorry, too soon?"

"Don't even joke about that, baby." He smiles, but it's weak. "I don't think my heart could take it."

"You don't need to apologize to me."

"Are you quoting me again?"

"Yes, but I'm serious. Can we put this behind us? Forgive each other and move forward?"

"Is that what you want?"

"More than anything in the world," I whisper.

God, the way he looks at me turns my insides to mush. Then he leans down and kisses me, and I sink into heaven feeling his gentle lips against mine.

Two months ago, I came to town looking for Ares for completely different reasons.

Five weeks ago, I wanted just one night with this man.

But one night was never going to be enough with him.

And now, a lifetime doesn't seem long enough.

It's hard to believe so much has happened since then—that I've found the love of my life.

How grateful I am that I learned the truth.

We break off the kiss when the doctor walks in. He's a man about forty years old with a kind face and a nice smile.

"There she is… you're looking a lot better. How are you feeling?" he asks in a clipped British accent as he picks up my chart and reads it.

"Like someone used my chest as a sieve."

"That's to be expected. You'll be sore for a few weeks, but you will bounce back as good as new. It was a close call," he says as he writes something on my chart. "Congratulations, by the way."

Slightly confused, I ask, "For not dying?"

The doctor chuckles. "Well, there's that. But on the other news."

"Other news?"

"You're pregnant. Five weeks to be exact."

EPILOGUE

ARES

The room is bathed in moonlight.

I stand at the end of the altar dressed in a suit. Beside me, Paw does his best to calm my restlessness, but he's not succeeding.

"I'm not nervous," I tell him.

But I'm lying.

I feel angsty because I want to see my girl. I haven't seen her since yesterday, which is the longest I've gone without her since she was shot, and I almost lost her.

I'm so in love with her it physically hurts.

But then, I like pain.

Like her, it's addictive, and I'm the willing addict. Every day I crave her touch, and every day she gives it to me, and it sends me further and further into my addiction.

"Relax, buddy. Your girl will be here soon," Paw says.

Across the room, I see my son in Cinnamon's arms—four months old and the most perfect thing in the whole fucking world. My nerves immediately calm. His name is Frankie, and the moment he came into this world, my life became so much more.

Today, my life will be complete when I make Rory my wife.

When she appears at the end of the aisle on Jack's arm, tears spring to my eyes.

She's so fucking beautiful.

Our eyes lock as she makes her way toward me, dressed in a simple white dress that falls elegantly around her figure. From a small crown in her hair, a trail of sheer fabric floats behind her. My heart is about to burst out of my chest, and I can barely breathe as I watch her.

Paw pats my shoulder. He's grinning. I glance around the room—everyone is smiling. Some of the old ladies are crying. Hell, even Earl looks like he's fighting back the tears. Beside him, Dolly curls an arm through his and nestles closer to him, her smile dazzling.

When Rory reaches me, I take her hand.

I'm never letting you go, baby.

"You're the most beautiful woman I've ever seen," I say softly.

She mouths, "Don't make me cry." Then she gives me a smile that melts my heart.

I don't hear the priest as he begins the ceremony. All I can hear is the pounding of my heart as this beautiful angel standing in front of me agrees to be my wife.

"Ares, do you have something to give Aurora?" the priest asks.

Removing the delicate chain with the crown pendant from my pocket, I drape it around Rory's slender throat and fasten the clasp. It's a Kings of Mayhem tradition. When a King takes a queen, he gives her his crown. Never in my wildest dreams did I ever think I'd give mine to someone.

"Rory, baby, I give you this as a sign of my never-ending love for you. Wear it, baby, and let the world know you're mine and that I am completely and utterly yours, now and forever."

I look into her lovely face. Tears glitter in her long lashes, and when she smiles, they spill down her cheeks. She's so damn perfect my breath snags in my chest.

"Thank you," she whispers.

From her right hand, she removes a band of black tungsten from her thumb and holds it to my ring finger. "Ares, I give this to you as a sign of my everlasting love. Please wear it with the knowledge that I am yours, and I always will be until I take my last breath. Be my king, and I will always be your queen."

She slides the metal along my finger to the hilt, and I let the tears spill down my cheeks.

"I can't wait to start our life together," she says.

I step forward and take my wife's face between my hands, and I kiss her.

Our life together.

It sounds so magical I can barely believe it's happening.

I didn't realize I was so lonely until she came along.

And then my son.

Now, I can't imagine life without them.

She smiles up at me and happiness wraps around my heart.

This woman has got me crazy in love.

And my future has never looked so good.

EPILOGUE

RORY

It's late. A million fairy lights twinkle in the poplar trees, and music drifts into the warm summer air. On the lake, moonlight is a silver ribbon on the dark water.

I take a break from the wedding reception and watch the guests from the little terrace overlooking the lakeside venue.

I watch with contentment as my new family and friends laugh, drink, and dance. It's only been a year and a half since I came to Flintlock, and in that time, they have become my everything.

At one table, Sheriff Pinkwater is engaged in conversation with Jack. Ares told me that when the FBI dug into who The Three were, they discovered three psychopaths who met in prison. Ares always suspected they weren't religious fanatics, and he was right. The seven deadly sins aspect of the murders were just theatrics. They were killers, and they wanted to get noticed. Their murders were less God and *all* ego.

I still feel a cold chill along my spine whenever I think about that night on the boat. About the quiet freak in the mask. About what could've happened. As a rule, I don't think about it too much now. I have too many wonderful things in my life to focus on, so I don't waste my time thinking about those loony tunes.

Just like I don't waste time thinking about my mom or Connor. Needless to say, I haven't been back to see them, and they haven't dared come looking.

I have a loving family now.

My son was born a week early. He was a big baby—nine pounds, fifteen ounces—and he was in a hurry. Ares delivered him in the back of my car three miles from the hospital.

And he has been obsessed with him ever since.

He's a good daddy. His kid is never going to know how it feels to not be loved by his father.

Farther along, at another table, Lacey from the Spicy Crawdad is in deep conversation with Wyatt, an old biker with a handlebar mustache and a gravelly voice. They think we don't know it, but they're secretly dating. It will be a cold day in hell before Lacey admits to having feelings. But they're there because I can see them now written all over her face as she looks longingly at Wyatt.

Speaking of romance.

On the makeshift dance floor, Gabe is dancing slowly with Cinnamon. They've been engaged for three weeks, and I have a feeling they'll be married by Fall. Apparently, she was the perfect antidote to his heartbreak, and he was the perfect elixir to her aversion to being an old lady.

Old lady.

Oh, my God.

I guess that's what I am now.

Ares' old lady.

A warmth spreads through me as I think about the man who owns my heart and soul completely. Every day, I wake up in his warm arms, and every night he sends me to heaven with his hot kisses and deep moans while his big hands roam my body.

When I think about what he did to me this morning, my body becomes warm, and my cheeks flush.

From the garden below, Bronte looks up and waves. I wave back, and the flash of platinum on my finger catches my eye, and I can't help but grin. My engagement ring is a band of diamonds and is the most beautiful ring in the world. But it's nothing compared to the diamond-encrusted crown hanging from the chain around my neck.

I reach up to touch it, and my smile grows wider.

Wearing Ares' crown is an honor, and it fills me with pride.

"That's what I like to see… my wife smiling," says the warm voice behind me.

Strong arms wrap around my waist. Gentle lips brush my shoulder.

"*My wife.* That has a real good ring to it," I say, turning in his arms to look up at him. I wind my arms around his neck. "Say it again."

He leans down and brushes his lips across mine. "My wife," he whispers.

His tongue slides into my mouth, and I melt against him, dizzy with lust. He could kiss me for a thousand years, and it still wouldn't be enough.

Earl clears his throat, and we reluctantly stop.

"Sorry to interrupt," he says.

He and Dolly are standing in the doorway, our son in Dolly's arms.

"Someone was beginning to fuss for his momma and his daddy," she says.

I take my son from her, and he yawns, then smiles up at me. "It's been a big day for him."

Frankie is the most adorable kid on the planet. But then, I'm probably biased. He has his daddy's features—dark hair, a hint of a dimple on the chin, long dark lashes—but he has my blue eyes.

"We were fixing to leave. You want us to take Frankie home with us?" Dolly asks. "Give you two some time alone?"

"No," Ares replies. He looks lovingly at me. "I think it's time I take my family home."

I look at him, surprised. "The party is still going strong. You sure you don't want to stay?"

His eyes twinkle across at me. "Let them dance. I want to go home and be with my family."

The affection on his face turns me to mush.

I ease up on my tiptoes to kiss him. "I love you."

"I love you too, little one."

With a grin he takes my hand and we head for home.

THE END

ACKNOWLEDGMENTS

To fellow authors, Talia Hunter and Kia Carrington-Russell, thank you so much for all the writing sprints, coffee dates and wise words. I'm so grateful for you.

To my betas, Stephanie Burdett and Rachael Cochrane, what would I do without you? (Please don't ever leave me!)

To my husband for NOT reminding me during the week of my deadline that I was actually on a diet and that wine was not allowed on said diet. You get me. That's why I love you.

To Amber, my amazing girl. Thank you for always cheering me on and reminding me that I've got this.

To Dozer, my main furry guy. You're so handsome and wonderful. Thank you for sitting by my side and giving me cuddles as I bled words onto paper.

To my readers and the bloggers who read and enjoy my words. I am so grateful for you. You make all the days of crying and yelling at my laptop so incredibly worth it! I love you, thank you xx

On a more serious note:

This book is a work of fiction, but as discussed, some situations are of a sensitive nature and deal with rape and abuse. While it is not detailed it is themed. So please don't hesitate to use the below numbers if you feel help is needed.

If you or anyone you know is in emotional distress or has been a victim of assault, please seek help or assist them to obtain help. Reporting the crime could possibly prevent another incident.

Crisis hotlines exist everywhere, so please don't hesitate.

If you live in:
USA call RAINN - 1-800-656-HOPE
Canada call 1.888.407.4747 for help
UK call The Samaritans 116 123
Australia call Lifeline Australia 13 11 14

PLAYLIST

We're An American Band—Rob Zombie
What It Takes—Aerosmith
Boyfriend—Dove Cameron
I'll Make You Love Me—Kat Leon
Pour Some Sugar on Me—Def Leppard
My Iron Lung—Radiohead
Hazy Shade of Winter—The Bangles
Harden My Heart—Quarterflash
Six Days (Remix)—DJ Shadow & Mos Def
How Much Can a Man Take—Big John Hamilton
Whitehouse Road—Tyler Childers
Day After Day—Badfinger
Sad But True—Metallica

CONNECT WITH ME ONLINE

Check these links for more books from Penny Dee.

READER GROUP

For more mayhem join by FB readers group:
Penny's Queens of Mayhem
www.facebook.com/groups/604941899983066/

NEWSLETTER

https://bit.ly/364AFvo

WEBSITE

http://www.pennydeebooks.com/

INSTAGRAM

@pennydeeromance

BOOKBUB

http://www.bookbub.com/authors/penny-dee

EMAIL
penny@pennydeebooks.com

FACEBOOK
http://www.facebook.com/pennydeebooks/

ABOUT THE AUTHOR

Penny Dee writes contemporary romance about rock stars, bikers, hockey players, and everyone in-between. Her stories bring the suspense, the feels, and a whole lot of heat.

She found her happily ever after with an Australian hottie who she met on a blind date.

Printed in Great Britain
by Amazon